The Monosexual

The Monosexual

A novel

Dean Monti

Lake Dallas, Texas

Copyright © 2024 by Dean Monti
All rights reserved
Printed in the United States of America

FIRST EDITION

This is a work of fiction, and is not intended to resemble anyone living or dead.

"I've Got You Under My Skin" from *Born to Dance*
Words and Music by Cole Porter
© 1936 by Cole Porter
Copyright Renewed and Assigned to Robert H. Montgomery,
Trustee of the Cole Porter Musical & Literary Property Trusts
Publication and Allied Rights Assigned to Chappell & Co., Inc.
All Rights Reserved
Used by Permission of Alfred Music

Requests for permission to reprint or reuse material
from this work should be sent to:

Permissions
Madville Publishing
PO Box 358
Lake Dallas, TX 75065

Cover Design: Jacqueline Davis

ISBN: 9781956440898 paperback
9781956440904 ebook

Library of Congress Control Number: 2023952539

For Julie

Chapter 1

(rip, rig, and panic)

When Vincent comes to, the first thing he notices is a long, shiny, silver post. Almost like something a very tall person might employ for hanging some very long trousers, but for the serif hooks jutting on either end of the T-shape at the top of the contraption. Attached to one of the hooks is a plastic bag, long and bloated, like a whale's condom or a carry-out sack for a submarine sandwich, but filled with a colorless liquid. The liquid is moving through a thin, hollow, clear plastic tubing that is connected to... *him*, as best as he can tell. He isn't absolutely sure, because he can't move his head. Or his arms. Or anything, really. But he is initially and primarily concerned about his head.

He isn't sure if his inability to move his head has to do with some restraining device—put in place by the same people who have connected him to a tube—or if he can't move his head because of fear or a lack of will on his part. He also harbors a third, nagging, improbable but persistent scenario: that perhaps he can't move his head because of some actual physical condition that prevents that from happening. Like, say, not having a neck anymore. Or a fully intact head.

He isn't at home. This much he knows for sure. The walls surrounding him are painted in drab seafoam green. Hospital green.

He's in a hospital room. But he has no clue how long he's been unconscious or any memory of how he got there. He believes it's daytime because he's woken up in a partially sunlit room. But it could be morning, afternoon, or early evening.

His head is facing the left wall. Without moving, he can make out the words on a poster: WHAT IS YOUR PAIN LEVEL? And just below it, there are drawings of faces that run the gamut from copasetic to cringing. Vincent is neither copasetic nor cringing, but nor does he feel *confident*, which is absent from the selection of facial expressions. The poster doubles as an advertisement for a pain medication. He appreciates being in a place that understands the value of pain medicine. The poster also doubles as a wall calendar. It tells him it's 1999. He knows he's nowhere near being in a place where he could party like it's 1999, but the year seems correct.

Vincent is aware, on some level, of being worried and scared, but he's also in an odd state of not *caring too much* that he is worried and scared. It is this forced sense of relaxation and self-acceptance so profound and so foreign to him that leads him to the conclusion that the colorless liquid dripping from above and into him must certainly be morphine. Vincent has felt the effects of morphine once before, some years back, in a bitter battle concerning a traveling kidney stone. He recognizes the cool, compulsory calm of sedation.

As time passes in the wake of his newfound consciousness—but he also can't see a clock to gauge how much time—he indulges in doing what he can do with his eyes. He can fix his gaze on small specific areas. He is even able to focus, if hypnotically and narcotically, on the plastic bag and the tube and the metronomic time it seems to keep as it keeps a steady drip drip drip into his arm. Or what he hopes is still something he would recognize as his arm, anyway.

He first registers the silent drip as a simple staccato in his head, but soon it begins to suggest a more rhythmic, ostinato phrasing and, ultimately, begins to suggest a more specific musical passage, and then a specific song with a specific singer.

Not just a voice, but The Voice. It is the talented Mr. Francis Albert Sinatra, accompanied by Nelson Riddle and his band of Intravenous Solutions, gently administering solution and song:

> *I've got you / drip drip*
> *Under my skin / drip drip drip*
> *I've got you / drip drip*
> *Deep in the heart of me / drip drip drip*
> *So deep in the heart*
> *That you're really a part of me / drip drip*
> *I've got you / drip drip*
> *Under my skin / drip drip drip*

It goes like this, chorus after chorus, for the first few hours or days or however long it is that makes up that initial post-traumatic episode of his life. *Post-traumatic.* It's natural to assume that whatever happened to him must have been traumatic. The telltale trappings of hospital infirming all about him. Morphine coursing through his veins. He might also be able to assume the most traumatic part of the trauma is behind him. He is, after all, in a hospital. He has not opened his eyes and witnessed any immediate peril—like his face pressed against the white dividing lines of a highway, or the fast-approaching horns of a charging rhino. Then again, a charging rhino might help him with geography. He isn't in Africa, or at the Lincoln Park Zoo in Chicago.

Chicago. He is from Chicago, isn't he?

But even though he can presume to be from the Windy City and under a doctor's care, he doesn't know what's left of him. Because his field of vision is limited, he doesn't know if he has a neck or how much of a body he has. If he is lacking a critical body part, anything more than a fingernail, then he feels he should be in a full-blown state of trauma, rather than feel that he was safely in a post-traumatic stage.

With each drip of intravenous solution, he considers the many possible permutations.
Head, but no neck or body.
Head and neck, but no body.
Head, neck and one arm for the intravenous tube, but no legs.
Head and body, no legs.
Head and legs, no arms.
Head and arms, no neck or legs.
She loves me.
She loves me not.
She loves me.
She loves me not.

I've got you / drip drip
Under my skin / drip drip drip

As a boy, Vincent had listened to Old Blue Eyes on thick vinyl record albums played on his father's Admiral stereo. So many times, in fact, that by the time the diamond cartridge had repeatedly navigated and etched the grooves of the vinyl ten, fifteen, one hundred times, the record had its own unique sound of imperfection. This is what remains in his memory. In an era of pristine CD sound, his mind can't help but fill in the crackles and skips of his youth.

Sinatra's music had frequently been a source of comfort to Vincent. Now, an adult in his mid-thirties, the same music evokes painfully bittersweet memories. Memories that can further damage his heart. A heart that, for all he knows, might literally be damaged.

But if the song wreaks havoc with his heart, it is also a healing, meditative mantra, one that keeps his mind off nagging images of broken, dismembered, or missing parts of the rest of his body, parts that remained frustratingly just beyond his ability to see and assess.

As the tune continues in his head, he becomes aware of another repeated, rhythmic pattern, beyond the imagined staccato of the IV drip. Something else is keeping time. It is his right index finger against his right thigh. He can now confirm that he has a working, mobile index finger on his right hand and sensation in his right thigh. These are encouraging bits of self-realization.

He inches his hand just a few inches left, to find out if his genitals are there. *Important.* As he does so, he feels as though he may have bumped against something familiar, although he may have overshot and grazed his other thigh. He can't tell for sure. He lacks a scintilla of sexual arousal. But if the fish weren't jumping and the cotton wasn't so high down south, he prays things are, at least, intact.

What is that song? Summertime. Is it summertime? No. It's not. Feels like summer, though. Hottish. Where would it be hottish? He glances around again to make sure the room is free of rhinos.

Something—again, he assumes it's the morphine—is keeping panic in a thickly padded, special delivery envelope with his name on it and saving it for him for later. Sooner or later, he figures, the fluid-dripping bag must deplete itself to the point of needing new dripping fluid, and the person in charge of fluid-dripping bags will tell him what has happened to him. He can be patient. Patience is his middle name.

No, it isn't. It's Albert. Vincent Albert Cappelini. Isn't it? Yes.

For a while, what seems like a very long while, nothing happens to Vincent except, possibly, the imperceptible wearing off of morphine, and with it, the slow but steady return of some connected and associative ideas.

The next thought that occurs to Vincent is that he does not know if it is a *good* thing that he has regained consciousness. Yes, he has come to. Inherently a good thing. But come to *what*? What life is he waking up to? Could things be so bad that a coma would be preferable?

He tries to move his eyes. Not his eyelids, just his eyes. And then he feels pain. Real pain. Pain of piano wires pulled too taut. Straining. Sharp, overtuned. Not exactly screaming pain, but his mouth is already pursed to form the words "more morphine," rehearsing it, in case he needs to suddenly shout it to a distant hospital worker. He shifts his gaze to the ceiling and unfocuses his eyes and this seems to relieve some of the pressure. He can hear (both ears seem functional), but only the muffled sounds of doors opening and closing, hospital (?) carts squeaking down hallways, voices that belong to strangers. Conversations out of context and with no laughter.

When Vincent closes his eyes again, memories are on the fringes of becoming less amorphous, more sharply defined. But he's not sure he's ready for that. So, he keeps his eyes open as long as he can, until a new round of fatigue overcomes him. Occasionally, when his eyelids flutter open after he's had them closed, he expects to see "fly me to the moon" written in little black letters on a yellow Post-it note stuck on the ceiling.

There is a reason for that. This is not due to head trauma or some ocular malfunction caused by an unknown blunt force. If he had been lying on his back in his *own* bed, in his *own* apartment, he could have indeed opened his eyes and seen "fly me to the moon" affixed to his ceiling on a yellow Post-it note above his bed.

It is this specific knowledge, this lack of a *fly me to the moon* Post-it note on the ceiling that convinces him that things are happening that are out of his control. Bad things, probably, but he tended to be a glass-half-empty person, or the kind of person who feels he has been given a faulty glass to begin with. A cracked glass, or a cup without a bottom (not to be confused with a bottomless cup of coffee, which he remembers is a fine thing indeed).

He is alive and breathing on his own. *Important.* He is not in any immediate pain. He is apparently under a doctor's care. He has at least one working finger, a responsive right thigh, a sense of rhythm, and maybe his genitals.

He does not know how much of a man is left of him, however, because he can't see his genitals. *Genitali obscuri.* Why does he pseudo-Italianize that thought? *Less important*, perhaps.

What else does he remember about himself? He enjoys a

quiet, early morning diner and a bottomless cup of coffee. *What else?* He enjoys an Old Fashioned on the rocks in the evening. Is he old fashioned? He likes classic films. The Marx Brothers. Frank Capra. Preston Sturges. He likes foreign films. Particularly Bergman, Kurosawa, and Fellini. He can't remember the names of the films he likes. Probably due to the morphine.
 Wait a minute. *Wild Strawberries. 8½. Duck Soup.* It's coming back.
 He likes the outrageous jazz stylings of the late multi-reed-man Rahsaan Roland Kirk who was blind and could play three saxes at once. Crazy song titles.
 "Half a Triple." "Slippery Hippery, Flippery." "Rip, Rig, and Panic." *Okay, random, but also pretty specific.*
 He likes jazz, in general. Monk, Miles, and Coltrane, vocalists like Ella, Nat King Cole. And Sinatra, of course. He can name every album Sinatra ever recorded. He can't do this at the moment, however. Probably the morphine.
 But he knows Sinatra is *important.* Important in general, but particularly to him. *Why?*
 Melissa likes Sinatra. No, she *loves* Sinatra.
 Important, yes. But too painful. *Why?*
 Never mind. It is a new kind of painful to abruptly remember Melissa. Her face, her eyes, her smile, her hair. Her head-to-toes. Her voice. Her *everything.*
 Think of something else, quick. Don't dwell on Melissa. What else is important? The pigs? No, not the pigs. Well, yes, maybe the pigs. The sunburned pigs had somehow gotten him here, to this hospital bed.
 Pigs on a hot tin roof.

Chapter 2

(pigs on a hot tin roof)

(A few days earlier, Chicago, February, 1999. Friday morning)

Fly me to the moon.

Five little words written in black ink on a little 2x3 yellow Post-it note.

When the simple little Post-it note isn't at home with him in Chicago, Vincent travels with it. So far, the note has graced his hotel bedroom ceilings in New York, Baltimore, St. Louis, Roanoke, Salt Lake City, Washington, D.C., and New Orleans. Within 24 hours the note will be above a hotel bed somewhere in sunny San Caliente, California, the location for a seminar on skin care and sun exposure featuring keynote presentations by leading dermatologists from around the world.

Giornale della Faccia, Italy's leading dermatology journal, has hired Vincent as a freelance writer to cover the event. All he has to do is write it in English—they translate it into Italian for their journal. And although Vincent can read very little Italian, he likes seeing his stories printed in a Romance language. He likes to think they are somehow better in Italian. He fondly recalls the first time he saw *verruche genitali* in an article he'd written. How sweet the sound. Much more lyrical—and far less menacing—than *genital warts.*

Vincent has, until recently, spent several years as a medical writer and editor at *Skinformation, the Skin Monthly*, a well-respected, nationally known medical journal for dermatologists, based out of Chicago.

Although *Skinformation, Giornale della Faccia, In Your Face, The Wart Report*, and similar niche-market medical magazines have no real readership beyond the confines of a dermatologist's overcrowded inbox, Vincent writes in-depth articles that are informative, accurate, and appreciated by his physician audience. And while he is not a well-known journalist in the larger world, he is, in the world of dermatology reportage—a world of rashes, alopecia, contact dermatitis, and the like—Vincent A. Cappelini's byline has become familiar and well-respected.

Vincent had steadily earned the respect of his boss, the editor-in-chief at *Skinformation*, a silver-haired, perpetually frowning dermatologist, Professor Donald Reeves. Dr. Reeves had his own personal skin condition—rosacea, which gave him an unfortunate, slightly bulbous, W.C. Fields nose, and cheeks like Bing cherries. But no one on staff ever spoke of his condition. Not while Vincent had worked there.

Vincent's abrupt departure from *Skinformation* came in the wake of a run-of-the-mill assignment from Dr. Reeves: go to Roanoke and cover a conference on sun exposure. The drill is familiar and simple. He attends seminars across the country, tapes the lectures on micro-cassettes, takes notes. Back at his keyboard in his cube, he could easily knock out a draft and fill out his story with what senior editors and well-meaning journalism teachers call "quotable quotes."

"Make sure you get quotable quotes," was the sole directive he'd received from Dr. Reeves about his Roanoke assignment. Vincent could be relied on to take care of the rest.

When Vincent returns from the Roanoke conference, he writes a good, comprehensive article about the seminar and about the dangers of sun exposure. He peppers the story with quotable quotes. All that is left to do is to embellish it with an interesting photo and caption.

During one of the lectures in Roanoke, one of the dermatologists had projected a slide that had caught Vincent's eye. In the aftermath of a flood in rural Iowa, several pigs from a hog farm (referred to as a "swine finishing facility") had found themselves stranded on the roof of a tin barn.

It may have been a question of priorities in a state of emergency, saving people before pigs, or it may have been that the pigs were simply unreachable. In any case, the pigs met their fate roasting on a hot metal roof under an August sun in Iowa with temperatures well above 90 degrees. These are hogs scheduled for slaughter, so a long, happy lifetime was never in the cards for them. But since they died a *slow death* from the heat, their plight was viewed—by the audience of dermatologists in Roanoke, anyway—as tragic. A photo projected on a screen at the seminar had captured the dead pigs, their shining pink hides glowing crimson under a bright sun.

Pigskin is tougher than human skin, Vincent learned, which is why they use it for footballs. Not that it's ever a choice, or something that's been tested—human skin has never been considered an option for footballs as far as he knew. The point, according to the venerable old dermatologist giving the presentation, was to graphically illustrate the intensity of the sun's harmful rays against the toughest of barriers.

"If the sun can do this to pigskin, imagine what it can do to human skin," the lecturer had said. A quotable quote if Vincent ever heard one.

The photo of the pigs is, Vincent thinks, just the sort of "wow" graphic that will complement his article.

To obtain a high-resolution copy of the photo, Vincent tracks down the dermatologist who gave the presentation in Roanoke and is put in contact with Dr. Barbara Borden. Dr. Borden was either a dermatologist from Iowa who specialized in veterinary medicine, or a veterinarian from Iowa who specialized in dermatology. Vincent was never sure which. She was from Iowa and had taken the photo of the pigs—that's all he knew.

After Vincent tracks down Dr. Borden and writes to her, she seems delighted and flattered and Fed-Exes a high quality copy of the photo of the sunburned pigs with a letter giving her blessings to use it. But there are two photos enclosed. One is of the pigs. The other is of Dr. Borden.

The photo of Dr. Borden is not a professional photo. Not a traditional professional physician's photo, a doctor in a white lab coat. Instead, she's sent him a glossy, 5x7 glamor shot. Something he imagines women might take to titillate and impress others—like a boyfriend, husband, or lover—or themselves. Very big hair. It surrounds her face and takes off in various directions. Hair that is neither red nor blond, but something created out of a bottle, and unnaturally orange, like the color of sharp cheddar. She is half-clad in a strappy, low-cut black dress (or slip?) that draws unwelcome attention to her breasts, so unnaturally and perfectly round they might be mistaken for a pair of bocce balls tethered to her chest. She also goes industrial strength on her rouge and lipstick. *Very smooth* skin. No expression. Nothing coy or haughty. No suggestively raised eyebrows, no seductive curl of a come-hither smile. He detects the telltale signs of too much Botox. It may confirm she's a dermatologist, then again, it may confirm she's a veterinarian in need of a better dermatologist.

A quick, casual glance at the photo might have given the average Joe the impression that Dr. Borden was sexy or attractive. Vincent, on the other hand, thought it all in extremely poor taste. What reaction was she hoping to elicit by sending this lurid photo to him?

"Whoa, what a juicy peach!" says a voice over Vincent's shoulder.

Giving the photo a once or twice over is Mitchell George Wallace. Mitch was Vincent's coworker at *Skinformation*, a fellow reporter and journalist, originally from Mobile, Alabama. Mitch sat in a neighboring cubicle and had a penchant for playing "Under Pressure" by Queen a little too loudly and a little too often. But apart from that, and apart from being a crude, if inept womanizer, Mitch wasn't a bad coworker to have.

Vincent never struggled too hard to crank out an article. But Mitch did, and Vincent was often called upon—often secretly at Dr. Reeves' request—to edit and sometimes rewrite Mitch's work. Mitch didn't really have a way with words, yet he never seemed at a loss for them.

"Babe-a-licious. Definitely."

"Really? You think she's pretty?" Vincent asks, turning the photo of Dr. Borden at different angles and squinting at it.

"Pretty? Give me one hour with her in a vat of olive oil and I'll squeeze the extra virgin out of her."

"Wow. Mitch. Cool it. She's a doctor."

"She isn't *my* doctor. Not that I wouldn't mind lowering my trousers for her."

"She's a dermatologist. Or she may be a veterinarian."

"Fine. I'll get on all fours for her and have a distemper tantrum."

"I don't see it," Vincent says, shaking his head. "Anyway, it doesn't matter, I can't use her photo."

"I can think of some uses for it," Mitch says, snatching the photo out of Vincent's hand.

For the remainder of the day, Mitch seems intent on proving Vincent is wrong about Dr. Borden. He acquires opinions from the male staff members of *Skinformation*. According to Mitch, all the men in sales, marketing, finance, graphics, and production all agree. Dr. Borden was *smokin' hot*. Maybe even *perfect*. Mitch tells Vincent that Dr. Reeves found the woman "unbelievable," though Vincent suspects Mitch has misinterpreted the adjective.

"I just don't see it," Vincent says, each time Mitch comes back around with the photo and his leering grin. "And it doesn't matter, anyway."

But the provocative photo has an oddly unsettling effect on Vincent. If the photo had been sent to impress him, or perhaps even titillate or allure him, it had missed the mark. So, there was that. But it also bothers Vincent that Mitch has amassed a none-too-scientific consensus that Dr. Borden is the embodiment of female beauty. He knows it to be otherwise. There is only one perfect woman in the world, and that woman would always be and could only be Melissa.

And although Melissa is not a current fixture in Vincent's life, he feels his experience with perfection qualifies him to make ultimate determinations about beauty. He feels compelled to defend it, in fact. It bothers Vincent that most men (albeit most men in his workplace) seem to idealize and prefer this magazine centerfold, plastic, manufactured idol kind of beauty.

"You're saying this woman is more perfect than Melissa?" he asks Mitch.

"Geez, Vince. What kind of question is that?"

Mitch backs off, tosses the photo of Dr. Borden on Vincent's desk and doesn't bring it up again.

Later, when it comes time for Vincent to write the caption for the photo of the sunburned pigs that Dr. Borden has provided, the metaphor of bacon on a frying pan leaps to the forefront of Vincent's mind. But he avoids this, knowing it's over the top and would be frowned on by the ever-frowning Dr. Reeves. Instead, he writes the simple caption "Pigs on a hot tin roof." A play on words with an assist from Tennessee Williams.

When Vincent is questioned about the slightly glib caption, he defends it on the grounds that it is an absolutely accurate, thoroughly literal description. As he explains to Dr. Reeves, the roof is tin, the tin is hot, the pigs are on it. Dr. Reeves lets it go, and the story runs as the lead in the next edition of *Skinformation* with Vincent's byline.

When it is published and Dr. Borden sees it, however, she apparently overlooks the content of the story, zeroes in on her pig photo and Vincent's caption, and takes umbrage. She writes directly to Vincent, in care of the magazine:

> Dear Mr. Cappelini,
>
> I am writing about an article you wrote which included the photo I allowed you use. The caption that ran with the photo was "pigs on a hot tin roof." My understanding was that you would not use this photo as a means to resort to a cheap laugh at the expense of the victims (the pigs). This was a tragic event and an important photo, and you have denigrated its integrity and mine along with it.
>
> Dr. Barbara Borden

Oddly, accompanying the letter is another racy photo of herself. It's similar to the first one. A little more cleavage, perhaps. Does she believe, in some oddly twisted way, that a second seductive photo will somehow underscore her credibility and bolster her argument?

Vincent's first reaction is to laugh it off. But, much to his chagrin, he notes that Dr. Reeves has been *copied* on the letter. After the inevitable summons to his superior's office, Dr. Reeves agrees that Dr. Borden has overreacted, but tells Vincent he is obligated to formulate a polite, considerate response.

The next morning, undertaking what he considers an inane task and a waste of his time, Vincent writes a polite and considerate response:

> Dear Dr. Borden,
>
> Thank you for taking the time to write to me about my recent article. It was not my intention to go for a cheap laugh or make light of the situation. I believed "Pigs on a Hot Tin Roof" was the appropriate caption for the photo, because the pigs were on a hot tin roof. I apologize, however, for any misunderstanding. I'm also very sorry about the pigs. I hope you will continue to read *Skinformation*.
>
> Sincerely,
>
> Vincent A. Cappelini

That might have done the job just fine, but after finishing the letter, Vincent thinks about the photo again. Not the photo of the pigs, but the latest cheesecake, cheese-haired photo of Dr. Borden. From his file drawer he retrieves her first photo—the one that Mitch and his male co-workers had fawned over. He places it next to her latest photo on his desk. Together the two photos side-by-side on his desk make him feel like he is preparing a spread for *Penthouse*. He feels that by sending him multiple R-rated photos of herself, Dr. Borden is *inviting* commentary. He begins typing again:

> PS: Putting aside the photo of the pigs for a moment, I'd like to address the other photos you sent, the ones of yourself. I'm struggling to understand why you sent them. Was it meant to impress me? I must tell you; I prefer natural beauty without an excess of lipstick and heavy make-up. I can't help but notice you're not smiling in the photo—was that a choice, or a physical impossibility caused by the preponderance of botulinum toxin injections to your maxilla area? Personally, I prefer a face that has the ability to show more than one emotion. Sad, happy, bemused, loving, silly, compassionate. I prefer natural breasts that don't remind me of Italian lawn bowling balls. And what's up with that orange hair? Even Halloween would not be an acceptable excuse for this appearance. I realize I may be in the minority and that many men find these traits appealing. I, however, am not one of them. In short, I concede you have a keen eye for pigs in distress, but not for things of beauty.
>
> Sincerely,
> Vincent A. Cappellini

It's mean-spirited and he knows it. Vincent doesn't like to be mean. Doesn't like this side of himself. He doesn't have anything against Dr. Borden, really. At one time he might have even seen, superficially, what other men saw in her photos. Before Melissa, that is. But as he writes down his thoughts, Vincent is thinking of Melissa and how Dr. Borden is the archetypal *anti-Melissa*. While semi-subconsciously articulating what he longs for in Melissa, he deconstructs what he believes are shortcomings in Dr. Borden. These vitriolic, personal observations find their way into his postscript in a pique of Vincent's sense of loss and frustration. He knows he should delete the post-scripted material before printing and mailing the letter.

But he doesn't.

Vincent is bypassed in the next stream of communication. He learns that Dr. Borden has called Dr. Reeves directly and faxed a copy of Vincent's unedited letter. Dr. Borden is now demanding a fate for him normally reserved for slaughtered pigs.

"Dr. Borden wants your hide," Dr. Reeves says, his frown so deep that Vincent thinks his forehead might cave in. His W. C. Fields nose seems about to explode on his face. "That's what she said. Your *hide*. She's been making all sorts of threats against the magazine and against you. She's aiming to make things very messy. The magazine has a reputation to uphold. You know that, Vincent."

"Am I being fired?"

"You think I *want* to fire you? You're my best reporter. It's ridiculous. But it seems to me you wouldn't have done this without wanting to get fired. Is that the case here?"

Vincent knows the answer. In an uncharacteristically reckless moment, he had allowed Dr. Borden to become the target of his own self-sabotaging behavior—something that Vincent had mastered in the wake of losing his precious Melissa.

While Melissa is running errands on a Saturday afternoon, Vincent is upstairs in the giant Tower Records on Clark, flipping through the latest releases in the jazz room.

Melissa seemingly appears out of nowhere. She is in the jazz room with him, standing next to a large poster recreation of Sinatra's Capitol album *Songs for Young Lovers*.

She approaches him and wraps him up inside her open, fur-hooded parka. She gives him the kind of tight, nestling hug that you give someone you won't be seeing again for a very long time. A big, down-filled security blanket kind of hug. She always does this with him.

"I thought you were out somewhere, getting 'everything' bagels today."

"*You* are my everything bagel, silly," she says.

So corny. But also, *so perfect*.

By the time the Dr. Borden pig scandal breaks, Vincent has not seen Melissa in more than a year. The last time was when she was walking out the door of his apartment, catching a taxi to O'Hare to board a flight to San Caliente, a coastal town in Southern California, to pursue a job opportunity in graphic arts. It isn't as simple as all that. There's more to it. It's ridiculously complicated. But the end result is the same. She's gone.

After getting fired from *Skinformation*, Vincent starts freelancing. He works from his apartment, freelancing for small foreign dermatology publications like *Giornale della Faccia*, and its German sister publication, *Gesicht*. These medical journals are always eager to have an experienced American dermatology journalist at their service. They don't know or don't care whether or not he is responsible for enraging a doctor over a pig photo. Dr. Reeves occasionally uses Vincent as a freelancer, but only when he is in a pinch, and always with a fake byline attached. Or no byline. Vincent no longer writes his own photo captions.

Freelancing is not, however, a secure, lucrative, or long-term gig for Vincent. His bank account is hemorrhaging fast. Grateful to be free of a nine-to-five job, one that opens a new window of freedom and availability, he lacks the financial means that will allow him to book a flight to the West Coast, let alone move to San Caliente and try to find Melissa.

And while freelancing gives him more time, it unfortunately leaves him with more time to think about Melissa. His apartment is replete with traces of her. Reminders of her are everywhere. Though he can barely take the emotional pain of discovering, say, one of her long golden hair follicles mixed with his own black medium length hairs in his hairbrush, he does nothing to remove these reminders. He keeps the most poignant reminder of Melissa taped to the ceiling above his bed.

Chapter 3

(fly me to the moon)

In November, 1966, John Lennon was invited by his friend, John Dunbar, to an exhibit at Dunbar's Indica Gallery in London. On display at the gallery was a conceptual-art show called *Unfinished Paintings and Objects*. The artist was a rather slight 33-year-old Japanese woman famous for pushing the far edges of art. Not an adherent of the traditional canvas and paint school, her art included things like transparent homes, imaginary music, and "underwear to make you high."

In a similarly avant-garde and imaginative vein, the artist invited visitors attending her London gallery show to climb a white ladder. At the top they would find a magnifying glass, attached by a chain, hanging from a picture frame on the ceiling. The viewer was compelled to use the magnifying glass to read a block-letter "instruction" beneath the framed sheet of glass. Lennon gamely climbed the white ladder that chilly November day, and saw the tiny, unexpected word. It said "yes."

Lennon would later report to the rock journalists and talk show hosts that if the message had been "rip off" or "up yours," he would have dismissed the art show and the artist. But it was the small, simple, positive message that impressed him. And it was under these circumstances that John Lennon met and fell in love with Yoko Ono.

They soon became John&Yoko. She went with him everywhere. Their inseparability was so intense that some would claim it caused a rift in the creative collaboration of *the* most popular and successful rock band of all time. But if one is going to make the argument that Yoko broke up the Beatles, one also has to acknowledge that it must have been one *hell* of a love to draw Lennon's attention away from the golden goose of rock music.

It is Melissa who tells Vincent the John Lennon story, and she's the one who decides to put a Sinatra spin on it. Melissa uses Vincent's fine-point Sharpie and writes the words "fly me to the moon" in small black letters on a Post-it note and affixes it to a spot on the ceiling directly above the bed in Vincent's Chicago apartment.

He discovers the note when he returns from a business trip in Baltimore.

The word hangs over them every time they make love. Sometimes, the *fly me to the moon* on the ceiling is obscured by Melissa's head and long hair as she sways ecstatically and moves herself slowly and rhythmically astride him. But even when he can't see the Post-it note, he is ever aware of—and reassured by—its presence. And, small as the Post-it note is, Vincent believes it protects their love, like a little private umbrella for two, from all the bad things that could ever happen to a couple.

After Melissa is gone, Vincent keeps the Post-it note on his ceiling, very sure—at first—that she will return to him. Months later, even as his confidence in the matter—and the adhesive on the Post-it note—begins to weaken, he keeps the note up on his ceiling. When the adhesive gives up, Vincent uses Scotch tape. Whatever it takes. The idea of taking down *fly me to the moon* seems an act of negativity so profound Vincent is convinced it could only ensure Melissa will never come back to him. Never call. Never send a postcard from California.

Vincent goes into a rapid tailspin without Melissa. Unlike Lennon in his "lost weekend" period, Vincent doesn't have the likes of Harry Nillsson, Ringo, and Elton John to hang out with and drink and carouse and play pool and behave like bad boys with until Melissa reappears. Unlike Sinatra, Vincent has no reliable Rat Pack pals, no Dean or Sammy, or even a Joey Bishop or Peter Lawford to help him drink whiskey highballs, throw craps, and debauch away his lonely nights.

Vincent's lost weekend is now in its thirteenth month.

Chapter 4

(monosexuality)

When Vincent finds out there is a dermatology conference happening in San Caliente, he's quite sure fate is knocking—make that *pounding furiously*—on his door and he immediately lobbies hard to score a freelance gig to attend it and cover it. It isn't easy. *Gesicht* turns him down flat. *Nein*. Too expensive to send a freelancer, they say. He reaches out to Dr. Reeves at *Skinformation*. Dr. Reeves is sympathetic, but says he already has someone assigned to the job. After several pleading entreaties, the editor of *Giornale della Faccia* relents, but only after Vincent makes a personal, long-distance call to Milan, stretches the truth a tad, and says that *Skinformation* plans to have *several* reporters there because it is such an important dermatology seminar.

"*Tutti devono partecipare! Evento molto grande!*" Vincent utters, raising his voice as effusively as he can while hoping not to sound as desperate as he feels. It works. A week later, he has a Trans-Lux Airline ticket in his hand.

One final detail looms large, however. Although *fly me to the moon* has become nothing short of a mantra for Vincent, *actually* flying—that is, getting on a plane and becoming airborne—scares him half to death.

The night before his trip to San Caliente, Vincent is on his bed in his apartment, looking up at Melissa's Post-it note on his ceiling, trying not to think about airports, flying, and 30,000 feet of nothingness under him. This prompts him to get off his bed and make sure he's packed his Xanax in his carry-on. He returns to his bed to look at the ceiling again and tries to think about *other* things.

Whenever Vincent tries to think about *other things*, he invariably indulges in myopic, self-indulgent reveries about his monosexuality. *Monosexual* is a moniker Vincent coined to describe himself when no other word seemed adequate. Demisexual, a sexual orientation in which a person feels sexually attracted to someone only after they've developed a close emotional bond with them, came close. But he doesn't care much for the word demisexual. He thinks it lacks a certain intensity, devotion, and sense of purpose.

Monosexuality is Vincent's self-appointed, glittering, gold badge of honor. A rare, eclectic, yet-to-be-discovered phenomenon that makes him special, makes Melissa special. Makes being *with* Melissa *extra special.*

He walks into the living room in his apartment and finds Melissa sitting cross-legged and barefoot on a zafu, a small, firm, plum-colored pillow used for sitting meditation. Golden hair in a tight ponytail. His Koss headphones are hugging her ears. She is plugged into his vintage Sansui stereo. Her eyes are open, and she smiles when she sees him, but her brow is wrinkled.

"What's up?" He increases his volume a bit to make sure she can hear him over the headphones.

"Something's not right," she says. "Sounds tinny, or just… wrong or something."

He tenderly removes the headphones from Melissa's head and places them over his own ears. *Sinatra at the Sands.* Track three. His own brow wrinkles. Something is indeed wrong. He follows the black spiral headphone cord to the output jack on the

Sansui. He sees that it is about an eighth of an inch shy of being plugged all the way in. He holds the plug between his thumb and forefinger, gives it a little push and it moves inside until it is snugly inserted inside the stereo input jack. Then he puts the headphones back over Melissa's ears.

"Now listen," he says.

Her eyes widen. He watches her face light up and her body reacts. He knows she is now experiencing the full ecstatic sound of Sinatra, with Quincy Jones' sweet, lush arrangements and Count Basie and his entire orchestra. All the horns. The throbbing bass, the crispness of the cymbals. All of it in full high-flying fidelity.

"It's amazing," she says. But just as quickly her astonished face melts and he sees tears forming in the corners of her eyes.

"What's the matter?"

"This is what it's like," she says, nodding her head. She straightens her posture on the cushion of the zafu as if the satori of enlightenment has just shot straight up her spine.

"What?"

"Being with you," she says. "It's like I've been experiencing life in mono, and now it's in stereo."

"Let me play it for you again, from the beginning," he says.

He resets the CD to the beginning of track 3. Then he picks Melissa up off the plum-colored zafu and leads her to his brown leather sofa. There, he gives it a little push and it moves inside until it is snugly inserted inside.

She keeps the headphones on the entire time.

In order to get to a place mentally that will allow him to board a plane, Vincent relies on a combination of Xanax, a temporary belief in a white-bearded God, and the support of his pilot friend Glenn Buck.

Glenn is not a monosexual, but a monogamous adult, and Vincent likes that about him. He's known Glenn since high school. Glenn went into the Air Force right after graduation,

Vincent stayed in Chicago, carving out a future in journalism. But Vincent received regular monthly letters from Glenn, postmarked from air force bases in Arizona, New Mexico, and overseas in Bitburg, Germany.

Glenn eventually becomes a commercial pilot and gets involved with several women who like to date pilots. Women tend to be attracted to pilots, rather than, say, *writers*, Vincent observes. But—after all Glenn's wild oats are sown, as if a time-to-mature timer has gone off within his libido, Glenn comes back home to Chicago, meets and marries Cookie, a petite, perky blonde who worked the men's fragrance counter at Nordstrom's and… *that's that*. Cookie was the next—but the *last*—in a long line of women in Glenn's life.

Glenn and Cookie often try to get Vincent over for home-cooked meals. He knows it's partly out of pity—because of what they know about Melissa being gone. But Cookie also makes an excellent bucatini carbonara. Hard for Vincent to resist.

Vincent can see that Glenn loves Cookie. He seems unlikely to cheat on her. But—like many other men—like Vincent before he became a monosexual—Glenn has retained the wandering eye of his Air Force days. Glenn is not above, for example, accessing the After Hours XXX-rated cable channel when Cookie is out of town (as Glenn confesses to him), nor is he immune from giving an involuntary grunt of approval when hair-flipping cheerleader posteriors are shaken on the sidelines in close-up during a Bears game on television. This is all to say, Glenn is a typical male. Glenn will look, but Vincent knows Glenn won't stray.

And that's fine for Glenn, Vincent thinks, even if it doesn't approach the majestic enormity of Vincent's monolithic monosexuality. A monosexual doesn't suffer from a wandering eye because… there's nothing to look at. It's well beyond an apples and oranges comparison. There's no one that *compares* to Melissa, no woman that ever could. So, there is no woman to make Vincent think twice, or even once. Looking and leering is for the common man. Not him.

Vincent exists in a self-defined, separate-from-all, romantic love exosphere, orbiting far above all those men who *thought* they knew what real love was. Somewhere near Jupiter or Mars, perhaps.

Fly me to the moon…

Monosexuality arrives in Vincent's life as a great cosmic remedy. It is the big, *oh, now I get it!* moment. Soulmate? Sure, but *way* beyond that. Something perhaps only animals mated for life would understand. Wolves and elephants, maybe.

And Melissa. She understood it all at some point. Or at least he thinks she did. Or hoped she did. When they first start dating, she expresses great admiration for his *concept* of monosexuality. She loves that he's come up with a special term to describe his devotion to her. She delights Vincent by saying things a monosexual would say. Like that time after they made love and she said:

Now I know what all the fuss is about.

And because Melissa is so romantically reciprocal, it's not a stretch to believe that she too is monosexual. It seems a logical conclusion. Vincent would have liked for it to be true. If they both felt *exactly* the same way—and more often than not, they did—they would be *mono e mono* and add up to *stereo* and have something Vincent might have liked to call, and probably would have called: *stereosexual* (again, so corny, but so perfect).

But—he never got to use this new name.

In the immediate wake of her absence, and long after that, Vincent found the whole business of sex and love—hearing about it, knowing about it, talking about it—extraordinarily painful. Now that he knows that a completeness of sexuality and two hearts beating as one can *actually exist*, the absence was intolerable. How or why would *anyone* ever let go of that once they had it? He can't fathom such a thing.

He's been living in a state of semi-denial for more than a year, hoping for several equally improbable things to happen. One is that Melissa simply returns. Unannounced, she is standing there in his doorway, just like the way she abruptly appeared in Tower Records. It's happened before, no reason it can't happen again. The other option: carry on without her. He's still banking on the first option. The second is impossible to consider.

But now there is a third option. Find her and get her back. He's waited 13 months. Not without good reason. Fear of flying may have been the least of it.

Vincent stares at the ceiling and tries to remember the name of everyone in Count Basie's orchestra. He'd done this before, partly to relieve stress, and partly to indulge it, in the wake of Melissa's absence. So he intoned the names: *Harry "Sweets" Edison, Al Aarons, Sonny Cohn, Wallace Davenport, Phil Guilbeau, Al Grey, Henderson Chambers, Grover Mitchell, Bill Hughes, Marshall Royal, Bobby Plater, Eric Dixon, Eddie "Lockjaw" Davis, Charlie Fowlkes, Freddie Green, Norman Keenan,* and *Sonny Payne* on drums.

This is what Vincent thinks about, lying in his bed, the night before he leaves for San Caliente, with *fly me to the moon* securely over his head. Ruminating about his monosexuality, naming everyone in Count Basie's band, packing Xanax—all of it is easier than thinking about flying.

Chapter 5

(the Bernoulli principle)

"Let's go over it one more time."

"Lift," Glenn says. "It all has to do with lift."

Vincent's friend, Captain Glenn Buck, senior flight officer of Trans-Lux Airlines, sits across from him in a dark corner of an early morning airport bar at O'Hare. Glenn isn't drinking. The FAA requires pilots to have, at minimum, an eight-hour window of sobriety before they get into the cockpit. Vincent is under no such regulations and is absently working a celery stalk around the interior of his second (or third?) Bloody Mary.

Glenn is doing Vincent a favor this morning. Not unusual. As longtime friends they did each other favors all the time. Vincent helped Glenn move his refrigerator up a flight of stairs to a new kitchen on one of the hottest days of the summer. And Glenn had helped move Vincent's brown leather couch to three different small apartments in Chicago over the years.

Today's favor is more on the intellectual and emotional side. Glenn, the experienced aviator, the ace of air buses, is explaining to Vincent the laws of physics regarding flight. It's not the first time.

Vincent is being reminded about the physical laws that keep planes in the air by a person whom he knows and trusts—and by someone who flies airplanes for a living. Glenn has successfully kept aloft and landed an array of aircraft, from F-15 fighters and bombers in the US Air Force to his latest job with Trans-Lux, flying commercial jets.

Vincent is keenly aware of Glenn's average work week—three days on, three days off. Which means that Glenn spends practically *half his life* in the air, a fact that astonishes Vincent. Glenn has spent more time in the air than Vincent has ever spent writing articles about blistering papules. If Glenn can reasonably assure Vincent it is okay to fly, it goes a long way.

It also helps that Glenn is dressed in his Trans-Lux uniform when he explains these scientific concepts. Something about the dark blue uniform and the captain's bars and the matching blue cap adds to the gravitas of what he tells Vincent about air travel.

It sometimes goes even further. Glenn's urban hubs sometimes coincide with Vincent's freelance assignment destinations; so, whenever possible, Vincent will arrange his schedule around Glenn's to ensure that Glenn can personally pilot him to his locale. A lot of the time Vincent flies standby on flights with Glenn. This started shortly after Melissa had left him, after he'd become a freelancer. He now often only takes the out-of-town jobs that paid enough to make it worthwhile and those that, furthermore, agree with Glenn's schedule.

The first time Vincent asked Glenn to do this, it was for a flight to Washington, D.C. Glenn had routes to D.C. that month and seemed delighted to do it. He appeared to like the idea of showing someone like Vincent, firsthand, what he did for a living, and so he arranged his schedule accordingly.

But on this occasion, just before Vincent's crucial, can't-miss, ultra-high-priority date with destiny in San Caliente, Glenn had been reticent, saying his schedule was filled with mostly eastbound flights.

Determined and undeterred, Vincent had gone directly to Glenn's house, pounded on his door, and then pressed him hard to accommodate. He avoided saying anything about Melissa.

"The thing is, I really need the money," Vincent said. "I really need to take this job. It's a huge dermatology conference."

"San Caliente? Really? It's nice but it's mostly a tourist town."

"No, this is big. The editor of the Italian dermatology journal called it *"evento molto grande!"* Vincent said, recycling his own made-up quotable quote.

"Vince, you know I don't mind flying you... but..."

"This is serious, Glenn. Are you going to help me with this, or not?"

Sitting in the Trans-Lux bar, Glenn expresses his surprise that Vincent wants to hear the entire physics discussion again; all the details about drag and lift, and arc and winds.

Vincent has most of this memorized and even has some of it transcribed into his journalist's notebook. But Glenn patiently repeats it for him. Bits and pieces come back to Vincent as Glenn explains it.

"Lift," Vincent says.

"That's right. Tell me again about... who's the guy? Bernstein."

"Bernoulli," Glenn says. "Daniel Bernoulli. In the 18th Century..."

"Bernoulli. Right. The Bernoulli Principle. Which states..."

"... which states that if air speeds up, the pressure is lowered. It relates to the shape of the wing."

"The wing, yes, because the air..."

"... because the air over the top has a farther distance to travel than the air underneath, its relative pressure is less. Similar to how water always runs downhill. The wing will move towards the least pressure. In this case, up."

"I thought water ran downhill because of gravity," Vincent says.

"Well, there's gravity, too. But in this case gravity keeps you up." Glenn pauses, then adds, "Of course, that's not always true."

"No, don't tell me it's not always true. That's not helpful."

"You've just got me thinking..."

"Well, think on your own time. This is my time."

"You see," Glenn says, "because air has to travel farther over the top wing, it must go faster. But if that were strictly true, planes couldn't travel upside down. Which, of course, they can."

"But planes don't fly commuters upside down to California."

"Not intentionally, no."

"Not *intentionally*? Jesus. Let's just stick with the basics. About why plane wings are shaped like they are."

"The principle of equal transit times?"

"No, don't go all that technical and mathematical jazz. That means nothing to me. Stick with simple."

"The faster the plane goes, more air flows above and below the wing. But the shape of the wing varies the air pressure above and below it. So, you get this difference in air pressure getting greater and greater, and once the lift force is more than the weight of the airplane—bingo. You're airborne. It's actually a very simple law of physics."

Vincent nods, like he understands. He doesn't really. But— it's okay. If he doesn't understand it exactly, the words still matter. Like the recitation of a prayer or a mantra. He sips on his Bloody Mary again.

"So… San Caliente…?" Glenn says.

"It's another conference on skin and sun protection. This symposium is called ICARUS. 'I Care About the Ravages Under the Sun.'" Vincent emphasizes the first letters of the keywords.

"Not sure I get it," Glenn says.

"Icarus. You know about Icarus."

"Flies too close to the sun. Bad things happen…"

"Right. Do you know about Daedalus?"

"No."

"Daedalus was Icarus's dad. He was—you may find this interesting—he was the one who had the original idea about flying. He invented the way for Icarus to fly, so that they could escape from the Labyrinth. Which he also built. For King Minos."

"Daedalus invented a means of flying?"

"Well, you know, only in a classic Greek mythology kind of

way," Vincent says. "I doubt any of this would have come up in your flight training. But in ancient times, within his own circle, Daedalus was considered a talented architect and engineer. The thing is, what Daedalus invented for flying didn't turn out well."

"No?"

"No, because he made the wings out of feathers and wax. Then he told Icarcus, his son, not to fly too low, because the water would weigh down his wings, but not too high, because of the sun."

"I have to tell you, that's a terribly inferior structural design," Glenn says. "But good advice, all things considered."

"Right, but Icarus forgot or ignored his father's advice. He flew too close to the sun. The wings melted and he plummeted back to earth. Fell into the ocean and drowned."

"Jesus."

"Well, you know. It's Greek, so you expect it to be tragic. But I think it's just a story about knowledge and power. You know, reaching too far beyond limitations, messing with nature."

Glenn thinks about this a moment, then shakes his head.

"I don't think that's the message," Glenn says. "It sounds like Daedalus had all the specs right, and Icarus ignored standard operating procedure. Of course Icarus died. If I came in low over the Great Lakes, I'd risk a water landing, too. We keep a cruising altitude of about 36,000 feet for a reason. And forget about the sun, you get past the stratosphere and into the exosphere and you're dealing with all sorts of adverse atmospheric changes. Outer space starts somewhere upwards of 400 miles high."

Vincent is listening, but words like *exosphere* and *outer space* distract him. *Jupiter and Mars.*

fly me to the moon...

"You get to an altitude where you risk severe stress to the structure of the aircraft," Glenn says. "What's Icarus thinking, flying near the sun?"

"Well, it's just mythology," Vincent says, trying to rein the conversation back in.

"Still. That's beyond pilot error; that's just plain stupid. And after his dad warned him. Nothing too high and nothing too low. There are good reasons for that. Did you know most of your migratory birds are migrating under 10,000 feet? And some Asian geese have been known to get up to 29,000 feet. You have to know what you can run into."

"Great, there's a new fear. Asian geese at 29,000 feet."

"We're not running into any geese," Glenn says. "That's why we're flying at 30,000 feet. To avoid all that."

"This Icarus story... it's just a story." Vincent says.

"No, I get that. It's just that Daedalus anticipated the hazards and issued the proper safety regulations and Icarus chose to ignore them. Don't blame the airline or the manufacturer because Icarus didn't follow the specs."

"Right," Vincent says, giving up. "The only reason I brought it up is because I feel like I'm tempting fate here *flying* to an event named after a person that flew and crashed into the ocean."

"I get that," Glenn says, "but we're not going to fly low enough to dip our wings in water or high enough to melt. You understand that, right? You know I'd never do that."

"Of course."

"And that's the whole story?"

"About Icarus?"

"No, about you. About San Caliente. I know you don't want to talk about it, but I feel sure this has something to do with Melissa."

Vincent knows that Glenn knows just about everything there is to know about Melissa. Knows she went to San Caliente and didn't come back. They rarely speak about it. Vincent rarely gives Glenn an opportunity to pursue discussions about Melissa.

"I told you, it's about the job. I need the job," Vincent says. "Freelancing is spotty. Good assignments are hard to come by."

"Look, I'm happy to fly you. I'm even happy enough to

request these routes in advance. I'm just concerned that we're not talking about what's really going on inside you."

"The only thing I'd like going on inside me is another Bloody Mary," Vincent says. "Look, this is on the level. I'm writing for an Italian skin disease journal, for Christ's sake. My article will probably be read by three dermatologists in a rowboat in Gorgana. But it pays my rent."

"Gorgana?"

"It's a small island off Tuscany."

"Dermatologists in rowboats...?"

"No, no, I'm just saying..."

Glenn backs off. "Okay. Fine. Will you be able to get out of the seminar and check out San Caliente?"

"Doubtful. I'm only there for a couple of days. When I'm not at the conference itself, I'll probably be holed up in my hotel room, typing up my notes. That's usually how these things go."

"You should spend more time with people, Vince."

"What are you saying? There's a ton of people coming to this thing. Dermatologists from all over."

"You know what I mean."

"Yes, I *do* know what you mean. And I'm telling you it's not necessary."

Glenn runs a finger over his brow, pushing his captain's hat up a little.

"I just want you to know, if there's anything I can do... Cookie and I... we both just want the best for you."

Vincent figures Cookie has probably put Glenn up to at least part of this. Especially the checking-in-with-him-about-his-feelings part. Glenn is a reliable friend, and they have pleasantly aimless conversations. But heartfelt talks are not Glenn's forte.

Still, he's glad to be reminded of Cookie. Beyond the concept of lift and the laws of gravity, Vincent likes the reassuring, stabilizing force that seems inherent in Glenn's domestic life. As cruel as life can be, Vincent doesn't believe fate would interrupt the life Glenn had with Cookie and the boys.

So, Vincent reasons, if he is on a plane with Glenn, he will remain safe from high winds, Asian geese, and other unforeseen disasters. Glenn always survives it, and being on Glenn's plane, Vincent trusts he will be a supernumerary survivor. He relied on Glenn as his friend, personal airborne chauffeur, and lucky rabbit's foot.

Glenn clasps his hands around the back of his neck, returns his cap to a professional forward tilt and leans back in his chair, seemingly wrapped up in his own thoughts. Then he leans into Vincent.

"Here's a thought. Did you ever think maybe you are like Icarus?"

"How so?"

"I don't know," Glenn says. "Extremes, maybe?"

"What are you talking about here? Let's drop metaphors for a minute."

"I'm saying that maybe with Melissa…"

"… okay, I was wrong. Let's go back to metaphors."

"I'm just saying," Glenn says. "Some of the things you talk about. Your idea of 'monosexuality.' Extremes. Melissa. Icarus."

"That's not metaphor. It's not even a complete sentence."

Glenn smirks and looks at Vincent with sad eyes. He gets sad eyes when the subject of Melissa comes up. Vincent hates this.

"Shouldn't you be gassing up the plane or something?"

Glen inhales deeply and lets out a great sigh. "Yeah, it's about that time."

They stand up and Glenn gives Vincent an overly ambitious hug, slapping him soundly on the back with his beefy hands to ensure it is properly interpreted as a solid, male-locker-room kind of hug.

"Okay, okay," Vincent says, already extracting himself from Glenn's clutches.

"Hang tough, Vince," he says.

"You know it." Vincent tries to sound convincing so that this part can be over quickly.

Glenn straightens his flight jacket. He raises his right fist in a solidarity gesture.

"*Bernoulli*, right man?"

"*Bernoulli*, yes," Vincent says. He forces a smile and weakly imitates the gesture with his own right fist.

"And Vince? Bernoulli was a real person. Not a Greek myth. You can take that to the bank."

"Yes, I knew that, but it's good to hear you confirm it."

Then Glenn goes to do what pilots do before a plane leaves the ground. Vincent never allows Glenn to talk about the nuts and bolts technical details of pre-flight preparation. Words like *pre-flight preparation*, *cross check*, and *cockpit* make Vincent too edgy if uttered in close proximity to the hours before take off.

Take off bothers Vincent, too.

There is still an hour before his flight. Plenty of time for Glenn's talk to wear off and for Vincent to entertain new doubts. Time to think about a dot on a map of Southern California and Melissa. Time for another Bloody Mary, he thinks, and maybe a Xanax, and several more silent invocations of the Bernoulli principle.

By the time he boards the airplane, his head is a thick plate of fusilli. He manages to find his seat, put on his belt, and find the in-flight music channel that plays jazz. His lights go out about four minutes into *Take Five*, during a drum solo by Joe Morello.

The next thing he knows, the flight attendant is rousing him awake on the tarmac in California.

Chapter 6

(burned)

As the taxi approaches the El Famous hotel, Vincent has a rare, momentarily positive reaction. The bright green palm trees, the hills, the ocean, the sun, and the inviting complexity of stucco and tile all seem like a welcome change from the flat grayness he's left behind in Chicago.

But as he gets closer to the hotel, he sees that it's not real stucco and actual tile, but merely the illusion of stucco and tile. Designers aiming for some sort of Spanish colonial casa or cozy mission have instead created a garish, white and orange, high-rise hacienda. Palm trees were in such abundance that he began to wonder if they, too, were manufactured. Clumped in such close proximity, they suggested a dense palm timberland rather than an aesthetic topiary design.

The taxi stops abruptly. Vincent and his luggage are deposited on a cobblestone drive (also fake) in front of the entrance to the hotel. It feels hot the moment he emerges from the cab. He is still dressed for Chicago, with a tweed jacket, khakis, and a thick, white, cotton shirt, and can now feel the sweat pooling in the small of his back. He walks up a promenade with his luggage, dwarfed by yet another canopy of palm trees. He expects the relief of air conditioning inside the lobby but doesn't get it. It feels no different than moving from sun to shade. Vincent tugs his luggage to the front desk and speaks to the young, golden-skinned girl behind the counter. She has a name tag that identifies her as "Miyako."

"I have reservations," he says.

"Wait until you see the rest of it," she says, soberly.

"Vincent A. Cappelini. I'm with the ICARUS seminar." Then he points, gratuitously, to one of the many ICARUS banners in the lobby promoting the event.

"*Dr.* Cappelini, yes," the woman says, and rapidly taps keys on her computer keyboard with long, manicured orange nails.

Rather than correct her about his title, Vincent keeps his mouth shut. The last time he'd been mistaken for a physician was at a Sheraton in Chicago two years earlier. The error garnered him a king bed with a memory foam mattress, a view of Lake Michigan, and a bottle of Prosecco chilling in an ice bucket. Why tell them he's a freelancing journalist? Doctors have it good.

"You're on the Presidential floor," Miyako tells him, handing Vincent a key with a heavy brass oval tag with a number on it. "803. Madison room. King bed."

Vincent repeats it all, mostly to himself, because it sounds too idyllic to be true.

"803. Presidential Floor. Madison room. King bed. Yes. Thank you, Miyako. And please hold all my calls." He affects an officious tone that he thinks might sound doctor-ish. Something deeper and more convincing than his own voice.

There are a few guests in the lobby, but he doesn't recognize anyone connected to ICARUS. Vincent doesn't know many dermatologists personally—most of his interviews are done by phone—but it's possible he might recognize someone from a professional headshot that accompanied a story he's written about them at one time or another. To avoid conversations, chance meetings, and awkward encounters, he tries not to make eye contact with anyone.

There is an ICARUS seminar registration welcome table set up in the lobby where he recovers a name tag already printed up for him:

HELLO, my name is:
Vincent A. Cappelini
Giornale della Faccia

Rather than affix the tag to his chest, however, he shoves it in the vest pocket of his jacket.

He declines an offer for help with his suitcase and drags it to the elevator. The elevator groans all the way up to eight, then Vincent pulls his bags down a long, dimly lit hallway. Other than the ascending numbers to guide him along, the only thing that gives him a sense of forward motion is the progressive series of presidential oil portraits on either side of him in the hallway. The portraits don't seem to be in any particular order, however. Eisenhower next to Adams, and so on. But at least he knows he's on the Presidential floor.

Vincent glances at room numbers and double-checks his key. *803.* At the end of the hallway he finds his room, situated amid portraits of Chester A. Arthur, Gerald Ford, and James Madison. He repeats his room number to himself a few more times, trying to both decode the information and also encode the number in his brain for future reference.

He pushes inside and immediately looks beyond for another door, one that will take him into his room, and then realizes he is already in it.

There is a king-sized bed up against one wall, but the rest of the room is only slightly larger than the bed itself. In the moat that surrounds the three sides of the bed are a nightstand with a phone and clock radio, a dresser, and television on a cart. No desk, no chair. He finds a small bathroom with a sink and stand up shower. He also finds a door that opens into a tiny closet where he shoves his suitcase, so he won't trip over it. The best way—perhaps the only way—to navigate the hotel room is to sidle, crab-like, in the crevasses surrounding the bed.

While he is no historian, Vincent remembers that James Madison, in addition to being the fourth president and a founding father, had the distinction of being one of the richest commander-in-chiefs, but also one of the shortest. Just a little over five feet tall. About the same size as his grandmother, he thinks, and a solid foot shorter than Lincoln, who was well over six feet tall. But even a short president like Madison would have issues with this room, Vincent thinks. He wonders if it is too late to secure the Lincoln suite, if there is one.

Above a wooden headboard over the bed there is an Andy Warhol-inspired multi-colored replica triptych of the James Madison oil painting he'd seen in the hallway. The odd grouping of pop art Madisons is the sole characteristic that makes the room "presidential," and by now, all hopes are dashed that he has scored a well-appointed suite, fit for dignitaries.

He sprawls on the bed, stabs at the phone and calls down to the front desk.

"Hi, this is Cappelini, 803," Vincent says to the man who answers. "This room is… it seems a bit small."

"Oh yes, Madison was very small," the man says. "Rich president but very small."

"Maybe you should have gone with the 'very rich' theme?"

"We don't have a floor with a 'very rich' theme, sir."

"No, of course, I understand that. But the theme of this room is… *what*? Unusual smallness? Some sort of inside joke about a man's proportion and size?"

"Oh no, sir. You misunderstand. You're on a good floor. It's the *Presidential* floor. All the rooms are based on presidents."

"Based on presidents. Based on their actual size?"

"All the rooms are actual size, sir."

"But the king bed…"

"Yes, you requested a king bed. Very nice, sir. Enjoy."

"Yes. Right. It doesn't work in this room. I'm just wondering if there's anything else available?"

"I'm afraid the hotel is full, sir. Big skin conference."

"Yes, I know. I'm part of that."

"Oh, you're one of the doctors?"

"Maybe. Does being a doctor make a difference?"

"Oh yes sir, I should hope so, sir. Doctors make all the difference in the world. Very helpful people."

"Right. So, I'm wondering what else you might... for instance, is there a Lincoln room?"

"There's no Lincoln Room on the presidential floor. The Lincoln room is on the Luxury Car level. Third floor."

"Is that...?"

"... taken, yes sir. There's also a Lincoln room on the New York Tunnel Floor, That's the sixth floor. Lincoln, Holland, and Queens Midtown... all very nice rooms. *Long* rooms. Not short like Madison."

"That sounds much better. But I imagine those are all...?"

"... all taken, yes sir."

"You know what? It's fine. I'm fine here."

What difference does it make? Vincent thinks, hanging up the phone and resigning himself to his quarters. He isn't going to be staying for more than a few nights. He crawls to the closet, pulls his suitcase onto the bed and extracts a spiral steno pad he uses for taking lecture notes. From inside the front cover, he gingerly peels off Melissa's Post-it note.

fly me to the moon.

When he stands on the bed, it yields unexpectedly under his weight, his feet disappearing into the spongy depths of the mattress. For a small room, the ceiling is incongruously high and it's a stretch for him to reach the ceiling and affix the note, particularly since it was already losing some of its stickiness. Still, after a few precarious, trampoline-like vaults, Vincent manages to smack the note up on the ceiling.

This foray into light gymnastics tires him to the point where the next logical move is to descend to the bed and lie on his back. He closes his eyes and opens them again, so that he sees the words as if they'd always been there.

"*Fly me to the moon*," he says, though his body is earthbound and leaden. He's still feeling the effects of his preflight intake of Bloody Marys and Xanax.

He reaches inside his jacket to make sure he has his wallet, an obsessive habit whenever he travels. When he opens it, he spies an old receipt buried deep inside the fold. This isn't a mistake. He saves a lot of old receipts—anything that connects him with a specific event having to do with Melissa. This one is from Mario's Pizza for $13.75.

Mario's. $13.75: Thin crust with black olives, mushrooms, and anchovies. Some Fridays it is pizza and marathon games of Scrabble; and sometimes it's pizza and marathon movie watching—usually classic, black-and-white films and foreign films. And sometimes it's pizza and marathon sex. But pizza is involved no matter what.

The pizza order never varies. Thin crust, black olives, mushrooms, and anchovies. The first time they order a pizza as a couple, they utter the exact same preferences in precisely the same order. He remembers this topping synchronicity as a watershed moment in their relationship. To be so perfectly attuned to the same tastes. Sure, it's good to be on the same page about the bigger issues in life. But aligning so exactly on something as important as pizza toppings, he thinks, irrefutably proves the existence of romantic perfection.

Vincent stuffs the receipt back into his wallet. As he does this, he notices Melissa's photo peeking out among a squeeze of credit cards. He's had the photo reduced to calling card size so that he can keep it in his wallet and look at it whenever he wishes to torture himself.

Don't look at it. Just don't look at it right now, he thinks.

But then he does. It's a photo he took of her. She is in a red sundress, standing in front of Buckingham Fountain in Grant

Park. Long hair tied back in a ponytail. Arms folded in front of her. A brown, wooden Tissot wristwatch he'd given her is on her arm, but otherwise no jewelry. The photo captures something about Melissa that is achingly attractive. The bemused smile, the soft brown eyes that always seem about to weep in anticipation of, or from the memory of an unknown pleasure. It is a special look that she conveys solely to Vincent. It's the way she arranges the lines, muscles and, seemingly, even the complexion and tone of her face in a way that seems *exclusively for him*. It is also the last photo he'd ever taken of her. October. Before the cold. Such a simple photo too, Vincent thinks.

It simply drives him mad.

He puts the photo back in his wallet and reclines on the bed again. He has more than seven hours before the ICARUS keynote lecture. A nap on the spongy hotel mattress, to offset his intoxicated head, seems the next logical option.

He tries to relax. But sleep seems impossible, and he soon grows restless. He tries not to be a smoker, but he keeps cigarettes handy, mostly when he's out of town. He's been carrying around the same pack for about six months. He goes back into his bag and retrieves one of the last two Newports from a half-crushed box along with a book of matches. The sting he feels at being given a fancy presidential suite and finding himself in a room not fit to inter a president justifies his resolve to ignore the no smoking signs. But he feels guilty enough about it to open a window.

Vincent traverses on his knees to the left side of the bed. He opens the blinds and slides the window up to its furthest stopgap halfway point. He can't see the ocean (he expects this latest drawback) but he has a decent view of the pool area between palm trees.

From his eighth-floor vantage point, he can see sunlight shimmering atop the aquamarine kidney-shaped pool, but no one is swimming in it. The surrounding area looks empty. Vacant deck chairs and loungers dot the perimeter. The sparseness doesn't surprise him. This is, after all, a conference on dermatology, melanoma, and skin care. What dermatologist would dare to bake and bronze in this environment?

Just as he is lighting his last Newport and leaning out the window, Vincent sees one person, a woman, face down on a pink towel draped over a chaise, tanning her back in the midday sun. The woman's long hair looks golden in the sunlight and obscures most of her face. She is wearing a bikini. Vincent squints hard and feels his chest tighten.

Melissa. It looks like Melissa. Melissa in her green bikini. Or was it teal? Whenever he had referred to it as "that green swimsuit," Melissa hastened to correct him. *Not green*, she'd say. *Teal.* Whatever color it was, it looks like the same green (or teal), bikini Melissa owns. The top is untied in the back. How many times had he tied and untied those straps for her? The bottom trunks hug a heart-shaped behind. Yes, he is eight floors up, and his eyes are not entirely clear, but… *that sure looks like Melissa's behind.* Her shapely legs are slightly splayed. *A Melissa trademark.* And didn't Melissa own a pink beach towel?

Although he can scarcely believe what he is seeing, he's also aware it's not unprecedented. Melissa has made unexpected appearances before. Once, when he'd spent what would have been a dreadful couple of rainy days holed up in a hotel in Baltimore, for a seminar on alopecia, Melissa had flown in unexpectedly. He found her waiting for him in the hotel coffee shop the morning after he'd arrived. A stack of waffles, a cup of hot coffee, and his beloved suddenly appearing before him.

Just couldn't be without you, she'd said.

To be here now, in California, at his hotel, by the pool is so unpredictably predictable of Melissa, particularly after so many months of silence and uncertainty. And it wasn't crazy. He was in San Caliente now, her neck of the woods. It wouldn't have taken much for her to have found out that the ICARUS convention was coming to town. She could have easily made a phone call or two to discover whether or not he was registered at the El Famous.

Yes, so like her, Vincent thinks.

But it would be unlike Melissa to repeat the Baltimore coffee shop routine. She would have felt compelled to outdo herself. This latest scenario made perfect sense—lounging outdoors, bikini-clad, patiently waiting for Vincent's arrival. Who else *but Melissa* would be audacious enough to brazenly sun herself poolside during a seminar on sun protection?

Vincent anxiously waits for her to turn over, so that he can, at last, see her face and confirm that all is right with the world again. He anticipates the perfectly sculpted nose and piercing brown eyes that will assure him that this is, without question, his Melissa. But she scarcely moves. Occasionally one of her legs will arch lazily in the air, then two legs crossing at the ankles, pedicured toes flexing, but beyond that, she gives no indication that she intends to turn onto her back and reveal herself.

Between the sun's reflection, the swaying of annoying palm trees, and his eyelids heavy from the Xanax, there is just no telling from his eighth-floor perch if he is seeing what he hopes to be seeing. If he could be afforded one touch, even blindfolded, he would know her skin. He would be sure. *One touch of her skin.*

He extinguishes his cigarette on the fake stucco exterior just outside his window, crawls off the bed, and sidles himself around it. There is no telling how long Melissa has been waiting for him poolside and Vincent is already anticipating that he will receive some good-natured grief for not getting down there sooner. He hastily grabs his room key, sunglasses, and some breath mints and dashes out of the room.

As he descends in the elevator, he begins to feel a radiant transcendence, electric angels and winged hearts around him. Whatever problems he's felt beset with are rapidly evaporating. His claustrophobic James Madison room, that had seemed such a downer, now seemed comic. He couldn't wait to show the room to Melissa. She will love the absurdity of it. He imagines a wild sexual reunion in a room with a spongy mattress. That was the magic of having Melissa in his life. With her, he can face anything, and without her, nothing.

Aware that he is in a hotel filling up with sun-averse dermatologists, Vincent might have felt compelled to make some concessions while poolside. Maybe roll down his sleeves and even invest in a baseball cap from the hotel gift shop. But he doesn't care anymore. He leaves his shirt sleeves rolled up and his head bare to the sun's rays. Besides, Vincent figures, it's sort of like sneaking into a strip club. Anyone else out in the sun would have to explain their *own* presence there.

When he arrives at the pool area, however, he finds himself more than just in the minority. He is alone. A moist pink towel still graces the lounge chair that he'd seen from his eighth-floor window, but its occupant has vanished. There is no bag, no purse, nothing left near the chair that he can rifle through. Just a wet towel. But since the towel is still there, Vincent reasons that its owner must be nearby and, moreover, will certainly return. He's anxious—the reunion has been delayed, and he doesn't know what he'll say to Melissa when he sees her—but it's not an entirely unpleasant anxiety. Or maybe the Xanax is helping to create a pleasant anxiety. It doesn't matter.

He wonders if Melissa is already aware of his arrival at the El Famous. She could have gotten situated poolside early and been waiting for hours and now may have gone on a break—perhaps to get a Diet Coke, or maybe a bite to eat, since it was already after noon. His own stomach growls, but he ignores it.

Turnabout would be fair play, he decides. Now *he* will be here, waiting poolside for *her. So perfect.* He brazenly removes his white cotton shirt. He's maintained a regimen of daily morning pushups in Melissa's absence. His skin is winter-pale, but not in terrible shape, he decides.

He and Melissa had once been ardent sun worshippers, but Vincent has been forced to keep his tanning low key ever since he started writing for skin magazines. When he'd worked full time at *Skinformation*, he'd been careful not to mention to his coworkers all those summer weekends with Melissa, both of them soaking up the sun's rays in adjoining lounge chairs out on the deck of his apartment. If questioned by coworkers on Mondays, Vincent would explain away his bronze tones by remarking that his grandparents on his mother's side were from the south of Italy and that olive skin was an inherited trait. Partly true.

"I tan very easily," Vincent would say. "All I have to do is walk to the drug store and I come back two shades darker."

They both tanned easily.

The sun loves me, Melissa says, poolside in a chaise at his apartment complex, wearing her Ray Bans and nothing else but her green (or teal) swimsuit.

The sun loves me more, Vincent says, from his neighboring lounge chair.

After a moment she speaks again. No, I believe the sun loves me more, she says.

No matter how much the sun loves you, it can't possibly love you as much as I do, he says.

That's so sweet, she says. She peels back her bikini bottom at the waist, just below her navel, offering him a brief glimpse of her progress, the cocoa brown of her belly against the lily-white skin below that hints at her private and pleasurable parts.

Impressive, he says. Maybe you're right. Maybe the sun does love you more than I do.

Maybe you need to come out from behind your cloud and beat down on me a little harder, she says.

I'll bear that in mind, he says.

He wonders if they are sharing the same metaphor. He doesn't ask.

Stripped down to his khakis at the El Famous pool, Vincent pulls a chaise lounge close to the recently occupied one with the wet pink towel and reclines on his back. Instantly he feels the heat of the intense West Coast sun on his stomach, chest, arms, and face.

It feels good, such a sharp contrast to the dreary cold and clouds he's come from in Chicago. He closes his eyes and waits.

When Vincent hears footsteps approach, his heart leaps once again, but when he opens his eyes, it's not Melissa. It's a woman with two young girl toddlers in tow, setting up camp not far from Vincent by the shallow end of the pool. They are all in brightly colored beachwear and matching, floppy, straw sun hats.

"California, right?" Vincent says to her.

Making conversation is uncharacteristic for him but reflects his equally uncharacteristically euphoric mood. When Melissa was in the forecast—a pleasant day, nice weather, and even friendly conversation—anything was possible.

"Isn't it marvelous?" the woman answers, beaming in response. She removes a large tube of sunblock from her beach bag and slathers each of her girls with a thick coat, while they impatiently hop up and down, anxious to jump in the pool.

"Are those your girls?"

"No, gosh no. I'm on nanny patrol. But not a bad gig, sitting by the pool, watching these little brats."

The little brats giggle at her remark, hop into the pool and splash around. The woman puts on a pair of Ray Bans, sits down on the edge of a lounger next to the empty lounger—the one with the moist pink towel—and starts inflating a beach ball. She is in excellent shape, Vincent notes. Maybe mid-to-late 20s, packed neatly into a black one-piece suit. Vincent watches as her chest heaves in and out as the beach ball begins to fill with air and take shape. She might have been the kind of woman Vincent would have fallen for, or at least have been distracted by, before Melissa. Now, however, she is nothing more to him but a pleasant, busty woman blowing up an inflatable toy.

"Are you here for that seminar?" she asks, between blows.

"Seminar?" Vincent says, feigning ignorance.

"Oh," she says, as if she's realized she's made a faux pas to an uninformed hotel guest. "There's some convention here at the hotel. ICARUS. 'I Can't Ruin Myself in the Sun' or something. It's some skin thing. A medical thing."

"Oh, yes, I saw the signs," Vincent says, not correcting her acronym or letting on what he is doing at the hotel. "No, I'm just waiting here for someone." He squints around the pool area again, looking for Melissa.

"I was hired by the hotel to watch these kids for a lady dermatologist who's attending the seminar," she says. The woman tests the tautness of the inflated beach ball and, satisfied, bounces it to the little girls in the pool who giddily splash after it.

"A dermatologist who lets her kids out in the sun?" Vincent asks.

"Provided we all wear plenty of sunblock," she says. On cue, she offers the tube to Vincent. "Maybe you should put some on?"

"Oh, no, I'm fine," Vincent says. "My ancestors are from Sicily. But thanks."

She nods, and starts applying the cream to her body, to her face, arms, and legs. She stops and appears to think for a moment before speaking again.

"I wonder... would you mind terribly putting some lotion on my back?" She smiles coyly, pulls her hair back, and hunches forward as if it were a foregone conclusion. "So hard to reach."

"Oh no, I couldn't do that," Vincent says quickly. It's a knee-jerk, monosexual reaction. He imagines Melissa rounding the corner in her green (or teal) bikini and forgetting how his monosexuality negated the possibility that his rubbing skin cream on naked, female flesh would be accompanied by any sexual arousal on his part. Melissa could be jealous—despite his devotion to her.

The woman shrugs her shoulders. "I understand," she says, nodding and smiling to herself. Vincent glances down at the blue-tiled ground and then looks up at her again.

"I mean, I *could* rub some on your back, it's not a problem."

Vincent picks up the tube of suncream from the blue-tiled ground, squirts some into his palms. He applies the cream, rubbing light crescents in the small of her smooth back. He intersects with her tailbone, glances against the fabric of her swimsuit, feels the nape of her neck. And he feels nothing. No unexpected tents in his khakis, no salacious thoughts, no lust. It makes him feel renewed pride in his monosexuality.

So much so, that Vincent feels it might be okay to share his pride with this stranger. "You see," Vincent says, mostly to himself, but also to the woman. "I don't feel anything when I do this. I'm unusual in that way. It's something I refer to as my *monosexuality*."

He is about to try to explain it further, as if expounding on it might impress the woman somehow, but the moment he utters his self-manufactured term "monosexual," he realizes it is a mistake.

"Oh, gosh," the woman says, straightening herself upright and out of his reach, adjusting the straps on her bathing suit, and looking around to make sure of the location of her children. "I'm sorry. I didn't mean to… I shouldn't have…"

"… no, it's okay," Vincent says. "I'm sorry, I shouldn't have mentioned it."

"No, I'm *very* sorry," the woman says again. "You needn't be ashamed. I don't judge."

"Oh no, I'm not ashamed. Actually, I don't think it's what you're thinking." He's not sure *what* she's thinking, but he decides it's best not to explain anything further. "Yes, of course, nothing to be ashamed of."

The woman seems anxious to busy herself with something other than the conversation with Vincent and begins to unpack her towels and lay them out on other lounge chairs. Pink towels.

"Are those… do those pink towels belong to the hotel?" Vincent asks.

"Yes," the woman says, defensively. "There's a big stack of them in the changing rooms. I was told there's no charge for them."

"That's fine," Vincent says. "But are they all… do you think they're *all* pink?"

"I'm sure I don't know," she says. "Maybe the men's towels are blue. I really have no idea. I just got here."

"No, the reason I ask is that I'm waiting for a woman to come back, and I thought this was her towel," Vincent says, indicating the lounger and the wet towel next to him. "She has a pink towel. Her own pink towel, I think. You didn't happen to see the person who was here, did you?"

"No."

"Green bikini swimsuit? Teal, maybe?"

"No, I didn't," she says emphatically, and she seemed unnerved again, the pleasant chat deteriorating fast, the amiability in her voice fading.

He figures the woman must be relieved when Vincent leans back, closes his eyes and stops asking questions. Periodically he will blink open a bleary eye and see the woman and kids in his peripheral vision, but the chaise next to him remains stubbornly vacant. The pink towel is drying rapidly in the midday sun and in danger of becoming just an anonymous pink towel, left by no one in particular.

Maybe it isn't Melissa's pink towel. *Doesn't matter*, he thinks. He still feels certain it was Melissa's supple body that he'd seen pressed against it. Surely it was Melissa's smooth, naked backside that he'd seen from his little James Madison room on the eighth floor. She'll come back for the towel. Maybe she's having a long lunch. He needs to be patient. Everything will be perfect in time.

Won't she be surprised?

All at once, the events of the day catch up with him. The flight, the exhilaration, the anticipation, the heat, the tranquilizers, the Bloody Marys. It's all melting Vincent down, reducing him, sautéing him in his own sweat, making his body seep—like pure butterfat, like ghee—into the cushions of the lounger. He isn't all that surprised when, after a short time, he begins dozing.

He is more surprised however, by how long he dozes. When he wakes up and looks around, he is surrounded by nothing but a lone, chirping macaw, a setting sun, and long palm tree shadows stretching like spider legs across the pool. The woman and her tots are gone. There is no pink towel on the lounge chair next to him. He looks at his watch. It is nearly four in the afternoon.

He assumes a hotel worker must have retrieved the pink towel while Vincent had been sleeping. But he can't imagine Melissa would have come and gone without noticing him there. As much as she liked playing games, she wouldn't have left him sleeping, taken her towel, and gone off to leave him guessing.

Or would she?

Melissa has more patience than Vincent when it comes to pulling off practical jokes. Still, it was difficult for him to imagine her delaying their reunion, particularly after they'd already been apart for so many months.

If Melissa is still at the hotel, there is only one other place she could be. Up in his little James Madison room. Maybe she charmed a hotel employee and wheedled her way inside. She was crafty enough to pull that off. Vincent puts his shirt back on—although it feels inexplicably tight—and takes the elevator back upstairs. He opens the door and his heart sinks. The room is just as he'd left it. Empty.

Vincent's mood spirals down quickly. It's like finding and losing Melissa all over again. His thoughts propel him into the spin cycle: *I think you're here, then you're not here* and on to *why aren't you here?* And ultimately *where the hell are you?*

He is so agitated that he feels uncomfortable in his own skin. But when he glances at his face in the mirror in the bathroom, he realizes the feeling is far beyond metaphorical.

There is a bright crimson flush across his face. He takes off his shirt, hangs in on a doorknob, looks in the mirror again, and sees a seriously similar situation painted on his chest, arms—everything above the waist, everything that has not been covered by his khakis. The fact that his genitals have been spared offers him little solace.

Vincent presses his index finger into his chest and releases it. A bright white crescent forms in its wake before the skin returns to its shiny, lobster tone. He stands in front of the mirror in sheer awe and disbelief for several minutes. What happened to that nice, transitional, Mediterranean bronze he'd been so fond of acquiring and boasting about? Sure, he has been sunburned before, but this is a luminous, ominous red—something he's never seen on his body to this degree. He is not merely rosy, not just red, he is... *vinaceous*. Even his earlobes burn hotly.

Already his thoughts are racing anew. There is the immediate problem, the physical sensation that he is still roasting under a bright, sizzling sun, now beginning to feel some pain when he moves. Soon he begins to feel pain whether he moves or not. *Showering is going to be a bitch*, he thinks.

The looming predicament is that he is due to cover the opening plenary of ICARUS in just a few hours. A full slate of keynote speakers talking about the harmful effects of the sun's rays. This level of sun exposure is definitely not something he can explain away to dermatologists with a prepared speech about having Mediterranean blood in his background.

He is *bright red*, for God's sake. It's a bust.

So now what?

Vincent decides to address the more immediate problem. What will help this sunburn? Nothing he has in his luggage, nothing in his room will combat it. He needs aloe vera, a body wrap with mint leaves, or maybe a complete skin graft. He remembers seeing a gift shop in the lobby. He needs to gift himself with a battery of topical coolants. And soon.

Vincent carefully eases his shirt back on, an act that feels distinctly counterintuitive and uncomfortable. When he exits his room, he looks left, then right, sees no one, and takes the elevator back down to the shop in the lobby.

It's California, so the shop is well-stocked with products for tanning as well as sunburn relief. He looks for something with aloe vera. The blue stuff. The green stuff is fine, but only the blue stuff, with lidocaine, will cool down his skin. He's written articles on this topic. Now he's putting it to the test.

Excess of one sort called for excess of another, so he takes *all* the blue stuff, five bottles, off the shelf in the gift shop. He puts four of them on the counter near the cash register and holds on to the last one, thinking he might apply it right now if no one stops him.

"Five of these, and a pack of Newports," he says to the cashier. He really wants to stop smoking. But not today. The girl behind the counter says nothing about his appearance or the volume of his purchase. Vincent counts this as a small win. Perhaps it's not as bad as he imagines.

As he is fumbling for his wallet, Vincent feels a tap on his left shoulder.

This is it, the thing Vincent has feared most. He's been spotted. He wheels around and is only momentarily relieved it's not a dermatologist.

"Wow. Someone surely overdid it." The Georgia drawl mixed with a dash of smarm confirms it's not a dermatologist but his former coworker Mitchell George Wallace.

Vincent faces Mitch, cradling the blue stuff and a fresh pack of Newports in his arms.

"They sent *you*?" Vincent asks. "I can't believe Professor Reeves sent you to cover this conference. I talked to him about it."

"I believe you are still *personas au gratin* in some circles," Mitch says.

"It's *persona non grata*," Vincent says.

Mitch's eyes widen as he gets a better look at Vincent.

"Oh wow," he says. "I was kidding, but man alive, you really *did* overdo it." The shock on Mitch's face doesn't help. Writing for medical publications had made both men fairly immune to disturbing photos of the very worst skin conditions on the planet. To Vincent's chagrin, Mitch even enjoyed looking at some of the more gruesome photos.

But now Mitch is looking at *Vincent's* face with the same thrill-house, horror-shock expression usually reserved for the truly unfortunate.

"God almighty. What's with the ultra-burn, man?"

Vincent's mind has already been calculating the best lies he can come up with in a pinch. He hasn't had much time to do this.

"I was just down by the pool for a few minutes… talking to one of the doctors," Vincent says. "I guess the sun got the best of me."

"I swear to God, I can feel heat coming off you like the hood of an El Camino," Mitch says.

"How bad is it, really, at a glance?" Vincent locates a mirror near a rack of sunglasses in the gift shop and stares at the image of a dangerously red-looking man. "Christ," he mutters.

"What were you thinking, man? I surely hope you don't expect to attend the plenary lecture tonight looking like that?"

"Of course not. I'm toast."

"Burnt toast, not to put too fine a point on it," Mitch says. "I believe it falls upon me to pick up the ball and run with this story."

Vincent can see the wheels turning behind Mitch's eyes. With Vincent out of the picture, the ICARUS story is Mitch's for the scooping. This matters little to Vincent at the moment, although he hates giving Mitch an opportunity to gloat.

"I need to get out of this gift shop," Vincent says.

"You need to get out of Dodge, man."

"Yeah, I know you'd like for that to happen. But I can't just pick up and leave."

"Let's get a drink," Mitch says. "There's a lounge just off the lobby. Nice and dark. Except I fear you might glow in the dark."

"Yeah. That's amusing," Vincent says. "Let's go."

Chapter 7

(the blue stuff)

The lounge is indeed dark, just as Mitch promised; the dim lights are mostly focused on gloomy, glossy, framed black-and-white photos of Hollywood stars who may or may not have stayed at the El Famous. Michael Rennie. Norman Fell. Telly Savalas. Vincent and Mitch plant themselves on a couple of stools at a tall table in a dark corner. Vincent tumbles his 16-ounce bottles of blue stuff out of the plastic shopping bag onto the tabletop, then puts a Newport between his lips. As he reaches for the lighter in his jacket pocket, he notes the lack of ashtrays and observes a few no smoking signs. He grunts his disapproval and keeps the unlit cigarette dangling from his mouth and lines up the shiny blue bottles in front of him.

"What am I going to do?" Vincent mutters to himself.

"I do have an opinion on that matter," Mitch says. "Something where perhaps we could both benefit?"

Vincent is only half-listening.

"I thought I saw Melissa by the pool," he says, peering into the dark corners of the bar.

"Melissa?" Mitch wags his head sadly. "You're losing it, man. And what's with the cigarettes? When did you start smoking again?"

"I didn't start smoking again. It's an intermittent thing. A travel thing. I have it under control."

"No offense, but I wouldn't call you a poster child for control, Vincent. Smoking, sunburned, unemployed..."

"As you can see, I'm not smoking this cigarette. Not that I don't want to. And I'm not unemployed. I freelance."

"Whatever. You're here working for another rag, I bet."

"*Giornale della Faccia.*"

"Spanish fascist magazines?"

"Not Spanish. Italian. And it's not fascist, it's faccia. *Face.* It's a well-respected journal in the Southern Italian dermatology community."

"Whatever, Bambino, I'm just saying, I can't help but feel you're wasting your talent. And yes, I acknowledge you seem to have a natural gift for journalism—but wasting it on freelancing for these small journals, jeopardizing your assignment by sitting in the sun too long. All this fucking blue stuff. Smoking..."

"Do I look like I need a litany of my failures? And when did bars become smoke free?"

"California's been smoke-free indoors for more than a year. I think it was January '98 round these parts."

"I thought California was supposed to be so laid back."

"You can lay back, just not with a cigarette in your mouth."

"Give me a break." Vincent leaves the unlit cigarette dangling from his pouting lip. Everything was better before January of 1998, he thought. He had Melissa in his life, *and* you could smoke indoors.

"I know you well enough to know you smoke when you're stressed," Mitch says. "Is it because you've been hired to write a story on ICARUS and you're out of the main loop these days? Or because you're burnt beyond recognition? I'm kidding. It's not so bad. Look, maybe we can work out a deal. I have a little preposition for you."

"It's *proposition*. Not preposition. And I don't need your propositions. I just need more blue stuff."

"Porn?" Mitch whispers.

"No, lidocaine gel. You know, it's good for treating sunburn."

"Sure, but self-medicating...?"

"Self-medicating? It's aloe vera with lidocaine."

"Right, but... abusing it in such large quantities..."

Mitch keeps badgering while Vincent fumbles around, trying to take the shrink wrap off a bottle of blue stuff. They are interrupted by the arrival of a cocktail waitress.

"Gentlemen. Welcome to the El Famous lounge."

"Ah, it's the lovely... *Paige*," Mitch says, uttering the waitress's name with overmuch emphasis and eyeballing the name tag pinned to her left breast. Vincent watches as Mitch lingers to gaze a moment too long at her chest, then takes in the rest of her, like a fox scoping out a henhouse.

He wonders if Mitch—always a male on the make—sees Paige dramatically differently than Vincent sees her. Maybe it's not so different, except Vincent, unlike Mitch, isn't thinking about how to get this woman into bed. Paige is a little over five foot four. She looks fit and wholesome in a California-health-food-and-yoga kind of way. Long, auburn hair tumbling down past the bare shoulders of a black sleeveless sweater. Shiny black stretch pants, slightly on the tight side but not unflattering. Low heels. She has a nice smile, even if it's being manufactured for her patrons. A good aura. Vincent is big on auras. Maybe dark or slightly sad eyes, Vincent thinks. Or maybe everyone's eyes look dark and sad in this bar.

She is pretty, he can admit this to himself. She's definitely someone who would have given Vincent pause—before Melissa. Vincent tries to recall the line from F. Scott Fitzgerald's *The Beautiful and Damned*. Something about women and beauty, and about a woman who was not beautiful for something as "temporary as her looks." Rather, "she was beautiful deep down to her soul."

He can't see Paige's soul, of course, and doesn't know her at all, yet he's confident Melissa possesses a deeper soul. It's a first impression, just a snap judgment. But like auras, Vincent puts a lot of stock into his first impressions.

"There's no smoking in here, I'm afraid," Paige says apologetically. "Sorry, not my rules."

Vincent drops the cigarette from his lips. There's no ash tray so he awkwardly stuffs the unlit cigarette into the vest pocket of his shirt.

Paige raises an eyebrow at Vincent's array of blue bottles. "You're also not allowed to sell your products in here," she says. "Skin care vendors are only allowed on the show floor outside Ballroom Three."

"Oh, no, I'm not a vendor," Vincent says.

"No, he's not a vendor," Mitch echoes. "He's just very heavy into the blue stuff. And I don't mean porn. I hope you didn't think we meant porn."

"I didn't…" Paige says.

Vincent cringes. It hurts to cringe.

"Just a little sunburn," Vincent says, feeling abashed. He stuffs the bottles of blue stuff back inside the plastic bag and sets it by his feet under the table.

"Mitchell George Wallace, just in from Chicago," Mitch says. He pulls a business card from the vest pocket of his jacket. He forces it on Paige who pockets it without looking at it. "We have traveled the highways and byways to reach your fair city."

"You didn't fly?" Paige asks.

"Yes, we flew," Mitch says. "But there were highways and byways on the trip over from the airport. Weren't there, Vince?"

"I remember highways. Not many byways."

"Chicago—if you don't already know—is an exciting, dare I say, sexy city," Mitch says.

"Yes, I'm familiar with it. Pretty cold." Paige says.

"Only half the year," Mitch says. "Actually, I was born and raised in Atlanta, as you might have gleaned from my accent. As you might imagine, a native Georgian knows a peach when he sees one. And I most definitely see a peach before my eyes."

"Well, that would explain the pit I feel in my stomach right now," Paige says.

Vincent smiles at this. He hasn't smiled all week. It stretches his face and the sunburn strings his cheeks.

"Sorry about Mitch," Vincent says to her. "He's pretty harmless, actually. Thanks for your patience."

"I'd be rightly delighted for you to be one of *my* patients," Mitch lobs to the waitress.

Paige stares blankly back at him.

"So, you're both dermatologists?"

"No. We're just journalists," Vincent says.

"Not *just* journalists," Mitch says. "We're looking to get the big C."

Paige looks at Mitch blankly, then at Vincent, who shrugs.

"*Connections*, baby," Mitch says. "We are all about making connections here. Perhaps you know if anyone really impressive hangs out in this bar?"

"I have yet to see evidence of that," Paige says.

Vincent smiles at this.

"Can I get you fellows something to drink?"

"*Circumvezas, por favor*," Mitch demands of the waitress, confusing her while embarrassing Vincent.

"No, no beer for me. I'm trying to wake up," Vincent says. "Maybe some coffee? And two glasses of ice water, please."

"Please excuse my compatriot. He's just being shy because of his limited budget."

"That's not true," Vincent says.

"Personally, I am always willing to push the limits of my generous expense account. Please tantalize me with your list of brews."

Paige generously goes through a long and thorough list of foreign, domestic, and local beer options. At the end of it, Mitch orders two Budweisers.

"A man with taste," Paige says, sighing.

"Thanks," Mitch says. "I've always said good taste comes from having the big C."

"Enjoy that while you can," Paige says.

Vincent smiles again. He likes this waitress. He likes that she can punt her sarcasm right over Mitch's head.

Paige smiles at Vincent again, turns coquettishly on her heels and goes to retrieve their beverages.

"Sweet little sports car, no?" Mitch says. "And most definitely looking to merge into my lane."

"No doubt," Vincent says vacantly. He shakes his head. "I don't know what I'm going to do. I'm going to owe *Giornale della Faccia* 1,200 words in about a week."

"Tell them they can read it when I write about it in *Skinformation*."

"That's nice. Thanks. That's very helpful."

"I *am* trying to help you, man," Mitch says. "Look, you don't need to worry about this. Listen to what I'm going to tell you. I found out ICARUS is videotaping the entire event tonight. I'm getting the tapes right after the conference."

"How are you pulling that off?" Vincent asks.

"You just never mind how; you just watch me."

"I'm not trying to steal any of your tricks. I'm just curious who would do that for you."

"The big C, man, Connections."

"I'd ease up on that 'big C' thing," Vincent says. "And how does this help me? Can I get a copy of the tape?"

"Hear me out," Mitch says. "What if I let you *borrow* the videotape? That would solve your problem, wouldn't it?"

"Why would you do that for me?"

"Well now, I'm not giving it away for nothing."

"I didn't think so. How much?" Vincent reaches inside his jacket for his wallet. "I don't have a lot of cash on me."

"I don't want your money."

"That's unlike you. What kind of shakedown is this?"

"I don't want to spend all night listening to boring lectures. I want to spend tonight filling up my Rolodex with some primo new contacts. Then I want to get invited to an after party in some rich dermatologist's suite in this hotel. Nosh on some fancy cheese and crackers and canopies. Sip some 50-year-old scotch."

"What about the plenary lectures?"

"I told you, they're taping the whole thing."

"You're going to rely on videotape? Watch the whole thing later?"

"No, *you're* going to rely on the videotape. Here's the deal. You watch the tape. You write up two versions of this thing. One fancy one with my byline and a plainer one for your Italian *magazine-o*, paisan."

"Why would I agree to that?"

"A bird in the tree is worth two in the bush, fella."

"No, that's not how it goes or what that means," Vincent says, shaking his head. He thinks again about how often—behind the scenes at *Skinformation*—he'd been recruited to polish and sometimes rewrite Mitch's sloppy drafts. Mitch usually got his facts right, but was weak on grammar, punctuation, and transitions.

"You want my assistance with your bad metaphors and clichés."

"Exactly," Mitch says. "Jazz up one version with some metaphors and clichés and shit like that. But nothing too fancy or cute. Just use some of those thirteen-dollar words you use."

"What about the version I turn in to my editors?"

"Your Italians are just going to translate it anyway, what difference does it make how it reads?"

This is true, Vincent thinks. *Giornale della Faccia* doesn't care much about literary flash and flourishes, didn't care what he turned in, so long as he turned in something newsy and accurate.

"So, you're not going to the plenary at all tonight?" Vincent asks.

"Oh, I'll be there long enough to meet and greet." Mitch says. "Get some face-to-face among the face doctors. Then I think I might come back here, chat up the lovely Paige. Why should I spend a night bored in the ballroom when I can be balling against a headboard? I've got a VIP room on the Senators floor."

"What is that? State senators?"

"No, Washington Senators. You know. Goose Goslin. Harmon Killebrew."

Thinking about his own tiny James Madison room makes

Vincent's face feel hot. Or hotter. He'd been thinking about discreetly opening one of the bottles of the blue stuff under the table just as Paige returns.

Mitch wastes no time. "Paging Miss Paige," he says loudly, feigning ignorance of her arrival. "Where is that lovely Miss Paige with our drinks?"

"Yes, I'm right here," she says, setting the beers down in front of them, plus two glasses of ice water, and a mug of coffee for Vincent. "I wasn't sure if you still wanted coffee, but there's no charge for it, so…" Paige smiles at Vincent.

He manages to smile back at her.

"Thank you."

"So how long are you working here, lovely Paige?" Mitch asks.

"All my life, it would seem."

"No, I meant tonight."

"So did I."

"Might I indulge myself in a confidentiality with you, Miss Paige?" Mitch asks. "You see, actually, I'm here on a very special assignment. My job is to get a flavor of this conference. I need to talk to everyone—from the doctors right down to the cocktail waitresses."

He sizes her up again with another long, leering look.

"Top to bottom," she says.

"You got it," Mitch says, warming to his own bullshit. "I'll probably be spending a lot of time here in the lounge. Getting the whole flavor."

"You're looking to get a taste of everything."

"Exactly,"

"Fantastic," Paige says.

"I mean, you know I really can't enjoy a cold beer unless you bring it to me in your hot little hands," Mitch says.

"I'll keep that in mind," Paige says.

"Keep 'em coming, sweetie."

Paige pauses momentarily and gives Vincent a private view of raised eyebrows and her eyes exaggerated wide.

As Paige walks back to the bar, Mitch nods smugly.

"Eh? Did I tell you?"

"Oh yeah," Vincent says. "Definitely into you."

Vincent takes hold of both beer bottles and rubs them along his forehead and temples. It feels good, but only as long as the glass is directly against his face.

"I can't drink that now," Mitch says. He yells across the room to Paige, requesting two more beers.

"I'm just cooling my face a little," Vincent says.

"You don't look great," Mitch says. "I hope your feeling poorly will not reflect the quality of your journalism."

"I don't think it will," Vincent says. "But I might be hallucinating. I thought I saw Melissa down by the pool."

Mitch hunches his shoulders and squirms in his seat. "Yeah. You told me that when we came in. You know that's not possible though, right?"

"Same swimsuit. Same towel. Well, maybe not the same towel. Do you know all the towels here are pink?"

"Uh no, I hadn't noticed." Mitch takes a long drink from his beer and shifts in his seat again.

"Same hair..."

"... but not the same person, obviously."

"So, you didn't see anyone like...?"

"... no, I didn't," Mitch says, putting a period on it.

It had been a mistake to bring up Melissa, Vincent thinks. Mitch never seems to want to talk about her. He seems angry about it, or perhaps he's jealous of the relationship.

Vincent would have loved for Melissa to suddenly show up in the lounge and prove Mitch wrong. But he knows Mitch is probably right. He probably didn't see Melissa from his eighth-floor window. The chances seem unlikely. And if Melissa was at the El Famous, they'd have intersected by now. He's going to have to get out and find her. He just needs a little time to collect himself. He's here for a few days. There's time.

"So, what *are* you going to do tonight?" Mitch asks, appearing increasingly eager to change the subject. "You going to hide out in your room so no one sees your uber-tan? Watch a little porn on the pay-per-view?"

Vincent thought about the tiny room again. "I don't know. I don't do porn."

"So, get out, man. This is California. When in Rome..."

"... take in the ruins?"

"That's what I'm saying. Buenos carpe dias, man."

"I can't. *Giornale della Faccia* didn't spring for a rental car. I'm stuck here."

"Oh, I forgot, you're... *freelancing*. Tell you what, man." Mitch reaches into his jacket and pulls out a set of keys with a round white tag attached to them. He tosses them and they land on the table in front of Vincent. "Take these and get out of here for a while."

"What's this?"

"Mustang convertible. It's nice. Cherry red with Jensen speakers and a spoiler package. Kick ass. Paid for by the company."

"Yes. I remember those days. But I can't take your car."

"I'm not using it tonight. I'm going to make the scene at this ICARUS seminar and then shoot right back here to the lounge for the rest of the night."

Vincent snatches up the keys and pockets them. Then he pushes his lower lip out and nods. "Just like that?"

"No catch, man. We're amigos, right? Colleagues. We used to work together. I'm just watching your back. Which, I hope looks better than your front."

"Come on man, what's the catch?"

"Hey, if you think of something you can do for the Mitchster sometime, I'm sure you'll return the favor."

"Ah, there it is. What do you want, Mitch? I want to get out of here, sure, but I'm not selling out my integrity any further. Not even for a Mustang convertible."

Vincent takes the car keys back out of his pocket and tosses them on the table.

"Integrity? Jesus. All I'm asking is that you throw me a number from that fat-ass Rolodex of yours."

Vincent has an excellent Rolodex filled with top-notch physicians. Good contacts are valuable. The more reputable and prestigious your sources, the more likely you are ending up with an article people will actually read.

"You want a contact? Is that all? Which doctor?"

"Not a doctor. Heather."

"Graphic design Heather?"

She's a woman Vincent and Mitch met at a publications trade fair in Chicago back when they were both working for *Skinformation*. Mitch had hit on her; Vincent had been along for the ride. But Vincent was the one who ended up with Heather's business card pressed into his palm. It happened to Vincent a lot when he was with Mitch, despite—or perhaps because of—Vincent's cool, detached, monosexual vibe.

"You know Heather about as well as I do," Vincent says. "I never called her."

"But you have her number. You've got an inroad."

"I thought you were all into Paige."

"Paige?"

"Our cocktail waitress. Remember her?" Vincent points subtly in Paige's general direction behind the bar.

"You're joking right? I'm still in California, I'm not in Chicago."

"Geez, you're a cad."

"A *cad*? Man, did you just fly in from a Renaissance fair?"

"Don't you ever feel like just… I don't know… sticking with one woman?"

"Why?"

Vincent shrugs his shoulders, wincing slightly as he feels the burn along his scapula and rotator cuff. He knows Mitch is happy in his pursuit of being a hit-and-mostly-miss lothario. Vincent is the unhappy one stuck on one woman—the one who had left him. Only a very special kind of person would aspire to that.

"Be straight with me. Do you want to call Heather because

you're actually fond of her, or are you just jealous because I have her number and you don't?"

"Oh man. Why do you have to be like that? What does it matter? You're getting a nice Mustang and a videotape of the conference."

It's true, Mitch is dangling many shiny baubles in front of Vincent. He also suspects Mitch wants to have all the dermatologists to himself and wants Vincent out of the picture when he makes his move on Paige—even if it means giving up his kick-ass, cherry red Mustang. He hates letting Mitch loose on innocent, unsuspecting Heather. But that would come later, when they were back in Chicago.

Right now, Vincent is in a jam. He looks around the room absently, weighing the decision. As the lobby fills up, more people are rolling into the El Famous lounge. Some of them have vaguely familiar, doctor-like faces.

Then Vincent sees a face more familiar than the rest. Hobnobbing in a group of people entering the lounge, he notices a woman in a low-cut lavender dress. He starts to sweat. It's Dr. Barbara Borden, the veterinarian dermatologist (or dermatological veterinarian), who has been after Vincent's hide.

He recognizes her from the photo she'd mailed him; the one that accompanied her pigs on a hot tin roof photo. If he'd assumed that she'd dolled herself up for the benefit of a glamor shot, he was wrong. She looks much as she had in the photo, showing a surprising amount of cleavage, and also going heavy on the rouge and lipstick. Plus, the flaming orange hair. While her men's magazine looks remain lost on Vincent, her gaudy sexuality appears to be working in her favor. Men are flocking around her. When she glances in Vincent's direction, he lowers his face.

"I have to get out of here," Vincent says.

"What's the matter?"

"It's Dr. Borden."

"*Borden?* Pigs-on-a-hot-tin-roof Borden? Where? Here?" Mitch wheels around to look for her. "Does she know what you look like?"

"I don't know. Don't turn around. Don't draw attention over here."

"Wow. Hotter than I remembered." Mitch says. "What's she doing here? Is she stalking you?"

"How should I know? It's California. It's February. All the doctors come out of the office when there's a seminar in California."

"Probably not good if she sees you sunburned, Vince. You know, the *pigs*..."

"Yes, you don't have to keep reminding me. I don't want her to see me *at all*. Alright, look. I'm out of here. When we get back to Chicago, I'll give you Heather's number. Whatever. What do I care?"

"Cool."

Vincent snatches the car keys back from the table and pockets them. He looks across the room. Dr. Borden is on the move.

"Can you please keep Dr. Borden away from me long enough for me to make a break for it? Go do that annoying, Georgia charm thing or whatever it is you do. Just don't tell her who you are or where you're from. And don't let her see me."

"Piece of cake, "Mitch says, squinting at her from afar. "Great hair."

"You *like* that hair? It reminds me of cheese puffs."

"I'd eat a bag of that and lick my fingers afterwards. Plus, her skin's so perfect."

"Lots of plastic, I think," Vincent says.

"It looks so smooth."

"Don't touch her, please, just distract her."

Mitch gets up just as Paige is returning with two more Budweisers.

"I've got to scoot right now, doll," Mitch says to Paige. "But if you're here later maybe we could make the scene."

"You want to make *another* scene?" Paige says.

Mitch nods at Vincent. "My associate will take care of the tab."

"You said my money was no good."

"Don't get cute, paisan. Later."

"Yeah, later, Mitch."

Mitch points two index fingers at Paige and cocks his head forward in a "I'll check you out later" gesture. Then, after giving Vincent what appears to be a victory wink, Mitch pushes his way into the crowd of doctors.

Vincent watches as Mitch successfully corrals Dr. Borden and the other doctors around her like Border Collies, deftly backing them toward the entrance of the lounge. But no further. They stand stubbornly in the doorway, gesticulating, guffawing, and blocking a clear exit. Vincent sits low in his stool and tries to hide behind the glassware on the table.

"What are you doing?" Paige asks.

"Oh," Vincent says. "There's someone here that I don't want to see. Or rather someone I'd prefer didn't see me."

Paige positions her darkly clad body close in front of Vincent, creating a visual barricade between him and the rest of the room. She is close enough that he picks up a combined scent from her sweater. Hops, gin, and Chanel No. 5.

"Better?" she asks.

"Thanks, that's very nice of you," Vincent says. Under temporary cover of Paige, Vincent plucks an ice cube from his glass and runs it across his forehead and temple. Next, he takes the two fresh, cold bottles of beer and runs them along his cheeks. When he's done, the heat on his face returns with doubled intensity. Paige seems only mildly bemused by these gestures.

"This isn't working," Vincent says.

"It works better if you drink them," Paige says.

Vincent puts the bottles back down on the table and pushes them away from him. "I can't, I shouldn't, drink right now. I'm sorry." With a flick of his hand, he motions for Paige to take the beers away.

"I can't resell them after you've rubbed them on your face. Health codes."

"Right. Right. I'll just…" Vincent reaches for his wallet, pulls out a twenty and puts it on the table.

"It's happy hour," Paige says.

"In what world?"

"No, the drinks. The drinks are two for one right now. A ten will do it."

"Doesn't matter. Keep it." Vincent's eyes dart ferret-like around the room.

"You're looking for a way out?" she asks, eyeing Vincent's furtive glances as she pockets the twenty in her slacks.

"Yes, but not the way I came in."

"I'm going on break," Paige says. "Do you still have your cigarettes?"

Vincent nods.

"Follow me," she says.

Vincent gets up, collects his plastic bag of blue bottles, and follows Paige. She grabs a backpack from behind the bar, then leads him through a dimly lit, gray concrete hallway and through an exit in the back. Soon they are outdoors, standing under the shade of fake palms.

All things considered, it's almost refreshing, Vincent thinks. He takes out his cigarettes.

"Smoke?" he offers.

"No thanks, I don't smoke."

"No, me neither," Vincent says. "Bad for you."

They both light up.

"Quite a character, your friend," Paige says.

"Yeah, he's a...character, that's for sure."

"You're both part of this dermatology conference?"

"We're both journalists, but for different magazines."

"You're not wearing a name tag. Did your friend call you Vince?"

"Yes, Vincent."

"Aren't you glad to be out of Chicago, Vincent?"

"Living in Chicago depends entirely on your disposition," he says. "If you're feeling good it's the best town in the world. If you're down, it can drag you way down."

"Wow," Paige says, pulling a long drag off her cigarette and widening her eyes. "That's one of the reasons why I got out of Chicago."

"Oh, you lived in Chicago. So, you know…"

"Yes. I guess it's not always so bad."

"No, of course not," Vincent says. But the only times he can recall about Chicago that weren't bad were the occasions that involved Melissa before she'd vanished.

"My shift is over in about an hour." Paige says. "If you'd like to…"

"I thought you… no, it's just that I thought I heard you tell Mitch that you'd be here all evening."

"I did say that, didn't I?" Paige says, a wink in her smile.

Vincent wrinkles his brow and rediscovers that wrinkling a sunburned brow is a painful thing to do. He tries to relax his face again.

"You're not big on name tags and I'm not big on pushy men," Paige says. "In fact, I hate guys like that. But I have to make my tips. Now you, you seem a bit more reserved."

"Might be sunburn and fever," Vincent says.

"I think a lot of women prefer that. Not sunburn and fever. A more laid-back kind of guy, I mean. I know I do. Anyway, it's a good thing."

That's all fine, Vincent is thinking, but why is Paige telling him all this? Why had she covered for him in the bar and abetted in his escape? Was she hitting on him? Red face and all?

Vincent required an inordinate amount of convincing in these matters. His obtuseness could be stupefying and annoying to women. At one point even Melissa tells him that she's prepared to whack him with a frying pan to knock sense into him and make him realize that yes, she really, truly, honestly is in love with him.

Paige isn't being all that aggressively affectionate. But she does seem to meet the criteria Vincent generally recognizes as early-stage flirtation. Even so, and cute and charming as she might be, Paige doesn't know what she's up against. She doesn't know that Vincent's heart is currently stuck in neutral, waiting for Melissa to put it back into drive. It feels self-centered and presumptuous to assume Paige is flirting with him or has an agenda that involves him. Still Vincent feels compelled to inform Paige before it goes any further.

"It's not that I'm so laid back, really. I'm a monosexual. It's sort of like demisexual. But more intensely romantic and devoted."

"No kidding?" Paige says, taking another puff on her cigarette and blowing it out slowly, appearing unfazed by his confession. "Who's the lucky girl?"

Vincent's eyes widen. "Oh, you know about...?"

"... Demisexuality? Yes. An emotional bond needed before you can have sex. I learned about it in an abnormal psych class at Loyola. What's different about monosexuality?"

"Like I said, it's more intensely romantic and devoted," Vincent says again.

"Well, you don't *seem* more intense. Not in a bad way," she says. "Is that a good thing that it's more intense?"

"You think it's abnormal?" Vincent asks.

"I didn't say that. I just said I heard about things like this in my abnormal psych class. It's unusual, but it's interesting. I'm not really in a position to judge anyone's personality. Except for Mitch. I'm pretty sure your friend Mitch is a classic narcissist."

"That assessment hardly requires a psych degree."

"So, what happened to you? Your skin, I mean."

"I was lulled by the warmth of the sun and fell asleep."

"It looks painful. But I like the sunburned look."

"You *like* it?"

"There's a certain... earthy ruggedness to red, swarthy skin."

"It's an affliction. It's not normal," Vincent says.

"Normal can be boring."

"Sure, but I'm just saying, it's not permanent. I hope not, anyway."

Vincent is talking about his skin, but he tries to weigh down his remark about impermanence with an anchor of subtext. He feels obligated to make his position clear. To hang tough with his monosexuality. "I'm just saying, don't get attached to it. My skin, I mean."

"I'm just talking, I'm not attaching," Paige says.

Despite all this, Vincent is still getting vibes. Maybe Paige is weirdly into sunburns. He's not really in a position to judge, either.

"So, um, where will you go in Mitch's little cherry red Mustang?" she asks.

"You overheard that, did you? I don't know where to go, I just know that I have to get away from here. From this hotel. You understand, it's not good for me to be seen sunburned at a dermatology seminar like this."

"Do you know your way around San Caliente?"

"Not at all. But I just figured I'd drive up along the coastline. Get some dinner. Come back later under cover of darkness."

Or so he is telling her, and himself. He isn't about to admit that he's already been thinking about cruising through the neighborhoods of San Caliente. Inhabiting the spaces where Melissa might be or might have been. Breathing the same air that Melissa is breathing or might have breathed. Hearing the same hum of traffic and melodious chatter of people that Melissa hears or might have heard.

He's also doesn't want to admit he is thinking of looking up Melissa's number or address in a local phone book, or that he may be thinking of dialing her phone number from a nondescript phone booth somewhere in close proximity to her, or quietly idling the cherry red Mustang in front of her house—once he locates it—after dark, when her lights are on.

"I carpooled to the hotel today with Rosalio, the barback," Paige says, interrupting Vincent's thoughts. "I was going to catch a ride back home with him, but if you're heading out, would you mind driving me? I live up the coast and I can guide you wherever you want to go. I could even show you a nice place to have dinner."

"I don't know," Vincent says. He mouths the words but his thoughts are elsewhere, obsessing about a blissful reunion with Melissa.

But he's also becoming less sure about how Melissa will react to his indomitable persistence for reuniting. He has to remind himself that things did not end well. It is obsessive, he knows this. He is, after all, nothing if not obsessed.

Perhaps he needs more time, he thinks. A little more time to heal emotionally (his heart) and physically (his face) before he seeks out Melissa again. He has a couple of days. But bottom line, right now, he needs to get out. Somewhere, anywhere but the El Famous hotel.

He glances at Paige again. She is providing Vincent a distraction and detour, one that could keep him from morphing all too soon into a desperate stalker. And whatever her motives, Vincent feels his monosexuality should effectively eclipse any romantic illusions Paige might have and help him maintain boundaries. He widens his eyes and shrugs.

"I'll be good, I promise," Paige says, perhaps intuitively reading his perplexed expression. She raises a pair of open, surrendering palms. "I respect your sexual... *identity*. Hands off. No judgments. Okay?"

"Do you *know* a good place for dinner?" Vincent asks.

Paige smiles and her eyes narrow. "I do. I have a change of clothes in my bag. Let me freshen up and meet you back here in 15 minutes."

"I'll freshen up, too. Better make it 20 minutes."

"Fifteen minutes," Paige says. "No one takes 20 minutes to freshen up in California."

Chapter 8

(fugu)

Vincent takes a service elevator to the eighth floor and squeezes inside the James Madison room. He strips off his clothes and seeks relief in the shower, but the sharp, sporadic jets of water sting like hornets as they pelt his face and shoulders. He retreats, dries himself gingerly with a bristly, coarse terry towel, then gets on the bed naked with his blue bottles.

He slathers the blue stuff liberally, pushing thick globs out of the tubes and onto his face, chest and arms. It provides some immediate relief but also gives his upper body an unnaturally smooth and purple cast, as though he's been dipped in raspberry Jell-O.

Although he has no thoughts of impressing Paige, an innate vanity prevails and—displeased with his gelatinous, alien-like appearance—he ends up washing most of the gel off his body again, wincing as he wipes himself dry again with the same harsh towel.

He mumbles to his image in the mirror: *Don't go out. Put the blue stuff back on, lie flat on your back in bed, and forget about the outside world.*

But then there is a rumble of hunger in Vincent's stomach. He takes another hard look at the dismal four walls that pen him in. He puts on a pair of khakis, then splashes water from the bathroom sink onto his red face and chest again. As the water drips from his face, he looks into the mirror once more.

They are in the women's department at Marshall Field's on a Saturday afternoon in October, helping him find a scarf for his mother's birthday. Melissa is good at this. She is savvy about colors and color combinations. It helps her in her work as a graphic designer, but it will also be useful today. He knows she will find the right item quickly, leaving them with spare time in the late afternoon for personal indulgences. Sex, of course, and maybe a quick stop somewhere beforehand for an Old Fashioned. She chooses a patterned silk scarf, something with autumn tones, black, gold, amber, and orange. Melissa drapes it across her black turtleneck sweater and stands in front of the department store mirror.

"This one's nice," she says.

"For you or for my mother?"

"For your mother, silly."

"It's perfect, but now that it's been on your body—I'll have a tough time seeing it on my mother." Vincent hugs her from behind. "It definitely looks good on you."

"I think *you* look good on me," Melissa says.

They stand there for a moment, looking at the scarf, but then looking at each other through their reflections in the quadrangle of Marshall Field mirrors.

"We look like we go together, don't we?" Melissa says.

"Sort of like a jigsaw puzzle," Vincent says. "You know, those pieces that—even before you connect them—you know they go with each other."

"It's not a puzzle when there are only two pieces," Melissa says.

He wants to agree. Or he doesn't want to disagree.

He doesn't say anything. Just hugs her tighter. Interlocking.

*

Paige has changed out of her dark hotel cocktail waitress outfit and looks fresh and relaxed in jeans and a sparkling white T-shirt. Vincent is in the El Famous parking lot, behind the hotel, leaning against Mitch's rented, cherry red Mustang.

"Your skin matches the car," Paige says.

"Not what I was going for," Vincent says.

He's not feeling his best, maybe even slightly feverish. His energy alternately sparks and flags. He can't tell if he's slowly improving, or slowly getting worse. Still, he's glad he made the decision to get out of his room because he also feels antsy. Like he needs to keep moving or whatever is ailing him will catch up with him full force.

He puts the top down—there seems little sense in avoiding sun exposure at this point—and Paige jumps into the passenger seat. She navigates them out of the parking lot and soon they are zipping south along the California coastline, with a crystal blue sky washing over them.

Paige looks over her Ray-Bans and punches buttons on the dash until she finds a radio station. She settles on a razor-like guitar that rattles the car doors. The guitar reaches a crescendo and there's a crash of drums and finally it is Blondie, growling "One Way or Another."

"You like the '80s?" Paige asks.

"Not while we were in the '80s, but it's fine now, I guess," Vincent says. Paige turns up the music and they are forced to shout over it, as the cherry red Mustang roars down the highway.

"How long are you going to be here, in California?" Paige shouts.

"Just a couple of days," Vincent says. "I was supposed to be here just long enough to cover this skin convention for an Italian magazine that hired me and then I was supposed to go home and write it up. But, as you can see, my skin is not presentable to any reputable dermatologist. I totally screwed this up."

"So, what are you going to do?"

"I don't know. I may have some options. I might be able to get my hands on a videotape of the lectures. But for now, I need to steer clear of the hotel."

"Where is your special lady friend? I assume you had one, the way you talked so passionately about your demiosexuality."

"Monosexuality," Vincent says. "It's more intense."

"Yes, sorry, I forgot. Is she back in Chicago? What's her name?"

Melissa's name has not come up yet. Vincent would have remembered uttering it, and the tightening of his chest that would accompany saying it aloud.

"Melissa?" His chest constricts on cue. "I'm not sure where she is, really. Actually, last I heard, she was here."

"In San Caliente? When was that?"

"Oh, gosh. I guess it's been over a year now," Vincent says as if he's unsure, although he practically knows the precise length of separation down to the hour, minute, and second.

"Does she know you're here?"

"Not yet. I mean, I don't even know if *she's* here. Not for sure."

"You haven't called, or…"

"No, I haven't done anything yet."

"Oh wow, so it's like that."

"No, it's not like *that*," Vincent says, although he isn't sure exactly what Paige means by the remark. "She came out here a while ago and didn't come back."

"Oh, so it's like *that*," Paige repeats.

"I guess. Well, no, not exactly. I don't know."

"Did you come out here hoping to find her?"

"Those who know me have told me it's not a good idea."

"But do *you* think it's a good idea? Or you can't help yourself because of your 'condition'?"

"I don't know."

"So, I'm guessing it was a bad break-up?"

"No. Well, maybe. And some other things."

"So, you haven't seen her in more than a year? I imagine that puts quite a crimp in your demisexuality."

"Monosexuality. There's really a *huge* difference."

"Sorry," Paige says.

"To answer your question, it's a problem, yes. Maybe we should talk about something else."

"You don't want to talk about it? Sometimes you sound like you want to talk about it."

"No, it's just hard, you know, with the convertible, and at this speed, and the music." He yells this a bit louder than the rest of his remarks, to emphasize the point. But even in an anechoic chamber on a remote island with no breezes, he'd feel equally at sea in this conversation.

"How do you like California so far?" Paige asks.

"Fabulous," Vincent shouts back. "I mean, I've only been here a few hours, but I'm sure it's fabulous."

But it isn't fabulous. It could have been fabulous. Gorgeous weather, a convertible, the California coastline, a lovely summer evening. Even the 80s music, now bouncing pleasantly along with "Love Plus One" by Haircut 100. All fine, except he is becoming increasingly aware that he is in the midst of a faux fabulous time with the wrong woman.

It isn't Melissa. Ergo—although he would not have used that word—he can't be enjoying himself.

He's also concerned that his physical malaise may be escalating, incrementally. It isn't just his face and shoulders and chest and the sunburn anymore, he is becoming inured to that discomfort, to some extent. It is his insides, mostly his stomach, that feels sick or hungry, he can't tell which.

When the queasiness subsides, the hunger rears up again. He hasn't eaten anything other than a bagel and cream cheese at O'Hare Airport early that day and imagines his stomach must be making noises which would have been clearly audible, had the '80s music and wind not been drowning them out.

When Paige points to an exit, Vincent takes it and is momentarily relieved to feel a sense of destination and the promise of nourishment. She directs him a few more miles along a long exit road that runs so close to the ocean that Vincent can feel the mist on his face. There is nothing but an orange, makeshift, plastic fence to prevent him from driving off the road, crossing a short stretch of beach, and ending up in the ocean. And after that, there is nothing but lots more water and Asian geese until you get to the Waiākea peninsula.

Paige points to a building on the right side of the road, facing the highway and the ocean. On the roof of the building—which looks like a refurbished barn with its weathered red planks covering the exterior—stands a splashy, larger-than-life, cartoon image on plasterboard, depicting an agitated, top-knotted samurai warrior wearing a baseball uniform. The samurai appears to be taking a mean, determined swat at an incoming fish with his sword. A white sign with splashy blue letters bears the name of the place.

"Slammin' Sammy Sushi?" Vincent says.

"Best sushi in California," Paige says.

"You're kidding, right?"

"No. There's this guy, Hideo Sakamoto, a Cubs fan originally from Chicago—well, originally from Evanston—anyway, he owns it. He's hoping to cash in on Sammy Sosa's name. Sammy has nothing to do with the restaurant directly, mind you. It's all Japanese baseball fans from Chicago. They're just using Sosa's name."

"Oh, sure," Vincent says, smiling as if he understands. But really, he knows very little about Sammy Sosa, or baseball, for that matter. He knows Sammy Sosa of the Cubs and Mark McGwire of the Cardinals were in a home run derby last year in 1998, and that both men were hoping to beat Roger Maris' record. He knows that Sammy Sosa's nickname is "Slammin' Sammy." He knows that the Japanese like baseball. But that's the extent of it. The idea of "cashing in" on a ballplayer having a good year seems ill-advised and short-sighted to him. But he doesn't voice his opinion about it.

Instead, he drives slowly through a noisy, crushed stone parking lot and puts the cherry red Mustang in park under a row of cypress tress.

Vincent expects the interior décor will be more traditionally

Japanese. He's been to sushi restaurants in Chicago, with Melissa, restaurants that attempted a semblance of Japanese aesthetic realism with paper lanterns, screened partitions and those indecipherable black-and-white hiragana brush paintings that Melissa used to suggest translated as "free sake tomorrow."

But the inside of Slammin' Sammy Sushi looks like an average sports bar, very much like he's been transported to the north side of Chicago. Large screen television sets are all tuned to a Cubs game in Arizona. Must be spring training or an exhibition game, Vincent thinks, since it's still only February. On the walls, behind deep glass frames, are all manner of baseball memorabilia, including bats, gloves, and jerseys. There is a framed jersey number 21, presumably belonging to Sammy Sosa himself, prominently displayed and backlit in a glass case on the wall.

The only hint Vincent has that he is not in an average sports bar is provided by the waitstaff. Men and women have been forced to dress up to emulate the incongruous, iconic restaurant logo. Neither samurai nor baseball attire, it works on some level as an amusing cartoonish image for the establishment, but transferred to real human beings it becomes, Vincent thinks, a bizarre hybrid. Blue and white Chicago Cubs stripes on their shirts and trousers, red kamikaze headbands, and samurai swords tucked into obis around their waists. The white socks they wear could have been absorbed by either aesthetic conceit, but since they are shod in authentic-looking wooden clogs, they look more like they've been plucked from traditional Edo Period Japan, rather than Wrigley Field. He assumes—or hopes, perhaps—that their samurai swords are fake, although he can't tell. Though Japanese-owned, much of the waitstaff is not Japanese, Vincent notes, further confounding the image. There is, however, a Japanese bartender, and a cluster of Japanese patrons at the bar, drinking tall Kirins from 16-ounce cans, their eyes glued to a large-screen television set.

"How are the Cubs looking this year, Hideo?" Paige calls out across the room.

"Hey, it's Paige," Hideo yells to the disinterested barflies. "I don't know, girl. Grace, Johnson, and Sosa are all looking good. But we're still down in the bottom of the ninth."

"Typical," Paige says.

"Hey, keep it down," a hardcore Japanese patron at the bar says in a low, growl. "Besuboru game on."

"We're going to head out to the terrace," Paige says.

"Nice night for it, doll." Hideo says. "Knock yourself out."

Vincent follows Paige to a door that leads outside to the terrace. No one is sitting at any of the outdoor patio furniture on the sun-bleached redwood deck.

"Not really a happening place, is it?" Vincent says, surveying the empty rows of dark, iron tables and chairs.

"It depends," Paige says. "There was a time you couldn't get a table inside, let alone out here on the deck. But that was back in the height of the sushi/baseball surge last year, in '98."

It occurs to Vincent that he may be a relic of past glories himself. His best years behind him. Days of Melissa. Smoking inside buildings. Things like that. He shakes it off.

"It seems a *very* specific niche restaurant idea, if you ask me," Vincent says.

"Well, it's off-season," Paige says. "But they still do remarkably well on karaoke nights."

All the Budweiser/Cubs umbrellas are down or at half-mast, but Paige erects one at a table near the edge of the terrace; a table that offers an unimpeded, spectacular scenic California view. Vincent can see surfers in the distance, cutting through rippling waves. A few yachts dotting the water. At least it's not the James Madison room, Vincent thinks.

And, short of being alone, he doesn't mind being alone with Paige, or rather he likes being alone with someone who hardly knows him, and away from others, away from the hotel, and Mitch and Dr. Borden, and all the dermatologists.

Paige pulls at a tortoiseshell hair clip on the back of her head, tumbles her long black hair out of a ponytail and lets it flow in the wind. She keeps her sunglasses on. Vincent keeps his sunglasses on, as well.

"You come here often?" he says, failing to come up with anything more interesting.

"I sometimes pick up some shifts here. Bartending when they need it," Paige says. "Hideo likes me because I'm from Chicago."

"You're a Cubs fan?"

"I'm not a big Cubs fan, no, but it helps to pretend to be, with Hideo. And he doesn't make his bartenders wear that ridiculous costume. Otherwise, there'd be no way."

"I can understand that," Vincent says.

"The Mai Tais are good. You like Mai Tais?"

Vincent looks around at the surfers, boats, and ocean. It seems wrong not to order a rum drink. "I might not say no to a Mai Tai."

"Finally. Something you might not say no to. That definitely calls for a drink."

A samurai baseball player emerges from inside the restaurant. Despite the details of the restaurant's logo, the waitstaff does not have to coif their hair into samurai top knots. Vincent thinks they must be grateful for that small blessing. Still, the server is forced to shuffle along in his clogs and it makes a harsh and ungainly clatter as he traverses across the redwood deck to their table.

"Princess Paige!" he announces, and then genuflects in front of her, dropping his elbows to the table and clasping his hands.

"Sir Nathan," she replies, with mocking regality. "Nathan, this is my friend, Vincent. Vincent, this is Nathan. Vincent's a writer for a medical magazine in Chicago."

"Brown from the Sun?" Nathan jokes, referring to Vincent's skin tone. "But more red than brown, I'd say."

Vincent hasn't assessed himself in a while and wonders if his condition has worsened since he left the hotel.

"I freelance at the moment," Vincent says.

"Vincent forgot to pack his SPF," Paige says.

"First day here," Vincent tosses in.

"Well you came to the right place to take our sweet little Paige on a date."

"Oh, well it's not..." Vincent says.

"No, we're not..." Paige says.

"No, we're just here for dinner and drinks."

"Best Chicago-style sushi on the coast," Nathan recites.

"What is Chicago-style sushi?" Vincent asks.

"It's like regular sushi, but we wear Cubs shirts," Nathan says. "You guys know what you want?"

Vincent looks around helplessly, then Nathan produces a menu from the folds of his obi. Vincent surveys the long, numbered inventory of exotic names. As he attempts to find something familiar, he surreptitiously pushes an index finger at another unexpected spasm in his stomach. He's already decided his system is not going to react well to anything cooked in oil or deep-fried. Chilled food seems best. Or better, at least. There is something about the ocean front environs that makes the idea of cold, raw fish and rice chased with an icy Mai Tai seem palliative, something that might potentially soothe his insides.

"Mai Tais, for a start," Vincent says.

"Definitely," Paige chimes in.

"Check," Nathan says.

Vincent struggles with the list of sushi choices. Paige notices his plight and leans across the table to assist.

"What are you looking for?" she asks.

"I don't know. Salmon or tuna or something? Maybe something I would normally eat from a can?"

"Boring," Paige says. She turns to Nathan. "How's the fugu today?"

"Fugu? I don't see it on the menu," Vincent says, squinting anew at the items.

"Fugu is not on the men-u," Nathan sings-songs.

"But I know you have it," Paige says.

"You sure you know what you're doing, Paige?" Nathan asks.

"Absolutely."

"Does this guy know?" Nathan asks, nodding to Vincent.

"He never really knows what he wants," Paige says, as if they've known each other for decades instead of hours.

It bemuses Vincent that she'd talk this way, but he also doesn't mind it.

"Princess Paige wants fugu, she gets fugu," Nathan says, shaking his head and wrinkling his brow. "Don't blame the management if you get 'fugged' up."

"Oh, that's original," Paige says. "I hope the fish is not as old as that joke."

"No, you know I'll bring you the freshest fugu," Nathan says.

"It's good?" Vincent interjects, perfunctorily.

"You've never had it? Oh, then you must," Paige says.

Vincent nods, though he still isn't sure it's a good idea or a terrible idea to introduce a new species of fish to his gastrointestinal system.

"Fugu for two," Nathan says. "Rest in peace. Back in a flash with your Mai Tais." He gets up from his knees and clatters on his clogs back inside the restaurant.

"So, you lived in Chicago?" Vincent says, not really asking a question but perhaps leading up to one. "How did you end up here? Not *here*, I mean, but in San Caliente."

After "come here often?" Vincent believes this is the most benign question he can ask, but he notices Paige reacts by blushing, and shifting in her seat.

"My parents own a beach house down the coast. They never use it themselves. Mostly it's a rental. So, I came to California. Just for a week to hang out. And…now I live here. Not *here*, but in the beach house, I mean."

"I don't understand. You never went home?"

"That story is a bit more complicated," Paige says.

"How so?"

Nathan interrupts as he arrives, nearly spilling two brim-filled Mai Tais in enormous blue glass goblets as he sets them on the table. "Your cocktails," he announces. "Everything good so far, Paige?"

"I was about to tell Vincent how I ended up in San Caliente."

"Mmm," Nathan grunts. Then his voice croaks out: "*The plane. The plane. The very bad plane.*"

Vincent supposes Nathan means to imitate Tattoo from *Fantasy Island*, but it sounds forced, bastardized, like a bad imitation of a bad imitation of Tattoo. Paige rolls her eyes in response. Nathan shakes his head at Paige and chuckles humorlessly to himself. "Poor, poor, Paige. Stuck in paradise. The fugu will be up soon. God rest your souls." He clatters away again.

"What's all that about?" Vincent asks.

Paige sips at her giant Mai Tai, takes a deep breath, and leans back in her chair.

"Are you a good flyer?" she asks.

"*Me?* Not in the least, no."

"Then perhaps you'll be a bit more sympathetic than others. My trip to San Caliente was my first time flying. Like, *ever*. I was already apprehensive about flying before flying. Then there was a major airline accident a few weeks before my trip, so that added to my stress."

"An air crash? When was that?" Vincent shudders. It could be sunburn and fever. It might be his own intense trepidation about getting on a plane. In any event, it's a hard shudder that nearly rattles his teeth.

"I don't remember. A little over a year ago, I suppose," Paige says. "So, I had *that* on my mind, and then I had the bad luck to get caught in a bad storm coming out here."

"Turbulence," Vincent says solemnly.

"A lot."

"Yes, I'm not fond of it, either."

"But more than that," Paige says. "It seemed to last forever—the pilot couldn't seem to pull out of it. Couldn't get above it or around it. At one point it felt like the plane hit a wall and we started diving, rapidly. Everyone was screaming. I thought, *this is it. It's over.*"

"Jesus Christ."

"But somehow... I don't know how... the pilot pulled out of it. And we landed, finally, in San Caliente. No harm to anyone. No physical harm, I mean. But I decided—long before my oxygen mask fell into my face and my coffee landed three rows up from me—that if I survived, I would never fly again."

"Wait. So, you just... *stayed here,* in San Caliente? Just like that?"

"Yes. At first, it was fine. I was staying at my parents' house on the beach and occasionally crashing with friends I'd made here. I barely needed to think twice about it. But when it came time for my return flight, I delayed it. I thought it was only going to be for a couple of days. Then I thought maybe another week. It kept going like that. Anyway, I kept extending it. And nothing was pulling me back home. Nothing important, anyway."

"Nothing back in Chicago?"

"No. I was unemployed and I didn't have an apartment to worry about. I'd been living with my parents in Oak Park until I made my next move. I was going to teach. I had resumes out all over the place. The trip to California was supposed to be just a nice little trip for myself before I came home, started interviewing, and then I'd start my life as a teacher in Chicago."

"What do you teach?"

"History. I'm certified to teach high school history. 20th Century. But then days turned into weeks, weeks turned into months..."

"... with you always intending to go back at some point?"

"Right. But after a while it became pretty clear that I wasn't making any plans to go home anytime soon. So, I stayed at my parents' beach house in San Caliente and started looking for work. And I knew how to tend bar. So, I picked up some shifts, then some steady gigs. Now that's what I do."

"What about teaching? Why don't you just teach here?"

"I don't know. I live here now but I often feel like I'm still waiting to go home. Although I'm not doing anything to make that happen."

"If you're spooked by flying—and I understand that—you

could take a bus… a train… rent a car… there are plenty of other options."

"Sure, I know. I guess I've lost my momentum. The longer I stay here, the more it's feeling like this is where I live."

"Do you think it's possible your fear of flying is incidental? Perhaps you don't want to face that next big step in your life waiting for you back in Chicago?"

"If you plan to psychoanalyze me, I need to be laying down."

Yes, Vincent wonders, where is this psychobabble to a stranger coming from? He is in no position to analyze the lives of others. But the entire time Paige has been explaining, he's been gulping down his Mai Tai on an empty stomach. He supposes that's what's making him uncharacteristically outspoken. He backs off.

"No. Not at all," he says. "Just saying what comes to mind, that's all."

"I know there are other options for getting back to Chicago, obviously," Paige says. "I used to think it was about getting over my fear of flying. Now it may be just a bad groove I've gotten myself in. You could be right. Maybe I *am* putting my life on hold, I don't know, really."

"Well, I mean, I wouldn't presume to judge," Vincent says. "If I had my choice, or if I'd had your experience, I'd probably never get on a plane again myself."

"So how do you do it?"

Vincent tells Paige about his pilot friend Glenn, parroting the laws of physics that he can recall. He repeats the principle of lift and mentions Bernoulli. "So, even when you're being tossed around in a storm, the laws of physics are still basically in your favor," Vincent adds.

"So, if you know that…"

"… well, knowing physics helps up to a point. What really helps is getting on flights where Glenn is the pilot."

Paige wrinkles her brow.

"Jesus. How does *that* work?"

Vincent explains how he arranges his schedule around Glenn and how if he can't manage it, he won't fly.

With this latest admission, Vincent can feel Paige's expression change, even behind her Ray Bans. It feels like disappointment. Beyond Vincent's suspicion that Paige might be looking for a date or companion, Vincent imagines she is also looking for a good reason to go back to Chicago. She might have preferred that he would have turned out to be someone who had overcome the fear of flying, and could be inspirational in that regard, rather than someone who is nuttier than she is.

"But that's just me," Vincent says. "Having Glenn fly me around, I mean. I can't say that's a good plan for everyone."

"Sounds like a terrible plan to me. Terrible for *anyone*. I think your pilot friend is enabling you, indulging you so that you don't need to face up to anything."

"Now who's psychoanalyzing?"

"I never claimed I wouldn't," Paige says.

"Look, I know you don't understand, and didn't want to say this, but it's more complicated than that. Someone close to me, someone I knew and cared about very deeply took a flight...and didn't come back. She didn't make it back."

Paige's face turns pale. "Oh my God. I'm sorry, I had no idea, obviously."

Vincent straightens in his seat and softens his tone.

"No, I'm just saying... she hasn't come back *yet*. Not *yet*."

Paige's face changes from looking aghast to looking dubious.

"You're talking about this woman you were involved with? Melissa? Getting on a plane to California and not coming back to you? That's *completely* different."

"Yes, perhaps. But..."

"... you can't let go of it, that's your problem," Paige says.

"Yes. I know that," Vincent says. "That's what I've been trying to tell you. I have no *intention* of letting go of it."

Paige shakes her head, looks around at everything and nothing and then reconnects with her Mai Tai. "I would swear, your face actually seems to expand, vertically when you talk about it," Paige says.

"It might be the sunburn," Vincent says.

"I've seen some long faces in my life, but yours is something else entirely."

"Why the long face?" Melissa says.

"Because I'm going to miss you while you're in California," Vincent says.

This isn't the second time. It's the first time. The time she'd only been gone for four days.

"Maybe I'm practicing my face when you're gone," he says.

"Show it to me again," Melissa says.

Vincent affects an exaggerated, hangdog expression.

"I'm coming back," she says. "I won't be gone long."

Vincent smiles and returns his face to its natural state.

"It looks exactly the same," Melissa says.

Vincent shakes the deja vu from his prefrontal lobes and makes an effort to relax his face. As best as he can, anyway. Any variations tend to sting.

"This might be my natural face now," he says, still half-lost or trapped in his daydreams of Melissa.

"No, your face changes when you talk about her," Paige says. "I think it's a shame that such a nice face can be so sad all the time. Aren't you having a good time? Not at all?"

"No, of course. It's not that. The Ocean. Seaside. Mai Tais. What's not to like? It's just that we're discussing some things that are hard for me. I told you before we came here that I…"

"You're a monosexual. Right, I know. You say that, but you're giving off vibes."

"Vibes? You think I'm giving off vibes? I don't think I am."

"You are. Women can sense it. I hate to talk about auras, but you're giving off an aura."

"That's not an aura, that's probably thermal mist coming off my body."

"Well, whatever it is, it's sending mixed signals. It's not saying yes, but it's not saying no definitively, either."

"Then I would say that my aura is misrepresenting me," Vincent says. "I apologize on behalf of my aura." Vincent takes a beat, strokes his chin and continues, thoughtfully. "You know, it's part of our biology that our complexion reddens when we are in mating mode. This may be what you're picking up on. Even subconsciously."

"Did you just say 'mating mode'? Did I hear that correctly?"

"What I'm saying is that when animals—animals in the wild—are stimulated, they may actually flush a bright red to send signals. I think perhaps my sunburn may be sending off a signal that..."

Paige interrupts Vincent and starts to speak, then checks herself and exhales deeply, as if she needs to release some pressure in her body.

"What is it?"

Paige wrinkles her nose and looks down into her Mai Tai.

"What?" Vincent says again.

"Nothing. It's like, this business of your being a monosexual. You talk about it like it's some special thing."

"It *is* a special thing. I invented it."

"So you say. But I think you're just one of those three classic bad choice guys women invariably encounter."

"I thought we were clear this isn't a date. You were just going to show me around."

"Yes, but you also seem determined to undermine anything nice that happens."

"I don't think that's true, exactly," Vincent says.

"You're Guy No. 3. The guy who hides behind the problems of his last relationship."

"I'm not hiding anything. Who are guys one and two?"

"Married, and too much back hair."

"But now you're talking like this is a date. I told you..."

"... yes, I know what you told me, but it doesn't change the fact that you're guy No. 3."

Vincent shrugs and shakes his head. "I'm sorry. I didn't try to mislead you. Honestly. As I said, it's more complicated than you know."

"Yeah. It always is," Paige remarks dryly.

Vincent searches for words. Not for the perfect words, just any words that might help him get through the next few sentences.

"She was...best thing...ever. Perfect...in every way. Then... gone."

"Thanks for the haiku, but that doesn't help," Paige says.

"It's all I can think to say about it."

"I think that's all you *want* to say. I think you're afraid if you say too much, I'll be able to poke holes in your perfect love story. I think that's what you're afraid of."

"I respectfully disagree," Vincent says. "I know it holds up and it's just that it becomes difficult to have to explain it nine different ways. But trust me, it's impenetrable."

"So now I'm obtuse," Paige says.

"I didn't say that. Look, maybe you're right. I'm just like all the rest. I'm guy No. 3. Just like you said."

"Yeah, you are, but you don't *think* you are," Paige says. She leans back in her chair and rubs her neck with both hands. "I need to avoid talking like this," she says.

"I thought this was *all* just talk," Vincent says. "What do you mean *talk like this*?"

"It's talking, but with checkboxes."

"Checkboxes?"

"Of compatibility. Figuring out if you're on the same wavelength. Such as..."

"Unmarried and no back hair?" Vincent offers. "I get it. Yes. This is probably not a good place for us to go, conversation-wise. I'm sorry."

"Can you put aside dating and matters of the opposite sex?" Paige says. "I'm not talking about all the physical things, and not all the deep things, but a lot of little, seemingly insignificant things. I'm talking about things like...he isn't a snob but wouldn't mispronounce February. He likes old Preston Sturges and Marx Brothers movies. He agrees that there are cat people and dog people but would feel shallow labeling someone a cat or dog person. Old fashioned at times. Drinks Old Fashioneds. Fatally romantic."

Paige has inadvertently nailed Vincent with a few uncanny and accurate thumbnails. Vincent doesn't like the feeling that he might be quite so transparent. So, he doesn't acknowledge it.

"Women actually do this?" he asks. "They make lists?"

But he's being disingenuous. He knows they do.

"Why me?" he asks. "Of all the men you can have..."

"Do you have their names? Just for reference," Melissa says.

"No, seriously," Vincent says. "I don't understand why I'm so special to you. I really don't."

"I'll think about it," Melissa says. "I'll get back to you next week."

The following week she surprises him with a neatly typed sheet, a numbered list of 50 reasons why she loves him.

Vincent looks them over.

"I don't see salsa dancing on this list," Vincent says.

"I didn't know you could."

"I can't, but you said you wanted to learn, so I would do it for you."

"Let's start taking lessons. It might make the next list. I'm shooting for 100."

"Where do we stand?"

"With salsa dancing? 51."

"I'll make some calls," Vincent says.

They talk about salsa dancing quite a lot when they are in a good mood. But it never happens.

*

Vincent blinks a few times under his sunglasses, as if it might make him more present in the moment. "So, now you're a cocktail waitress?" he asks.

"Another gratuitous question to steer the conversation away from something you don't want to talk about." Paige says.

"No. Well, yes, maybe," Vincent says. "I'd like to steer away from me and back to you for a moment. I'm just saying… you bartending… you living here and thinking about teaching back home in Chicago. It all seems a bit helter skelter. Or is it still not cool to say 'helter skelter' in California?"

"I'm just trying to have a nice, non-dating conversation with you," Paige says. "I didn't expect to be picked apart."

"Nor did I. And I've only just met you."

"Are you *glad* that you met me?"

"I'm not sure how you mean that. I'm here…"

"Don't bowl me over with enthusiasm. Besides, you don't even seem all here."

"Well, no, I'm *not* all here. I admit that. This isn't a date, and…"

"I know this isn't a date," she cuts in curtly. "You don't need to keep reminding me."

"Look, I'm sorry," Vincent says. "I don't think I'd be the best company for you on a normal day. But today I have more immediate concerns on top of my ongoing malaise. I have this sunburn, I have the ICARUS conference on my mind, I'm definitely in the land of lost love being in San Caliente, and now the Mai Tais have gone to my head because I haven't eaten since I was at O'Hare Airport in Chicago this morning."

As if on cue, Nathan shows up balancing a large tray and sets down two bright white platters and two more giant Mai Tais. In the middle of each platter there are thin-sliced pieces of unappetizingly gray and opalescent-looking raw fish. The only thing the meal has going for it, Vincent thinks, is that it looks reassuringly like fish and looks fairly fresh. Adjacent to the main course, drawn on each of the white platters in dark miso paste is a small skull and crossbones.

"Fugu. You have my condolences," Nathan says, and returns to the kitchen.

"I imagine all this exaggerated drama about this fish is good for business?" Vincent asks.

Paige doesn't reply. She seems to be waiting for him to start.

Vincent picks up his chopsticks and in an uncharacteristically adept move, picks up a large mouthful from the row of raw fish pieces in front of him and practically swallows it whole. It feels good, and he digs in again. Whenever he looks up from his food, Paige is looking directly at him, as if waiting to catch his eyes, or pierce through his sunglasses. But now, much to his surprise, she is smiling again. At him, or at the arrival of sushi. Or at the prospect of him eating the sushi, maybe? Because of her sunglasses he can't tell which.

It's an engaging smile. Paige is witty, like Melissa had been. Sometimes her retorts even remind him of Melissa's feisty nature, or something Melissa might have said, but embodied in a different package. He wishes, wistfully, that he could be having this experience pre-Melissa, before he knew of her existence. He thinks he might have even enjoyed it in more naïve times, as one enjoys rowing a rowboat before ever experiencing a luxury yacht.

"Eat up," Paige says. "I think I can help you with your sunburn. I've got something back at my place."

"Thanks, but I've got my blue stuff back at the hotel. It has lidocaine. I bought just about every bottle they had in the gift store at the El Famous. I should have brought some with me. I suppose what I should do is drop you off, get back to the hotel and apply it liberally."

"You know why they sell that blue stuff at hotels? Because it's for tourists. I'm talking about something made from real aloe vera from my own plants. From the source. Uncut. I also use fresh mint leaves from my mint plant for Juleps. And my homemade skin cream has yogurt and a few other natural ingredients. And a bit of Balsam of Peru for esthetic purposes. But, honestly, it's very basic, homeopathic stuff. Best cure you'll ever find for a sunburn. Unless you see a dermatologist."

"Well, you know I can't do that at the moment. But I missed the part where you changed your major from History to Chemistry."

"I'm a mixologist. I experiment with different mixtures."

"Ah. So, you think you can cure my sunburn with an amateur bartender's homemade remedy? You know that I've written for medical journals. Peer-reviewed *dermatology* journals. I've spent a good part of my career debunking miracle wonder creams like the one you just described."

"I bet I can surprise you," Paige says. "I just need a guinea pig."

"A guinea pig. A victim, in other words."

"Sure, whatever," she says, without smiling. "Eat up. We should try to get to my place by sunset. I've got a nice view of the ocean from my balcony, where I have most of my plants. You can watch the sunset, have a drink, and I'll take some cuttings from the plants, mix it up and get you feeling better."

"That's quite an agenda. And a tall order, besides. Do you meet that many men with sunburn that you have to keep medicinal plants around you at all times?"

"Aloe is good for a lot of things. You know that. And I use the mint in juleps, mostly. I'll make you one."

"So... mint juleps, aloe vera, yogurt, Balsam of Peru, and a cure for my sunburn, that's your plan for me?"

"Unless you have another plan?"

"I need to finish my fugu."

"I'm impressed that you had any at all, you don't need to overdo it," Paige says.

There's not much on the plate, and Vincent has been eating like a famished cougar taking down a gazelle. He isn't sure his stomach likes it. Rather than digest, the food seems to keep moving around as if the fish is so fresh it's swimming in his stomach. Still, he keeps stabbing with his chopsticks and stuffing his mouth.

"You're not eating yours," he says, stabbing at Paige's platter with his chopstick.

"I guess I'm not as hungry as you."

It seems a waste, he thinks. Paige's plate remains largely untouched, while Vincent's plate shines white against the sunlight as he picks off the last pieces of fish and gobbles them down, washing it all down with slugs from his second giant Mai Tai.

"Do you want mine?" Paige asks. She doesn't wait for an answer and shoves several more pieces of fish onto his plate.

"If you really don't want it," Vincent says, and digs into Paige's portions of fish. "It's really not bad at all."

"Glad you like it," Paige says.

"So, what is fugu?" Vincent asks. "It's not fishy. Tastes a bit exotic."

"Blowfish."

"Blowfish?" Vincent's eyebrows extend up above his sunglasses. "No. You're putting me on. It's poisonous, isn't it?"

"Not entirely. But I'm impressed how you're tearing into it."

"I'm sure I've heard that it's very dangerous," Vincent says. He now envisions something evil darting around in his intestines, waiting to strike.

"When it's prepared correctly, it's a delicacy, not a death sentence," Paige says. "The most important thing is how it's gutted. They have to make sure the poisonous parts are separated from the toxic parts. The toxic parts are worse than cyanide. No cure."

"Is that a fact?"

Vincent begins to feel light-headed.

"Only licensed sushi chefs can prepare it. There's a minimum of two years training."

"And you feel confident that the chef here...?"

"Here? Oh, of course. Randy is certified in fugu."

"*Randy*? I'm trusting my deadly fish consumption to someone named *Randy*?"

"I *think* Randy's in the kitchen tonight. I just assumed he was. He *must* be, he's the only one certified. They wouldn't allow anyone else to handle fugu."

"Oh, well...that's fine then," Vincent says, sighing heavily, rubbing his head with one hand and his stomach with the other.

"Are you sweating?" Paige asks.

"A little. I think it's just that I'm not used to this California weather," Vincent says. He removes his linen napkin from his lap and dabs at his forehead. What had, moments ago, tasted not so fishy in his mouth and had felt only slightly uncomfortable in his stomach now tastes quite fishy and very much at odds with his stomach.

Vincent finds himself also rethinking Paige's remark about needing him as a "guinea pig." It had sounded harmless and jovial enough a few moments ago, but now it gives him pause. He is with a relative stranger, eating a strange fish she ordered up especially for him. Fish that she has barely touched herself.

"What'll really kill you is the price," Paige says. "An exotic fish like this, prepared by a licensed chef—presumably, I mean. It's not cheap."

"Oh, gosh, I didn't think to ask…"

"It's something like $120 for a few slices."

"One *hundred* twenty…?"

"For each plate. These were pretty good-sized portions. I'm still surprised you finished it all. That's very brave of you."

"Oh, wow," Vincent says.

He feels a seismic quake of nausea accompanied by considerable after-tremors in his stomach.

"You know, I might have been better off with salmon or tuna," he says. "Or even a hot dog."

"I'm joking with you. I hope you don't think I would make *you* pay for this," Paige says, reaching under the table for her purse. "I just wanted you to try something new and different."

"I can't let you do that," Vincent says, "I can't allow you to pay." He reaches into his back pocket, pulls out his wallet and puts it on the table. He carries a fair amount of cash on trips, for unforeseen emergencies, but fears the fugu dinner might wipe him out entirely.

"Put that away," Paige says. "I get a big discount on food because I work here sometimes. And the drinks are on the house."

"Still, I don't think…"

"Are you worried that you'll *owe* me?" Page asks. "Like I might feel I can have my way with you back at my beach house?"

"I wasn't thinking that, but…"

"As you're so keen to remind me, *this isn't a date*." Paige says, putting a stack of twenties on the table and anchoring them with a bottle of soy sauce. "You can put those thoughts out of your head."

Vincent knows she's likely teasing, but he's still not even 50 percent sure of her motives.

He recalls the mad-serial-killer-women types he's seen on investigative reports on A&E. Women that seem perfectly normal but actually hate all men or, at the very least, all men that remind them of their abusive boyfriends, husbands, and fathers. These women commit oddly unique crimes like stabbing men with high heels, super gluing their testicles together. Homicide by an exotic poisonous fish seems to fit this category.

He is currently dining somewhere along the California coast where nary a soul would know how to find him. He is driving a car that isn't registered to his name. If something happens to him, it might be a long time before he is traced, or worse, identified through dental records. And since he hasn't been super vigilant about keeping his dental appointments, he imagines this will further complicate the identification process.

Paige seems normal; then again so had many of those women on the A&E investigative reports. Those women were safely behind bars. But then he thought of another show, *Unsolved Mysteries*. That's the show to which he should have been paying more attention. Knowing about women who have *already* been caught won't help him. It would be better to know if there were any unsolved blowfish murderers *at large*.

He weighs the prospect of further endangering himself by going off with Paige to her beach house; driving to some *even more* remote location and allowing himself to be alone with this relative stranger, a woman who will encourage him to rub some of her homemade aloe-mint-yogurt-Balsam-of-Peru and-*who-knows-what-else* on his body. Possibly some kind of rare, muscle-atrophying topical lotion and a formaldehyde face wrap.

He wishes now he hadn't made that reference to "Helter Skelter."

His face feels hot again. Or hotter.

"Shall we head up the coast to my place?" Paige asks, snapping her purse shut, wrapping her hair back in a ponytail and clipping it up again.

"I'm not sure I'm feeling all that well," Vincent says.

"Then we should probably keep moving," Paige says, humorlessly.

Vincent nods, if not robotically then not in complete control of all his moving parts. Primarily the parts that are affecting his ability to make sound decisions or disagree.

"Sure," he says. "Let's go."

Chapter 9

(ghosts and albinos)

They leave Slammin' Sammy Sushi and head further south along the California coastline. Paige has her hair tied in a ponytail again for the ride and plays with the radio as Vincent drives. They don't say much during the drive but Paige points to things. Surfers, boats, maybe a whale—but they can't be sure. She eventually points to a trio of small bungalows dotting the shoreline and Vincent pulls onto another exit road, then down another long gravel driveway.

"Which one?" Vincent asks, nodding to the three bungalows.

"Last one on the left," Paige says. "The others are vacant."

The place is a second-floor walk-up, propped up on thick-beamed wooden stilts moored into concrete. Might have been safer to keep it on the ground, Vincent thinks, but ostensibly the height increases the ambience of the ocean front. A fairly recent coat of turquoise has been applied to the siding.

There is a vintage blue VW bus in the lot. Maybe 30 years old, but it looks like it has been restored and kept up. It seemed well-placed next to the bungalows, like a prop in a documentary about free-spirited Californians in the late 1960s.

"That's yours?" Vincent asks.

"That's Chrysanthemum," she says. "She leaks a little oil, very unreliable, so I carpool a lot. But I love that little camper."

"You name your cars?"

"This one I did."

"Do you camp?"

"I don't. Well, sort of. I sleep out in it, in the parking lot near the ocean. I pretend like it's camping."

Paige leads Vincent up a flight of creaky, intimidating wooden stairs. Inside, the bungalow is more homey than touristy. There are no stereotypically fake watercolor prints of boats on the wall, no lamps shaped like anchors. Instead, it is contemporary retro chic. An impressive and expensive McIntosh stereo receiver in a glass cabinet. A comfy-looking camel-colored sectional arranged adjacent to a rattan table and rattan chair. A framed mosaic mirror on one wall. A large tropical fish tank gurgles in one corner of the room. A framed photo on the wall of Miles Davis that Vincent recognizes from the cover of *Tutu*. Black-and-white, his perfect face against a dark background, eyes dead serious, no attitude, looking vulnerable and dangerous all at once. Strong, yet fragile. *The Prince of Darkness* and *Man Walking on Eggshells*.

"You like jazz?" he asks.

"Yes. I like all kinds of music, she says. "But I really like this picture."

"It is a great photo," he says. "Great place."

"I pay my parents a modest rent and keep it up," Paige says. "The Miles print is from a gallery in La Jolla. That's my one indulgence. That, my stereo, and my tropical fish. The rest was furnished by my parents." Paige kicks off her sandals and walks barefoot across a hardwood floor to a wooden crate of CDs to search for something to play. "Oh, and my bed. I love my bed."

"Nice," Vincent says again. He doesn't ask further questions about the bed.

"I love it," he thinks he hears Paige say.

The music that pours out of the speakers sounds to him like Lyle Lovett, so he thinks she may have said "Lyle Lovett," rather than "I love it." But Vincent doesn't ask.

"You like this?" Paige asks over the music.

"It's fine, fine," Vincent says, part of him wanting her to turn the music down a bit so he can hear her, but not down so low that he'd need to fill in the quiet it would create.

Vincent parks himself on her rattan chair and lets his eyes wander around her place. Paige walks over to him, stands before him, arms akimbo.

"Okay," she says. "I believe I promised you a mint julep. And something soothing for that burn?"

Paige has Vincent stand up, slips off his sunglasses and together they examine his outer layers in her mosaic mirror. His image is distorted, or at least he believes it may be.

"Is it possible I've gotten redder?" he asks.

She puts her index finger on his head and rotates him slowly, as if she is dialing an old rotary phone, then regards him with a frown.

"Mmmm. I'd like to say I've seen worse, but I don't want to lie to you," Paige says. "Come with me, the deck is just outside my bedroom."

Vincent had already started following Paige but stops when she says the word "bedroom." He looks around her living room for another door or something to help him to avoid, or maybe at least delay going into her bedroom. He stops and kneels next to the 20-gallon fish tank, perched atop a bronze credenza.

"This is a nice tank. You like tropical fish?"

"Sure," she says. "Come on. We're going out to the deck."

"Hang on a sec," Vincent says. He glances inside the aquarium and observes a bed of white pebbles, a miniature Ferris wheel and a few fake palm trees, like miniature versions of the palm trees he'd seen back at the El Famous hotel. The fish tank is well-kept, very clean. In fact, it seems too clean. There doesn't appear to be any aquatic life in it.

"What do you have in here?" Vincent asks. "I don't see any fish."

He has managed to momentarily deter her. She returns from the hallway and joins him at the fish tank.

"Let's see," Paige says with a sigh. She gets down on her

haunches next to Vincent and put her head next to his, peering inside. "If I remember, I've got ghost shrimp in here and some albino frogs."

"Ah. Very funny," Vincent says, staring into the pristine tank.

"No, I'm not kidding. Three ghost shrimp and two albino frogs."

"Ghost shrimp and albino frogs," he repeats, as he gazes more deeply into the tank, trying to detect any movement. "Set against a bed of white rocks."

"Exactly."

"It's a tad... monochromatic, no? I've never heard of ghost shrimp. Do you have to dip them in batter before you can see them?"

"Don't be silly. They're right there. Two on that rock there, in the middle..."

Vincent squints harder.

"Oh. Okay, yes," he says, as he stares at something he suspects is not a shrimp or frog, but just another white pebble. He's still not sure if this is a put on. Nothing in her voice indicates it.

"Do they use the Ferris wheel much?" Vincent asks.

"They may. But I haven't seen that," Paige says.

"Too bad. It might make it easier to see them if they took a little ride now and then. What are their names?"

"They don't have *names*," Paige says, as if he's daft to suggest it.

"You named your VW camper, but you don't name your fish?"

"They're just for show. I just like having them in my tank because they're interesting," Paige says.

"Is that why *I'm* here?" Vincent says. "Just to make things interesting?"

"You're the one who wants to talk about my fish tank," Paige says.

He ignores her response and continues with his intellectually lame opinions on the value of aquatic christening.

"It just seems to me that by not naming them, you're denying them their individual identity," Vincent says.

"I hadn't thought of that," she says. "I guess I prefer not to get emotionally involved with my fish," she says. "Can we continue this on the deck? We're going to miss a perfectly good sunset." She stands up.

Vincent remains in place, still kneeling at the fish tank. Stalling. Not wanting to see or possibly be asked how perfectly good her bed might be.

"It's nothing to do with getting involved," Vincent continues. "The thing is, if one of these creatures dies in this tank without identity, the others won't be left with any sense of self, apart from the group that will motivate them to keep going. One dies, and they all learn to die—because they're a group, not individuals. That's their learned behavior."

As Vincent is manufacturing this drivel, he's aware he's being overly pedantic. Channeling the Discovery Channel and *Psychology Today* through the sieve of his own neurosis. But if the anonymity and plight of the tiny creatures troubles him at all, it's not as troubling as the thought of having to go through Paige's bedroom to get outside.

Paige listens to him without blinking. She kneels down next to Vincent again. "So now you're suggesting that I'm killing my fish…"

"… by not naming them. Yes, possibly."

"Quite frankly, I doubt I can tell them apart."

"Well, you wouldn't say that about human twins or triplets."

"I might. But they're not human twins or triplets, they're aquarium decorations."

"I think you need to give them all names and hope that when you're addressing them that you get it right. At least some of the time."

"By that reasoning, if I get it wrong, won't I risk hurting their feelings by accidentally calling one by the wrong name."

"I suppose," Vincent says, momentarily glancing down at the floor. "Then again, I've read that fish have an attention span of about three to four seconds, so I suppose nothing's ever really going to stick, anyway."

"How about Emerson?" Paige says, brightening. "As a name, I mean. You know, Thoreau, Emerson… Walden Pond and all that. Like a quiet place of contemplation."

"Yes, I get the idea," Vincent says. "Which one?"

"Which one?"

"Which one are you calling Emerson?"

"All of them."

"All of them? Oh. You mean like naming them all George, like George Foreman did with his boys?"

"Yes. That way I won't risk offending them no matter what I call them. They will all appreciate being called Emerson."

"Well, for about three to four seconds, anyway," Vincent pitches in, somberly. "With their limited attention span, and all that, I mean…"

"… yes, I understand. Do we have this crisis with my fish all settled, then?"

"I think so," Vincent says.

Their faces are close, close enough that Vincent can feel the heat from Paige's face, or perhaps it's a heat boomeranging off his own sunburned face. He wonders if she feels it, as well, and wonders if she may be wondering the same thing. But he doesn't ask. He stands up.

Paige leads him down a narrow hallway. There are candles on the wall along the way and she lights a few of them as she comes to them. He guesses they are clove-scented because he is momentarily reminded of his dentist's office. They finally arrive in Paige's bedroom, and, unable to help himself, he steals a surreptitious glimpse at her comfortable room and large fluffy bed, covered with bulging ebony throw pillows. More candles grace her nightstand and she lights them. It concerns him that she is creating "mood" and "aura" in an environment normally reserved for pajamas or less. But just as quickly as she lights the bedside candles, she leads him out the French doors off the bedroom onto her balcony.

There is, in fact, nothing to see from her wooden deck but the shoreline, miles of ocean, and a sun that got glutinously redder, sucking in surrounding light and bulging against the horizon.

There's a pair of matching wooden Adirondack recliners on the deck, and a small plastic tray table, but the deck area is largely defined by Paige's plants. There are scores of green and leafy things in earthen pots; a few of them flowering. Vincent can't distinguish a mint plant from an aloe plant. He possesses a cursory recognition of some well-known poisonous plants from having written dermatology articles on skin conditions caused by plants. Poison ivy, poison oak, poison sumac. Wood nettle plants. Paige's plants do not resemble any of these, however, and it puts Vincent slightly more at ease.

"So, you like gardening?" he asks.

"Not particularly. But I like having plants. I hope you're not going to make me give them all names."

"No. I won't," Vincent says, as he settles into a deck chair.

Paige leans down and begins inspecting her collection of flora, caressing and squeezing certain leaves, bending over the plants in her bare feet, concentrating intently, carefully pulling off some select leaves. For his skin potion, he presumes.

She stands and faces the ocean, stretching out her arms, fists full of leafy greens, gloriously backlit by the descending sun, appearing to Vincent like a leafy goddess. "What do you think?" she asks, looking out at the vista.

"Very nice," Vincent says, referring to the ocean and sunset. But what has momentarily captured his attention, to his surprise and shame, is Paige's heart-shaped behind, tightly outlined against her faded blue jeans.

Checking out her ass? This isn't who he is.

He turns his gaze away, feeling a traitor to his monosexuality and experiencing a Melissa-induced pang of guilt. He stares off into the sunset trying to detach himself, putting himself far out to sea.

Paige turns around and faces him with her handful of leaves.

"This ought to do the trick," she says.

"Trick? What trick?" Vincent says, feeling as though he's been caught in a lie he hasn't uttered. Or worse, caught admiring the shapeliness of Paige's piriformis muscles.

"It's just an expression," she says, cocking her head at him quizzically. "Why don't you try and relax. Sit here and enjoy the sunset. I'll be back in a couple of minutes."

As she disappears, the CD changes and he is left with a sunset, an ocean, and faint strains of a song by The Four Tops from the stereo inside. As he idly half hums and half sings along he begins to realize the song that he is half-humming and half-singing is *Baby I Need Your Loving*. Once Vincent realizes what he is humming/singing, he stops humming/singing it.

That's fine, I'll just ignore that, he thinks.

His stomach is still queasy and he's developed a dull, throbbing headache besides, all of which he's blaming on the sunburn, in addition to nagging thoughts about the possible ill effects of ingesting potentially lethal blowfish at Slammin' Sammy Sushi.

He is also feeling the specter of guilt looming over this date-but-not-really-a-date tableau. He can feel Melissa rolling in with the tide, like a brine-soaked mist from the ocean. Within the synaptic vapor is the persistent, yet insipid hope that Melissa is indeed in close proximity here in San Caliente. If not at the El Famous hotel pool earlier in the day, then somewhere else. But nearby. *Somewhere*. He hopes Melissa has been trailing him this entire time and is about to burst through the French doors. Give him hell for being with Paige.

Bring it on, Vincent thinks.

He'd welcome it. Have it all out, explain to Melissa the absurd series of consequences that caused him to be here in a woman's beach house, get past an awkward farewell to Paige and then split with his beloved Melissa. Still time for he and Melissa to enjoy this perfect sunset, find a beachside motel, and consummate make-up sex.

Vincent stands up, looks out into the ocean again, this time hoping to see an incoming boat, or a seaplane, coming to rescue him.

Save me.

But all he sees is sand, surfers, and the occasional, indifferent gull wheeling along the shoreline. He sits back down in the Adirondack chair, feeling heavy and anxious.

The music from inside has transitioned from the suggestive Four Tops to soothing Cat Stevens. It's "The Wind" from *Teaser and the Firecat*. A bittersweet, and evocative song, but one that makes him feel more in his element.

Paige appears again, her arms loaded with a wicker tray, carrying two drinks that he supposes are mint juleps (the mint sprig is the giveaway), and a clear Ball Mason jar that contains something gelatinous, aqua in tone. He regards the jar dubiously, since it has a similar blue color as the blue, over-the-counter stuff he'd purchased from the El Famous gift shop at his hotel. Not exactly the same blue, but very close, he thinks. He wonders if Paige hasn't poured some of it in a mason jar to make it look homemade and is just pulling his leg about all the rest.

The music changes again and Vincent recognizes "Blue in Green" by Miles Davis, from the album *Kind of Blue*. It seems suspiciously and coincidentally cued up for the occasion, but he doesn't say anything about it.

"You just whipped up this concoction?" Vincent asks. "Just now?"

"Of course," she says. "Now let's get at it."

"Let's get at it," Vincent repeats, in a lower, less enthusiastic tone.

"Unbutton your shirt." Paige makes the demand in a clinical tone and, after a brief pause, he acquiesces.

The image of Melissa's face returns, raining down on Vincent's consciousness, all thunder bursts of disapproval, precipitations of disappointment, and droplets of disdain. In his mind he snaps at Melissa.

You'd just have me suffer with this sunburn, wouldn't you? Even though you're not here to help me with it yourself and aren't here to stop this from happening.

This nonverbal tongue lashing doesn't make the phantom Melissa disappear, but it makes her a tad more oblique.

"Taking off my shirt now," he announces aloud to the fading image.

"Yes, that's the idea," Paige says, snapping Vincent back into the reality of the moment. She is kneeling beside him, wiggling her fingers impatiently in his face to receive the garment from him. "*Focus*. Unbutton, please."

"Right, right," he says. Like ripping an old bandage from a hairy arm, his burned torso makes the shirt removal painful, but once his chest hits the air it feels momentarily cooler, and for this he is grateful.

"Oh wow," Paige says, eyeing the hot, glowing flesh. "Your shoulders, your chest... I may need more of this stuff. Look at you... your stomach... your..."

"... it stops at my waist," Vincent says, tracing a boundary finger along his belt line.

Paige unscrews the top of the Mason jar. Vincent immediately leans forward to dip his hand into the shining blue goop, but she nudges his hand away.

"You have to let me do this," Paige says.

Vincent fails to note on which word she has placed her emphasis in this demand.

It could have been:

You *have* to let me do this (as a person with a fetish for someone with sunburns might say when they wish to experience the condition firsthand). Or it might have been: You have to let *me* do this (positioning herself as one better qualified than he to apply the gel).

Regardless of the inflection, he wonders what kind of woman would eagerly anticipate this? No woman—and certainly not an (empirically) attractive woman like Paige—could be so desperate to get a man to remove his shirt and touch him that she would resort to spreading a mysterious mix of mint, aloe, yogurt, and Balsam of Peru on his sensitive skin.

Paige is different from other women Vincent has met in his life (before and after Melissa). There are no bells and whistles going off. He isn't getting any choirs of angels or Vatican smoke signals. But the vibe he's getting is mostly positive. Paige seems super nice, and she's being super nice to him.

Is this what flirting looks like nowadays? Vincent wonders. Maybe. Maybe not. Perhaps she is just being nice because she wanted a ride home. Or maybe she didn't have any motivation at all. Maybe she just liked him.

What kind of people are *those*, anyway? It seemed impossible for Vincent to reconcile his hard-nosed cynicism with his healthy sense of doubt. But, ultimately, he doesn't argue and lets Paige proceed. The CD changes again and it is now Charlie Parker with Strings. "Everything Happens to Me."

Paige dabs into the jar with her nimble fingers and begins softly applying her special treatment to his forehead and cheeks. She caresses the balm over Vincent's face, carefully, methodically, not unlike a blind person might trace the outline of a person's features to get to know them. The physical effect is the epitome of contrary sensory feeling. There is the pain of having his raw skin touched but also the cooling relief of the balm. He is having one of those uncomfortable yet exquisite moments of wanting to say "stop" and "don't stop" all in the same breath.

He keeps his eyes closed so that she can do her job, but occasionally he opens them and, unlike a blind person, awkwardly meets her gaze dead on.

Then her fingers are on his sensitive neck, then down to his pectorals. The balm goes on like the first layer of paint on a sun-bleached Kansas barn. Bristle-brushed, even with Paige's soft bristle fingertips.

Slowly, imperceptibly, Paige's touch is beginning to cross over into a sensation more pleasurable than not. As she moves across his chest, his nipples distend and harden, much as he would prefer they wouldn't. As Paige fingerpaints across his stomach he involuntarily sighs with a satisfied, guttural grunt. The frown that has been on Paige's face as she empathically endured his oohs and aahs, now gives way to a smile of accomplishment. A canary-fed cat smile.

"Better?" she says.

"I suppose," he says. He tries to keep it clinical. "So, there's mint... and aloe..."

"Balsam of Peru..."

"Balsam of Peru, yes. And what's the slippery part of it?"

"Partly yogurt," Paige says. "But I expect you're feeling the Kalahari melon seed oil."

"Kalahari..."

"... pure, Kalahari melon seed oil," she says.

"I don't recall you mentioning that before. Where do you get Kalahari melon seed oil?"

"From Kalahari, silly."

"No, I mean you, personally."

"It's not as hard as you might think," she says.

"What makes it blue?"

"Food coloring."

"So, totally unnecessary food coloring."

"It looks more soothing. Do you think that that blue lidocaine stuff you buy is naturally blue? Blue is the color of relief. The question I have for you is: *is it working*?"

It *was* working. Perhaps too well, Vincent thinks. Touching his face, chest, and nipples is as about as intimate as nearly anything he can think of. He supposes it would have been even *more* intensely personal if the situation was reversed, and he was touching her face, her chest, her nipples. He momentarily imagines her erogenous zones reacting to the touch of cool Kalahari melon seed oil. But she isn't reacting that way because he isn't touching her, and silently chastises himself for momentarily thinking about it.

"I've, um... I've never really done anything like this," Vincent says.

"You mean to tell me you've never had a mixture of aloe, yogurt, fresh mint leaves, Balsam of Peru and Kalahari melon seed oil smeared on your body?"

"Maybe some sailors, once, when I was in the Navy," Vincent says, trying to make *any* joke, however lame, to lighten what is beginning to feel distinctly *intimate*. Paige dips her fingers into the jar again. But when her hands move down to Vincent's stomach and abdomen—which are equally afflicted and therefore no less in need of relief—he puts his hand over hers.

"It stops there," he says.

Unfortunately for Vincent, it doesn't stop there. It does for Paige; she rolls her eyes and obediently puts up her hands in surrender. But just below his abdomen, things are continuing. Expanding. Initially, Vincent attributes the unexpected arousal to some completely involuntary biochemical aberration. What other explanation could there be? He hopes the natural tenting of pleats in his khakis will hide it. Paige doesn't appear to notice anything and if she does, she doesn't say anything, and for this he is extremely grateful.

She sighs and wipes her hands on a terry cloth towel. "Let's move on to part two."

"Part two?" Vincent says, his voice betraying new apprehension.

"The juleps."

"Ah. The juleps."

"Another first for you?"

"No, I've had juleps before," he says. He is about to say "in the Navy" again. But he is distracted.

Juleps. Another summer evening. Another rooftop deck. Another body of water. Melissa's 28th floor Chicago apartment that looks out on Lake Michigan. Sitting outside on her deck on a balmy, summer-like Saturday in early May. Lounging on loungers. His shirt off. Her in a white cotton blouse and shorts. A pitcher of juleps. The television on, just inside her living room. The 123rd running of the Kentucky Derby. Horses at the gate.

"I do believe they are finally starting," Melissa says, with an affected Southern drawl.

"And I do believe it's fah too nice outside to be inside watchin' people on horses," Vincent says, matching her drawl for drawl.

"I do declare, you may be right. But it's powerful hot in this sun." She unbuttons the top three buttons on her white cotton blouse. Vincent admires the soft valley that appears, the wonderful alabaster skin, the promise of simple delight.

After the pitcher of juleps, they decide to go inside, to have sex on her smooth leather couch. They miss the Derby. Vincent hears about the winner later during a recap.

Real Quiet.

Vincent stares down into the julep Paige has mixed for him. He downs it quickly, while wondering if phantom Melissa can see through his troublesome khakis. He wonders again if Paige has detected anything. His mind and body are tag teaming like wrestlers in the ring; alternately grappling, thrashing, and body slamming through conflicting thoughts and sensations. Is it the memory of Melissa in her unbuttoned white cotton blouse that has made the blood rush from his head to his penis, or the loving touch of Paige's fingers? He hopes it is the former, fears it is the latter. Another tag off.

Paige's CD player revolves again and lands on a new CD.

Oh no, Vincent thinks.

"Sinatra? You like Sinatra?" he asks.

"Doesn't everyone like Sinatra?" Paige says.

But it wasn't just any Sinatra. It was *the* song. *Their* song.

I've Got You Under My Skin.

"Is something wrong?" Paige asks.

"This song… it's just… oddly timed, that's all."

Paige smiles and looks at her hands. Vincent guesses she's thinking that he's referring to the fact that she's been under his skin, literally, with the ends of her fingers.

"Oh, right," she says. "It wasn't planned. Now you need to sit still for a few minutes or two with this stuff on, soak it in."

"Sit? You mean sit *still*? Not talk?"

"Yes, we're going to just sit. Relax. Calm. Meditate. Enjoy the Sinatra."

"Enjoy the Sinatra," he repeats.

Vincent imagines himself submerging to the bottom of Paige's fish tank, deep under the white stones, among the Emersons, invisible in a liquid narcosis of silence.

Longing to be in a place where he can't hear the song.

Chapter 10

(the Super Cannoli)

"Who's up for a song?" someone yells from the far end of the room.

Vincent is upstairs in the party room of Paisano Pasquale's. His annual office Christmas Party, December 1997. Coworkers, colleagues, and strangers. Red wine, martinis, and grappa. Antipasto platters, baked ziti. A giant cannoli filled with smaller cannoli.

Paisano Pasquale's popularity, size and success makes it a prime location for large company functions, like the *Skinformation* staff dinner that Vincent feels compelled to attend each year. The company had reserved a private party room on the second floor of the restaurant every year Vincent had worked there. He and all 29 of his coworkers were expected to attend. Spouses and dates were optional. Vincent had gone stag. If he had managed to corral a date during the holidays (and he had not), the last place he'd have taken her to would have been a work-related function like this one.

The writers, editors, dermatology physician advisors, and graphic designers all drink too much grappa, get loud quickly, and eventually sing a lot of insipid, inappropriate, and insensitive parody songs: "Rudolph the Rosacea-nosed Reindeer," "It's Beginning to Look a Lot Like Eczemas," and "Basal Cells" (sung to the tune of "Silver Bells").

The downside of not bringing a date is that Vincent is forced to interact more directly with his coworkers. In the office, as a writer and editor, he can keep mostly to himself. When compelled, he can converse on easy, universal topics, like construction causing traffic problems, or the miserable weather—one could always talk about the road construction or weather in Chicago. When his coworkers are not drinking or singing, however, and are forced to talk socially and not talk about work, it often falls flat. It usually comes back to the weather, the roads, and what everyone simply *must* watch on HBO.

Vincent consciously seeks conversations with extroverts, people who can do the heavy lifting, conversationally. *Skinformation* is rife with extroverts, and on this night it's Vincent's coworker Mitchell George Wallace, who has corralled a seat just to the left of him and is boasting about how much he lifted at the gym the night before.

"The 220 curl is a cruel bitch," Mitch says with serious, almost convincing bravado. "You have to work up to it." He mimes the motion in miniature with a forkful of ziti, an action that countermands and eviscerates any macho posing he might have been trying to evoke.

Mitch is not even talking to Vincent; he's broadcasting his alleged feats of strength to any women within earshot at the table. Vincent's unspoken task in this scenario is to nod at Mitch's accomplishments and make little noises as though he is impressed by it all, so that the women might be sent swooning, or so Mitch hoped. Vincent has never actually seen this tactic succeed.

Half-listening and not talking, Vincent is in compulsive sipping mode; his elbow in a perpetual state of bending. He is mostly drinking dry martinis and knows it's a road that will lead to a nasty hangover, but…oh well…office Christmas parties come but once a year.

Vincent's head grows increasingly buoyant, and his visits to the bathroom to clear his head and relieve his bladder are frequent and necessary. But he also welcomes opportunities to excuse himself from this party he wants no part of.

"Who's up for a song?" one of his coworkers yells again.

No one knows it, but Vincent has an excellent singing voice, and is an accomplished Rat Pack vocal mimic, as well. But he reserves this talent for personal moments; daily showers, solitary commutes in his Fiat. He prefers to do his crooning alone in his apartment with an Old Fashioned in a rocks glass and his Koss headphones snug around his ears.

When a new employee group song seems inevitable, Vincent takes it as his cue to make another quiet exit from the party room and stands up.

"Again?" Mitch says, when Vincent gets up to excuse himself. "You're going to miss the arrival of the Super Cannoli."

A dessert tradition at these holiday parties, and the pinnacle of the evening, the Super Cannoli is an eight-pound, tubular pastry torpedo, large enough to have the company's *Skinformation* logo recreated in blue and green icing on its side, and filled with enough smaller (comparatively smaller) cannoli to feed the entire *Skinformation* staff, and then some. Even Vincent will admit it is impressive to see it brought forth by several waiters, carried in like Cleopatra on a palanquin and set down ceremoniously on the glossy white tablecloth amid much exaggerated gasping and applause. "Save me a cannoli," Vincent says. "And a regular coffee, if they come around. I'll be back."

In the downstairs men's room Vincent takes care of business and then vainly checks himself out in the mirror and muses silently to himself about the drab predictability of the holidays.

He tugs at his Hugo Boss sports jacket, straightens and tightens his crimson tie, and brushes his trousers free of stray crumbs he might have collected during dinner. He checks his white shirt for any signs of marinara sauce. Everything seems in place. He always dresses well, but these are also the only *nice* clothes he owns. Frequently dry cleaned, this outfit travels with him to dermatology conventions across the United States, then hangs in his closet the rest of the year waiting for the office Christmas party. Vincent begins to think he should wear it more often because it gives him confidence. But that might also be the dry martinis.

"Not so bad," Vincent says to his reflection in the mirror. "Tell me again why you aren't dating anyone?"

The martinis have also increased his desire for a cigarette. He is not a regular smoker and is perpetually planning to quit entirely. He smokes when all feels wrong in his world, quits when things are going well. Lately, he's been out of sorts more often than not, so the odds are not in his favor for a smoke-free holiday.

Tonight, Vincent had picked up a pack of Gauloises at a specialty tobacco shop before coming to the restaurant. A cigarette, particularly a long French cigarette, will buy him a few extra minutes before having to jump back into the fray of his colleagues upstairs. Vincent turns a corner out of the men's room and walks into the neighboring restaurant bar, searching for matches, an unlit cigarette dangling from his lips.

It is not unusual for Paisano Pasquale's to pipe in Rat Pack favorites over their sound system. But when Vincent hears Sinatra singing "I've Got You Under My Skin" the moment he enters the restaurant bar, it seems like the tune has been magically cued up just for him. Like his very own walk-on music, his theme song. Later, he will interpret it as introductory music for the next scene of his life. The curtain rising on his Act II. And an overpowering sense of *now this happens.*

The bar has surprisingly few patrons, but there is an attractive woman sitting alone at the other end of the bar, sipping a martini.

Vincent would later remember it as a thunderbolt; some powerful force that turned his head in her direction and kept it there, squarely. If there had been one of those big hand of God index fingers in the vicinity, it would have broken through the ceiling of Paisano Pasquale's and pointed directly at this woman.

Lo and behold. *This one.*

He would later describe it (to anyone who would listen) as a tableau that unfolded like the scene when Tony meets Maria at the dance in *West Side Story*. Everything around Maria fades into gauzy soft focus. It is the same for him now. There is only this woman at one end of the bar, Vincent at the other end, and a beautiful Sinatra song floating between them.

I've got you under my skin.

In any other circumstance, even with a sense of initial attraction, he might have merely smiled in her direction. But the cosmic otherness of the moment causes Vincent to instead give her a quizzical look at first, rather than a smile. As if to say: *Do you sense the same thing I sense happening here?*

The woman's reaction surprises Vincent even further by mirroring the look back at him. There is no hint that she is annoyed at being stared at, only the same bemused look on her face that seems to respond, *Yes, what's happening here?*

Vincent does not stop for matches at his end of the bar, but continues walking directly toward her. He doesn't break his glance. As he nears her, and she is filling the entire frame of his vision, he feels light-headed taking in her beauty. This time he's certain it's not the martinis. She is perfect. She is wearing a shimmering gold sweater and jet black, leather slacks. Her golden hair is shoulder length. Fine in texture, but it shimmers. A deep scarlet has been impeccably applied to her lips and fingernails.

Out of nowhere, emboldened by her beauty and/or by the booze, he begins to sing to her. Not loudly or boisterously, but rather in that intimate way Frank Sinatra used to sing to women swooning in the front rows of nightclubs in the late 1940s, making them feel the song was being sung only for—and only to—them. He'd have never done it if he hadn't felt a) sure that he could pull it off effectively and b) inexplicably certain it would charm her.

"So deep in my heart, that you're really a part of me… I've got you, under my skin."

The woman's lips move in sync with Vincent's, but she doesn't sing aloud. When he finishes his chorus, he sits down on the stool next to her.

"Vodka martini, two olives," he calls to the bartender without breaking his eye contact with the woman.

"Same," she echoes.

The unlit cigarette is still dangling from Vincent's lips.

"Don't you need a light?" she asks.

"I don't smoke," Vincent says, absently putting the cigarette in the vest pocket of his sports jacket.

He receives his martini from the bartender, raises a glass to her and takes a self-satisfied sip. She returns the toast.

"Your Sinatra's really good."

"Thanks," he says. "I went to Francis Albert Academy for Boys."

"Ah. That would explain it."

"Six years. I was held back twice for gambling and consorting with mobsters."

"I'm so sorry."

"It wasn't so bad. The school had an outstanding lounge. And there was an Angie Dickinson Finishing School just up the road."

"I went to Barnard," she says. "It's a pretty well-known women's college."

"Yes, I've heard of it," Vincent says. He fears she might be too smart for him. Or he too dumb for her.

She smiles and for a moment looks at everything around him, everything except him, as if looking at a frame to see if it fits the picture, rather than the other way around.

"I love those Sinatra songs," she says, looking around the bar and the restaurant as if she can see and feel the music embracing her. She moves gracefully in her shimmering gold sweater. He stays motionless, and when she faces him again, he is right there in front of her.

"I have to tell you, I've been watching you all night," Vincent says.

"All night. You mean for the last forty seconds since you walked in the bar?"

"No, I've been around."

"Where?"

"The men's room. I've been hanging out in the men's room all evening waiting for the right person to come along."

"Well, that could be your problem," she says. "Didn't anyone ever teach you how to pick up women?"

"By the nape of the neck? Oh, wait, that's kittens, right?"

"Depends on the woman," she says.

"Fair enough," Vincent says.

He takes another sip of his martini and settles back into his barstool. "Excuse me for expressing a cliché…"

"I bet you're good at it."

"Is there a new and improved way to say, 'what's a nice girl like you…?'"

"Wow. You really weren't kidding about clichés."

"No, seriously," he says. "I can't fathom a woman like you being alone at the bar. It's incomprehensible to me."

"What makes you think I'm alone?"

"I don't know. If I were Sherlock Holmes, I might point to the telltale accumulation of toothpicks on your cocktail napkin. The Virginia Slims in the ashtray."

"Maybe my boyfriend doesn't drink. And maybe I'm dating a guy who likes a nice long women's cigarette."

"I think I'd like to meet this man."

"I don't think that would be a good idea."

"You're right. I have a much better idea. How about if I'm your date for the evening? We're both dressed nice, sitting here together. I bet we look fantastic together."

"You'd better hope you're not my date for the evening. He's late. That doesn't sit well with me."

"Oh, I've walked into a blind date."

"How did you know it was a blind date?"

"Because if he knew what you looked like, he wouldn't dare be late."

"Exactly," she says, acknowledging the compliment and raising her glass to him.

"So, how will this work? Your blind date, I mean."

"It's a dating service. They match you up, you meet in a restaurant…"

"… and watch the sparks fly."

"I don't know about that. But the dating service has a good reputation. Based on interests and backgrounds, we're supposed to be 83 percent compatible."

"Why would you settle for less than 100 percent?"

"I'm trying to be realistic."

"I feel like I'm at 94 percent already. What do you say?"

"I think you're slightly drunk."

"A minor detail, I assure you."

"The dating service thinks we'll be very good together."

"I think *we're* good together," Vincent says. "You and me. In fact, I'm sure of it."

"I don't believe anyone can be so sure, so quickly," she says, feigning a standoffishness that is coquettishly charming. She reminds him of a character in a Jane Austen novel. Someone of that ilk. Someone who would be likely to use the work *ilk*, in fact. And correctly.

"We both like Sinatra…" he says.

"Lots of people like Sinatra."

"We both like martinis."

"Lots of people like martinis."

"We both think you're beautiful."

"Well, there's that." She smiles again.

"So where is Mister Mystery Date?"

"I was supposed to meet him here at 7:15. Now it's what… 7:30?"

"You were supposed to meet him here? At this bar?"

She nods.

Vincent takes his eyes off her long enough to glance around the room. He spots a man at a corner bar table by himself, smoking a cigarette and nursing a Heineken. Slightly heavy. Slick. Thin hair oiled back over a mostly bald pate, torso a bit large. Too many buttons open on his shirt for any season, let alone December. A glint of gold chain strangling his thick neck. Vincent sees him look at his watch, but he also appears to be very much in his own world, waiting for something to come to him, rather than seeking something beyond his immediate space.

"There's a guy in the corner over there, waiting for someone, too," Vincent says, rolling his eyes left and indicating the man in the corner. "Someone or something."

She glances over her shoulder, and quickly assesses the man in the corner.

"Oh dear. That may be my guy."

"Him? No. He's not your guy. I'm your guy."

She squints in the man's direction again. "He seems nice, I guess. Could he really be Mister 83 percent...?"

"If so, I'd say he left at least 75 percent in the car."

"Maybe he thinks I'm the one standing *him* up," she says.

"What are you going to do?"

"I have to say something to him. Meet him, have dinner with him."

"No. No, no. You don't want to do that."

"I have to. I don't want him to think I've stood him up."

"No, you can't meet him. That would be a disaster. Once he meets you, he won't want to let go of you. He'll be heartbroken if he can't see you again. You don't want to do that to him."

"You're exaggerating."

"On the contrary. I'm speaking from personal experience."

"What are *you* doing here, anyway?" she asks. "At this restaurant, I mean."

"Fate. I'm sure it's fate. Well, fate, and I'm attending an office Christmas party upstairs. I'm with *Skinformation*. I'm a writer."

"Really? I do layout for some of the medical associations in the city. I'm a graphic designer for Klein and Company on Dearborn."

"I bet you're a good graphic designer. I noticed a symmetry

to the way you laid out your toothpicks on the napkin. Have you been here a while?"

"At this bar?"

"No, in Chicago."

"Just a couple years. Before that I lived in San Caliente. In California."

"Ah. Sunshine and palm trees. Is that more your style?"

"If I'm happy, I can be happy anywhere."

"That's very optimistic. I like that."

"Aren't you optimistic?"

"I became more optimistic when I saw you sitting here at the bar."

"Aren't you afraid you're missing out on your office party?"

"We're anticipating a giant cannoli. But otherwise…"

"A giant cannoli?"

"The Super Cannoli. It's the Taj Mahal of Italian desserts."

"Geographically mixed metaphors confuse me."

"It's very simple. It's one gigantic cannoli, with a lot of normal-sized cannoli in the middle. And then there's all that good stuff inside. Sweetened ricotta cheese, nuts, citron, chocolate bits. It's the best dessert in the world and it doesn't come along very often. *Molto delizioso*. In fact, I feel certain you need to *see* this cannoli."

"I think you should go back upstairs to your party," she says. "That sounds special."

"It is special," Vincent says. He looks at her again, head to toe. "But you seem very special, too. I wouldn't want to walk away from the Super Cannoli of women."

"That's supposed to be another compliment, right?"

"It is. Trust me."

"Thank you, but honestly, you should go back upstairs. I have to have dinner with that man."

"You must be kidding."

"No. I have to. But I do want to see you again."

"You do? When?"

"Come back in an hour. I'll know in the first 45 minutes if there's anything at all to this blind date."

"And if there is?"

"Are you worried?" she asks.

"I'm not sure I like this plan," Vincent says. "I mean, apparently, you have all sorts of shared interests that you're about to share. I'm concerned about this 83 percent business."

"What happened to the confident man I met a few minutes ago?"

"I wasn't sure if you were going to take me seriously."

"Listen, if that man's 83 percent can make me forget all about you, then you're not worth my time."

"I still don't like this plan."

"When you come back in an hour, I will be here. And he won't. I can almost promise you that. But I want you to feel confident about it. I want you to know that after you let me go, I'll be here again to meet you. What's more, I want to know that *you'll* come back. I want to know that you think I'm worth waiting for. Otherwise, what are we doing, right?"

There is nothing in her tone and certainly nothing in her eyes to suggest that she is joking. Still, he shakes his head in amazement.

"I just met you, right?" he says.

"Is that how it feels to you?"

Vincent rubs the nape of his neck. "No. It doesn't. Does it feel that way to you?"

"No," she says. "I really don't know *what's* happening here. I only know that you'd better be back here again in an hour."

"And you'll be here."

"You know I will."

Vincent stands up and polishes off the rest of his martini.

"It's Vincent, by the way. Vincent Cappelini." He holds out his hand and she shakes it. It feels good.

"Melissa Taylor," she says.

"Gosh, now I have so many more questions," Vincent says.

"You're a writer, go write them down. I'll be judging them."

"That's a lot of pressure."

"Let's see how you do with that."

He takes a few steps away, pauses and turns around to face her again.

"Where do I stand now? Eighty-five percent? More?"

"Bring me back a cannoli and we'll talk," she says.

By the time Vincent returns to the party upstairs, most of his coworkers have already left the gathering. Those that remain are mingling in small groups, devouring the carcass and insides of the Super Cannoli. Mitch is sitting alone, digging into one of the smaller, interior cannoli.

"Jesus, Vince. Where the hell have you been?" He points his fork at his dessert. "You don't know what you're missing."

Vincent's head is still downstairs in the bar, the image of Melissa burning into his soul. Like a hot iron brand that didn't stop at the surface, but went right through, irrevocably, eternally. *Under his skin.*

He quickly retrieves two fat cannoli from the larger cannoli and puts them on a double paper plate, then covers them with a napkin.

"Atta boy," Mitch says. "Taking a few for later."

"Indeed," Vincent says, smiling. "I think my life is about to change."

"They really are good cannoli," Mitch says.

"No, I'm saying my actual life is going to change. It's already changing."

"For better or worse?" Mitch asks.

"I think so," Vincent says.

Chapter 11

(pause)

"You look so lost in thought," Paige says. "Tell me, what is it?"

"Nothing," Vincent says. He downs the rest of his latest mint julep in one gulp.

"Do you want me to turn off this music?" Paige asks.

"No."

"Do you want me to play it again?"

Chapter 12

(replay track 3)

"Let me play it for you again, from the beginning," he says. He resets the CD to the beginning of track 3. Then he picks Melissa up off the purple zafu and they make love on the sofa again. She keeps the headphones on the entire time. It's a long cord.

Paige runs the back of her hand across her forehead. She blinks. She seems unsettled.

"What the matter?" Vincent asks.

"I'm feeling light-headed now," she says. "Maybe all the work."

"Work? Did you have a long shift today?" Vincent asks.

"That's not what I meant by work." Paige stands up. "Do you mind if I go inside and lay down on my bed for a few minutes? You're welcome to join me."

She doesn't wait for his reply.

Chapter 13

(Kirsten)

"Do you mind if I go lay down on the bed for a few minutes?" Melissa asks him.

"Of course not," Vincent says.

She disappears into the bedroom. They had been discussing Kirsten and San Caliente again.

"I suppose you should go," Vincent says. "At least check it out."

"It would be nice to see Kirsten, again," Melissa says. "We were very close."

Kirsten had been a big part of Melissa's life before Vincent. After college, the two women had shared an apartment in San Caliente. After Melissa moved to Chicago two years ago, she'd still make frequent trips to the West Coast to visit Kirsten. But once Melissa and Vincent had gotten together, she hadn't been back. Instead, they had frequent long-distance phone calls.

"We were very close roommates. She was very tidy."

"I can be tidy when I put my mind to it."

"And there's a really good opportunity for me at the company where she works."

"Designing album covers."

"Designing CD covers."

"So, do you intentionally design the graphics smaller than albums, or will they make them smaller for you?"

"I know you're joking, but there is an art to it."

"No, I know. It does sound like a good opportunity for you. But…"

"…but it's California," Melissa says.

"San Caliente, to be exact. It's like 2,100 miles away."

"Do you just know things like that?"

"No, I had to look that one up. I didn't think you wanted to go back there."

"I didn't think about it much. But now this job opportunity has come up. Wouldn't you move there to live with me?"

"California? No."

"No? Just like that? But you can write and edit anywhere, can't you?"

"Maybe, but… we're dug in here."

"Can't we dig into California?"

"I don't think it's safe to dig into a place that's already in danger of sliding off the map."

"I know you don't actually believe that."

"I got that from *you*. You're the one who always says that about California."

"Yes, but you never believed it."

"Well now I think you may be right. And I can't bear the thought of us sliding helplessly into the Pacific."

"Can't you talk about this seriously?"

"No, I can't."

He couldn't.

"I think I should go to California, check into this job and realize I'm not missing anything there," she said. "And I want to see Kirsten again."

"But what if the job is appealing?" he asks. "What will you do then?"

"I'll come back home, and we'll talk again."

*

The evening before Melissa leaves for California, after she retreats into his bedroom to lie down, he gets up from the kitchen table, walks to the stereo and flips through his collection of CDs. He has the Sinatra disc in his hand, has it poised within inches of the CD player. Then he stops, puts it back among the others and sits back down at the kitchen table. Sinatra is his pocket ace. He wants to wait and use it at just the right time when he really needs it.

But that doesn't happen. He won't play "Under My Skin" again until after Melissa has left the apartment for a pre-dawn flight, and the kitchen is empty. He wonders if playing the song while she was still there might have made her stay. And if she could just come back to him, it'll be the first thing he would do.

Play the song.

Chapter 14

(friction)

The CD changer skips on ahead to another random disc. Al Green. "Love and Happiness." Vincent had felt a pain in his gut when the Sinatra song had started, but an even more profound pain flares up when it's over.

He closes his eyes for a few minutes, and when he opens them again, Paige has returned from her bedroom and is sitting directly across from him.

"You came back," he says.

"I actually thought you might join me."

"In the bedroom?"

"I just thought we might be more comfortable there. Don't worry, I'm giving up on any crazy ideas of intimacy. I'd prefer it if you'd just talk to me. You seem like you're a million miles away right now."

"More like 2,100 miles. Give or take."

"So, talk to me," Paige says. "I'll listen."

"I was thinking about a nice time I had once," Vincent says, with slight exasperation slipping out in his tone. But it's all out of his mouth before he realizes he's saying it.

"Oh," Paige says.

"Not that this *isn't* a nice time," Vincent says. "I really mean that. I know it doesn't always appear that way. It's just difficult for me to enjoy some things. Sometimes."

Paige leans back on her rattan chair.

"Let me ask you something, Vincent. Is there anything we can do that would help you *not* think about her?"

He doesn't answer.

"I see," she says. "Pretty serious, I guess."

"Pretty serious," he mumbles back. He pauses. He's afraid if he starts talking about it, he might not be able to stop. He holds himself to a few words. "She might be here. Somewhere. In San Caliente. I don't know."

"Then why aren't you with her? Or trying to find her?"

He looks at her helplessly and shrugs.

"I'm sorry," Vincent says. "You're right. I probably shouldn't have come here."

"I didn't say that," she says. She stands up, abruptly. "I'll be right back." She takes his empty glass and goes back inside.

Nice job, Vincent thinks. This nice woman had seen to his immediate needs in a very caring way and he repays her by getting lost in thoughts of a life with another woman. When Paige returns, she is still rather stoic. But she has also brought him another julep.

"Try this one," she says.

"This one? What's different about this one?"

"Have I steered you wrong yet? Just try it."

He puts the glass to his lips and gives it a cautious sip. It has a different taste from the first drink. Not better or worse, just different. "What did you put in it?" he asks, now drinking it without hesitation.

"Just a little something extra," she says. "Don't worry. It has an herbal remedy in it. Sort of like an aspirin to go with the balm."

"Sure, thanks. Might help relax me."

"Well, let's not go overboard," she says.

He detects some irritation in her voice, and downs the rest of that drink. But now he feels a burn, as if—in a delayed reaction—the walls of his esophagus have been incinerated.

"Oh my God," he gasps. "Is that tequila?"

"It's an herbal drink with a little tequila," Paige says. "The burn is good."

"I thought we were trying to get rid of burns. Jesus."

"This burn is good for you," she says. He doesn't think she's speaking spitefully, but there's no longer traces of joy or playfulness in her voice. She talks to him like an attending nurse.

"I don't always do well with tequila," Vincent says, then clears his throat a few times to avoid a coughing fit.

"So," Paige says, in a tone that suggests gears are about to switch, "do you have a picture of this woman? I bet you have a photo in your wallet."

"You don't want to see it. Do you really want to see it?"

Paige doesn't respond, just stares at him.

Vincent reaches in the left rear pocket of his khakis for his wallet. It's not there. It's also not in the complementary right rear pocket. And although he would never keep his wallet anywhere but these two places, he pats himself down frantically, though it pains him to pat himself anywhere.

"You don't have your wallet?" Paige asks.

"No. No, I don't. Where…?"

"Could you have left it at the restaurant?"

Vincent replays his last moments at the patio table on the deck outside Slammin Sammy Sushi. He's about to pay, he puts his wallet on the table. Paige insists on paying. He gets up.

"I think I left it on the table," he says. "Damn it."

"Look, don't worry about it," Paige says. "I'm sure they still have it."

"I have to go get it."

"I'll call over there for you. I'm sure Nathan found it and will hold onto it for you. Don't worry."

"No, I should go get it now. All my identification is in there, my credit cards, cash…"

"And the photo…"

He nods. "Yes. And my picture of Melissa. There's only one of them. It's not that I want to leave. I mean that."

"Then don't leave."

"No, but I really *have* to. There's the wallet, and the sun's going down, and I'm still not feeling well…"

"I could go with you," Paige offers.

"That's nice of you, but, you know, it's totally out of the way. The restaurant is on my way back to the hotel."

"I could stay with you at the hotel, if you like."

"My hotel room at the El Famous is super tiny. We'd both be stuck on the bed all night."

"Well, I wouldn't want you to be 'stuck' in bed with me. I'm sorry I offered."

"No, but you know what I mean."

"Yes. I do. And I certainly don't need to see that picture anymore. I think I get the picture."

Vincent's shirt is still off. Paige puts a hand to his chest. He looks down at her soft hand against him.

"Paige… thank you. Thanks for all this. For taking care of me with the balm and the juleps and having dinner with me."

"This sounds very much like a farewell speech."

"Just for now."

"'Just for now?' When do you think I would see you again? It doesn't happen if you don't make plans."

"Look, I'm only here for two days. That's one strike against us."

"So, that's it? One strike, and…?"

"The truth is, I *would* like to see you again," Vincent says.

And it *is* the truth. Now that he's about to leave Paige, he's not sure he likes the idea of leaving it like this, and he's not liking the idea of not seeing her again.

"I don't know. Maybe when this is over, and my head is clear…"

"That doesn't sound like a realistic goal," Paige says.

"That's fair. I know. It's just that this other thing… this other woman. She left me."

"Yes, you've made that very clear," Paige says. "It was some time ago as I understand it."

"Yes, that's true, but it's more complicated than that. I felt like I wanted to tell you about it, but then I feel like I shouldn't talk about it and be in the moment here with you."

"I like one of those ideas," Paige says.

"I've been experiencing the whole thing again during this trip, and I don't know what I think anymore."

"I'm here to listen to you."

"I know, and I appreciate it, really. I've been burned, Paige. Not just the sunburn. Juleps and Kalahari melon seed oil aren't going to fix what's inside me."

"No, you're absolutely right," Paige says. She slaps her hands on her knees and stands up. She screws the cap back onto the Mason jar full of blue balm and puts it in his hand. "Keep using this stuff. It'll help. It won't cure everything that's wrong with you, but it will help your skin heal."

"Thank you," Vincent says.

"So, is this really goodbye for good?"

"I don't know, Paige."

"Because I'd hate to think that all that was keeping us from really connecting with each other or seeing each other again was a faded photograph in your wallet."

She reaches for him again. This time, instead of touching his chest she hooks his beltline with her index fingers and pulls him closer. He feels his body against hers. Inexplicably, it seems she is radiating even more heat than he is.

The music in Paige's beach house has stopped and there is nothing to replace it but thundering silence.

Her chest presses against his pained, sensitive skin and—to his surprise—he doesn't care. It makes him wince, but he welcomes it. His hips are in contact with her hips. Parts of his body that have escaped the burn are in contact with hers. And it's not unpleasant. He suspects Paige must feel his reaction, because she pulls him in, even closer.

This has to be a mistake, he thinks.

But it isn't.

His monosexuality has been tested to the limit and is now

betraying him. Perfection, and his idealized notions of love—these things are crumbling before him. He can't deny it but also can't let it go any further. He breaks their embrace.

"I have to go," Vincent says, pulling away from Paige. He grabs his shirt and pulls it back on. With all the slick stuff on his body, it sticks like flypaper.

"You're not even going to wash that stuff off before you go?"

"It's fine," he says, buttoning his shirt hastily.

"I can make a call. Your wallet will be okay. The photo will still be there, I promise."

"No, I should leave. I have to leave."

Paige lowers her head, nods, turns away from him and walks out to the edge of her deck, facing the ocean. He can't tell if she's crying. He can't bear to know right now.

He leaves her silhouetted against a dying sun on her deck as he makes his exit. Mason jar in hand, past the ghost shrimp and albino frogs, and the print of Miles Davis. He nearly trips down her wooden stairs in his rush to get back to the rental car.

Chapter 15

(mystery karaoke)

Vincent motors back up the California coastline, cursing himself all the while. Along with his sunburn, there is now a burning sensation in his stomach and esophagus. As it grows dark in San Caliente, he's in a dreary, bleary, debilitated, and slightly feverish state, fighting off a touch of tequila and whatever else is churning inside him, squinting as he drives along the highway, searching for the Slammin' Sammy Sushi sign.

Sooner than he expects, the not-to-be-ignored, giant, illuminated billboard with the samurai in a baseball suit, brandishing a sword, appears toward the next exit.

Vincent turns down into the familiar little valley and sees the restaurant loom up before him. He brakes when he gets to the gravel parking lot and dust flies up around him.

In and out, he thinks. Then he'll go back to the hotel, lie on his back, and try to recover and figure out what the hell has been happening to him today.

Unlike earlier that day, Slammin' Sammy Sushi is now crowded, and, instead of a handful of patrons, there is now a preponderance of people. Couples and tourists, it seems, but mostly Japanese men. The music is loud. Elvis Costello and the Attractions are pumping it up so hard that Vincent can feel it in the souls of his shoes. As he muscles his way to the bar, he notices a different person is tending it. A tattooed, muscle-bound type in a T-shirt and baseball cap.

"I think I left my wallet here earlier," Vincent says, having to yell to be heard over the crowd and Costello. "I think I need to talk to Nathan."

"I think Nathan is out back," the bartender shouts back. "I'm a little jammed up now, as you can see, but as soon as I can get a break here, I'll check."

Vincent taps his foot but tries to be patient while the bartender fills drink orders. Glasses and beer bottles clink and clank around him in a menacing staccato. He wonders if another drink might counteract the tequila or whatever was in the julep, or whatever is attacking his system. Anything to help him feel less pain. He orders a cold Kirin. As it runs down his throat it is momentarily refreshing, or gives, at least, the illusion of momentary refreshment. He realizes he has no wallet, and therefore no money for the beer, but he hopes to remedy this very soon.

Abruptly, the music at the bar stops and Vincent overhears different music and a familiar song coming from another room. He wanders over, pushes aside a thick red curtain and pokes his head in. Inside a room lit with flashing lights, neon, and decorated in red, textured wallpaper, "Witchcraft" is playing loud and clear over a small set of speakers. Well, loud, anyway. Clear might not be the best way to describe it. Frank Sinatra's dulcet tones have been replaced by the voices of two Japanese gentlemen with microphones, performing atop a podium. There's a DJ in the back and a host of others are gathered around, shouting and laughing. He is interrupted by the clatter of Japanese sandals and then feels someone give him a solid nudge from behind.

"Hey, you're back. Just in time for karaoke, man!"

"Nathan," Vincent says, recognizing the waiter from a few hours ago. "No, I'm not here for karaoke. I left my..."

"... your wallet. No, I know about that, Paige called a few minutes ago."

"She did?"

"Yes, she told me to look for you. I thought it might be yours. I have it in the safe in the back office."

"I appreciate it, thanks."

"But since you're here and have your wallet, you should hang for a bit," Nathan says. "The party's just getting started."

Vincent is becoming increasingly annoyed and distracted by the two Japanese gentlemen, decked out in tight black suits and red ties, making a mess of Sinatra. Struggling through the song lyrics, stumbling and missing at every stanza. The duo are being alternately cheered on and berated by a small crowd of similarly dressed Japanese businessmen near the stage.

"Wow, I don't want to be mean, but—can't they read?" Vincent asks.

"It's mystery karaoke night."

"Mystery karaoke. What does that mean?"

"You don't get to look at the words. They're blacked out at the bottom of the screen. You have to sing it right without seeing the lyrics."

"Which they are clearly failing to do." Vincent observes.

"Yeah. Most people fuck it up. But it's good for a laugh. Brings in customers."

"But they're ruining this song. They're destroying Sinatra."

"There's a prize for people who can sing the tunes without missing a word," Nathan says.

Vincent watches as the two Japanese businessmen look at each other helplessly, both of them equally inept. They make up words, put together phrases that don't rhyme.

"This is pitiful," Vincent says, shaking his head in disbelief. "What's the prize?"

"Free Mai Tais for a month."

"Wouldn't do *me* any good," Vincent says. "I'm out of here soon. Back to Chicago."

"How about Paige?"

"Paige?"

"Yeah, Paige. She's in here all the time, picking up shifts, hanging out. You could give it to her. Nice girl, Paige. Don't cha think?"

"Yes. She's nice," Vincent said. "Um. Just curious. How come *you* aren't dating her?"

"She's very friendly, but hard to get close to. She kind of walls herself off to most men."

"Really? She didn't do that with me."

"Then you must be special. I know she's looking for a certain kind of guy. I don't know who that is, but I'm not it. Plus, I have back hair. But you and Paige looked like a pretty good match."

"What are you talking about? I don't imagine you can tell that much just by serving us drinks and some poison fish."

"Sure, I can," Nathan says. "I've never seen Paige so animated with another guy. You shouldn't pass that up. I hope the fish didn't mess with your innards, man. You never know with that stuff."

Before Vincent can consider these remarks further, Nathan is nudging him and turning him around.

"See the chalkboard up there?" Nathan asks. "Those are tonight's songs."

Vincent had already peripherally noticed the chalkboard when he came in. Now he regards it more closely, through hazy, squinted eyes.

"It's Mystery Sinatra Night," Nathan says.

Vincent looks at the song list. And sure enough, there it is, like it has been waiting for him to arrive. Written on the chalkboard just below "Witchcraft." A white scrawl of letters with the name of his song. Their song.

"I've Got You Under My Skin," he says.

"You know that one?"

Without singing, Vincent begins to rapidly recite the lyrics to Nathan, like a mantra he's been invoking for years.

"Hey, sounds like you know *all* the words." Nathan says.

"Oh hell, it's a piece of cake."

"Well, what are you waiting for? Get on up there, man."

"Me? No, I'm not feeling well. I need to go."

"But you know *all* the words. One song, man!"

"No, no."

But despite his protests, Vincent has already begun to put himself in performance mode. He pulls at his sticky shirt collars and pushes his fingers through his hair. *Yes, I need to do this*, he thinks. It seemed important to get up there so that no one else takes the stage and crucifies his sacred hymn.

Still, Vincent shakes his head in the negative again, until he hears the Japanese duo butcher another line of "Witchcraft". The two men giggle. There are a few boos from the crowd.

"Oh, for God's sake," Vincent says, in disgust. He downs the rest of his Kirin in two gulps, hands his glass to Nathan and marches up to the podium.

There is a round of applause, as if the audience hopes he's come there to save the day. The Japanese men abashedly surrender the podium, smiling contritely at Vincent.

The emcee, a balding, aging hipster failing to look young in black leather pants and a red silk shirt, grabs his microphone. Next to a Casio keyboard the emcee has a console where he can cue up the music. He hits a button and the opening bass line of Queen's "Another One Bites the Dust" crackles over the sound system.

"Better luck next time, boys," the emcee says to the retreating Japanese gentlemen. "Thanks for playing."

Vincent figures he can just grab the mike and do his thing, but the emcee seems determined to do his schtick before the next tune. Vincent stands on stage, stoically, and waits.

"Hi, I'm charismatic Kenny Coxswain on the Casio keyboard," the emcee says. "I'm your emcee extraordinaire here at Slammin' Sammy Sushi's."

He plays something on the keyboard—almost jazz, but with no swing, rhythm, or syncopation. Vincent imagines it may be the emcee's own self-penned theme song.

"And welcome to Mystery Sinatra Night! Who do we have here?"

"Um, Vincent," Vincent says, unprepared for obligatory banter.

"Is that your full name, Vincent?"

"Vincent Albert Cappelini. And I'm ready to go," he says impatiently.

"Well, hold on now. Hold on," the emcee says, then shouts out to the crowd. "We've got Vincent Albert Cappelini here tonight. Sounds like this Italiano thinks he can knock off Frankie tonight. What do we think, folks?"

Vincent hears one lone person whoop and applaud. Nathan, he imagines.

"Are you in from out of town?" the emcee asks.

"Yes."

"Where's home, Vincent?"

"Chicago."

"Chicago! The wiiiiindy cit-eye!" In a flurry of fingers, the emcee imitates the swell of a giant wind on his organ then picks out the first eleven notes of "Chicago, Chicago, (That Toddling Town)."

"You know, Vincent, they named this place after Chicago's own Sammy Sosa."

"Yes, I know that," Vincent says.

"You betcha. I was from the wiiiiindy cit-eye myself. That was before my operation. They removed the stupid part of my brain and I relocated here to sunny California." And again, lightning fast, after a flourish of descending chords, he bangs out the beginning of "It Never Rains in California" on the keys.

"No, but really, Vincent, I hope you're finding your stay in California agreeable. Have you had a chance to get out much, check out the local cuisine?"

"Here. I've eaten here. That's it."

"Wise choice, my man. We have the finest sushi in the world here at Slammin' Sammy's. You like raw fish?"

"Yes. Sure," Vincent says.

"Kind of surprises me."

"Why is that?"

"Cuz you look kinda overcooked, pal!" The emcee hits a button on his console and the sound of a drummer's rim shot echoes through the place. He follows this up with "Burn Baby Burn" on his keyboard.

"Have you put anything on that sunburn, Vince?"

"Yes. I did." Vincent says. "Could we just go ahead with...?"

"...no, but seriously, Vincent, you should take care of that. Hey, what kind of sushi did you have?"

"I had the fugu."

"I beg your pardon?"

"The blowfish."

"Blowfish!" The emcee hits another button on his keyboard and a big foghorn sound erupts, followed by a *wah wah wah* in a vague representation of disapproval. "No, but seriously folks, freshest sushi in the world here at Slammin' Sammy Sushi."

"Actually, I'm not feeling all that great. I'd like to just do the song."

"Well, I'm not surprised. You may be cooked on the outside, but I bet you're not raw when it comes to music. You gonna take a stab at Frankie for us tonight?"

"Under My Skin." Vincent says.

"All righty. Lemme just cue that up and we'll see what you've got."

The emcee finally gives Vincent a look as if to say, "whenever you're ready." He nods back.

The room falls silent for a moment.

The music starts and Vincent raises his head, confidently. Then he proceeds to nail it. Emotion wells up in him, as it does whenever he hears the song, but now he uses it, releasing the emotion through his voice.

He sings as if Melissa is standing just outside the room, and that, by singing this song, she will emerge through the red curtain at the back of the room, walk up to the podium, and she and Vincent will embrace while the crowd cheers.

And with that in mind, he nails it. All the words, letter

perfect. There is nothing in life he does better than this. Perfect tone, perfect intonation, perfect Sinatra, sung only for Melissa. But it's nothing more than that. Melissa doesn't emerge through the red curtain when he finishes.

But others do, eager to see the face behind his stellar performance. At first, it's more Japanese businessmen, then other faces appear. When he finishes the song, tenderly and exquisitely as he ever has, he receives a riotous round of applause.

He descends from the podium and is greeted by the charismatic Kenny Coxswain, who clutches his chest in exaggerated -heart-attack style.

"Oh! How about that, folks? The red man, Vincent Albert Cappelini. Give it up." Many in the room cheer anew. More people enter the karaoke room through the red curtain. The emcee extends the gift certificate to Vincent, snaps it back to tease him, then gives it to him for real, and pats him on the back.

"You also get this," the emcee says, pressing a small brown, wrapped package into Vincent's hand.

"Okay, thanks" Vincent says, shoving the package in his front jacket pocket.

As Vincent walks back down into the crowd, the emcee cues up another Queen song "We Are the Champions." A yin to the yang of "Another One Bites the Dust."

Vincent's former contenders—the Japanese businessmen—are lined up along the wall in the karaoke room. There must be a dozen or more of them, all dressed in tight black suits and red ties. They are muttering a lot, muttering in a huddle. Finally, the circle breaks a bit and he can see that they are holding a tray filled with shot glasses.

Vincent tries to walk past them as he makes his way through the room, but they intercept him. They had initially appeared somber and serious as hell when they were huddled together, but when they greet Vincent they smile broadly. The two Japanese gentlemen who had lost to Vincent in the karaoke contest are smiling the broadest.

"Very good. You sing good," one of them says.

Others are shaking Vincent's hand and patting his back. All

smiles. One of his karaoke competitors takes a shot glass off the tray and presses it towards him.

"What's this?" Vincent asks.

"Kamikaze!"

They all repeat it loudly. "*Kamikaze!*"

"Oh, no, that's not a good idea," Vincent says.

But before he can politely refuse, they are already raising their glasses and toasting. He tries to remember what's in a kamikaze. Vodka and lemonade mostly?

"Mr. Frank! Mr. Frank!" they cheer.

It dawns on him that they are referring to Sinatra. But he doesn't know if they are calling *him* "Mr. Frank" or if they are toasting the master himself.

Even after the Mai Tais, juleps, herbal tequila drink, and beer that created a miasmic vortex amid the fugu in his stomach, he feels compelled to oblige them, and downs the shot amid another collective chorus of "kampai!"

Whatever it is, it's not vodka and lemonade. It burns all the way down, but worse than Paige's julep and herbal tequila drink, and in a more chemical way than the distinct hard alcohol taste he expects. It tastes mechanical, or diesel, if such a thing is possible. It doesn't seem to bother the Japanese a bit.

"Jesus," Vincent mutters, barely able to hold it down. His eyes water. He immediately feels blurry again. Feverish.

Immediately after Vincent downs the drink, the Japanese businessmen drop their festive nature and become stone-faced and serious.

"You never sing here like that again, Mr. Frank," one of them says. He is baring his teeth, crooked ones at that, but he doesn't appear to be smiling.

"What's that? Oh, sure. Of course." Vincent says, and he chuckles nervously, taking it as more of a tongue-in-cheek plea than a warning. But they are still not smiling. Had he shamed them? Put an end to the fun they'd had, attempting to warble mystery karaoke?

Though he is taller than any one of the Japanese gentlemen, they are menacing as a group, like jackals, and he no longer feels safe around them. He mumbles a word of thanks and moves away from them. He's afraid to look back.

He's relieved to see Nathan at the back of the room. Vincent had never high-fived anyone before, but he responds to the call when Nathan puts his hand up. He gives it a good slap.

"You're the man," Nathan says. He hands Vincent his wallet. "Everyone knows it now. You are the man."

Vincent opens his wallet, checks for his money, driver's license, and the photo of Melissa. All are still there. He hacks through his teeth, still choking on whatever was in the kamikaze shot. He is feeling increasingly odd, as if he is losing control of himself. As though he might faint or suddenly blurt out obscenities.

"You okay, Vince?"

"I'm fine," he says. "Listen, can I give this gift certificate to you, to give to Paige?" He puts it into Nathan's hand.

"Why wouldn't you give it to her yourself?"

"I don't know if I'll see her again. Just please give it to her the next time she comes in," Vincent says. "Tell her thanks and tell her I owed her a drink."

"What else did you get?" Nathan asks, pointing to the small brown-wrapped package in Vincent's hand.

"I don't know what this is. Maybe you know?"

"I might know, but I can't say. You just need to take it."

"Sure, right," Vincent says. He tries a smile, but it must have looked gruesome because Nathan's smile fades away when he sees it.

"You look very... *shiny*. Like, pale, but still red at the same time. It's weird."

"I think I need to get back to my hotel and lie down," Vincent says. "Listen, thank you again, and take care of yourself, Nathan."

More people have filtered into the karaoke area to check out what all the fuss is about. Another person stops Vincent just as he is about to exit the karaoke room.

"You're the man," he tells Vincent.

"Yeah, I know. I'm the man."

"No, you're the man. You're the man who interviewed me in Baltimore. Aren't you Vincent Cappelini?"

Vincent steps back and looks into the familiar face and gleaming bald pate of a noted dermatologist from the Southern California area. Vincent had met and interviewed Dr. Hugh Flemming at a dermatology meeting in Baltimore, some four or five years ago. At that time, the doctor was just emerging as someone to know in the vanguard of cosmetic dermatology.

"Dr. Flemming. Yes. Hello."

"Vincent Cappelini. I didn't know you were out here on the coast. I saw your former colleague Mitchell Wallace at the El Famous. Are you here to cover the ICARUS event too?"

"Me? No. Well, yes. Sort of."

Dr. Flemming takes Vincent by the shoulders and turns him toward a neon light. "Good God," he says, giving him a clinical, appraising look. "What happened to you?"

"I accidentally fell asleep by the pool at the hotel."

"You look shiny."

"I put some... homemade balm on it."

"What were you thinking? You need to get that treated. You should come see me. Or any of the skin specialists here. Well, you're in the right place, anyway. Several dermatologists from ICARUS are here tonight."

"Here?"

"Dermatologists love karaoke," Dr. Flemming says. "I think after the lectures were done, a lot of them started migrating here from the hotel."

"Here? I appreciate your concern, Dr. Flemming, but I really need to get out of here. It was good to see you again."

As Vincent moves away from the angry Japanese karaokeists and toward the exit, he sees more dermatologists coming in.

Chapter 16

(cheddar)

Just outside the red curtain of the karaoke room, people have begun to swarm around Vincent. He recognizes faces here and there. Some people he's seen in the pages of *Skinformation* and other dermatology magazines. There are people he knows and some that he has interviewed over the years. A Mohs surgeon from West Virginia, a hospital director from Illinois, an alopecia expert from Upper Montclair, New Jersey. And still more start to form a crowd around him.

Some of them have apparently accompanied Dr. Flemming and are now pumping Vincent's hand, patting his back, confirming with him that it was his Sinatra rendition of "Under My Skin" that they'd heard as they walked in.

"Are you with *us*?" the Mohs surgeon asks him.

"Us?" Vincent asks.

What is the correct answer here?

Dr. Flemming steps in on his behalf. "This is Vincent Cappelini. The journalist from *Skinformation*."

"Used to be," Vincent quickly adds. "Now I freelance, mostly."

There follows a lot of head nodding, and a cacophony of "oh, right" and "yes, of course, didn't recognize you," and "great job up there." No one mentions his red face and shiny skin, which is a relief, but he also notices most of them are half in the bag and have probably wasted no time boozing at the bar while he'd been performing.

Caught up in a whirlpool of dermatologists, Vincent repeats "thanks" and "good to see you" as many times as he can muster, all the time pushing his way forward, hoping to find a break in the crowd where he can make his exit.

He faces a sea of undulating faces, mostly men. A lot of leisure suits, sportcoats and cigars. Some are offering him a shot, which he politely refuses. He moves forward again, nearly stumbling in the crowd and directly into a woman. He isn't sure what presses against his face first, the breasts that threaten to tumble out of her tight, purple, off-the-shoulder gown, or the flaming red cheese curl hair that porcupines out of the woman's scalp. Then he is face to face with Dr. Barbara Borden—the physician who had threatened to skin his hide over his "Pigs On a Hot Tin Roof" story. He feels dizzy.

"Oh, excuse me," Vincent says, hoping Dr. Borden won't know, recognize, or remember him.

Her eyes have a lifeless, drunken glaze over them. And otherwise, she is expressionless. Nothing conveys recognition. He looks for signs of malice. He doesn't see any. He needs to stay cool. Even though his photo sometimes accompanies his byline in the articles he writes, he figures it is unlikely she will recognize him, particularly with his fire engine face and haggard look. He starts to walk away, but she gets in front of him again.

"Where do you think you're going?" Dr. Borden says—closer to a reprimand than a question.

"I'm just... I just stayed to sing one song," Vincent says. "I left my wallet here earlier and came to retrieve it. I'm late. I really have to go..."

Somehow, by determination, physical strength, or sheer force, she manages to curl her left arm around Vincent's shoulder and neck, lasso him, and pluck him from the crowd. He winces, feeling all his skin irritations as one big painful flash. Dr. Borden's right hand is tautly curled around a Collins glass filled with ice and some sort of pale brown liquid. He notices long, imitation cheddar, manicured fingernails that match her hair.

"I caught your performance," Dr. Borden says.

"I'm not a performer," Vincent says. "I just do the one song. It's just a little karaoke competition."

"You must stay and have one drink with me." She presses her own drink toward him.

"Oh. No. Thank you. I've had enough tonight."

"But I bought this drink especially for you," she says.

Not wanting to anger her, or find out if she is already angry, and still not sure if she knows who he is, Vincent takes the glass from her and takes a small sip. He detects bourbon. He hopes that's all it is, anyway.

"Wow," he says, feeling the liquid scorch his lips and throat. "Yes, that's just what I needed. Thank you. Now if you'll excuse me, I think I see some people I know back there…"

"… you have a *wonderful* voice," Dr. Borden says, staggering slightly.

"Thank you, that's very kind, but…"

"I just love Frank Sumatra," she says, slurring and transforming the Chairman of the Board's name into an Indonesian island. "I would love it if you would sing it just for me."

"No, I couldn't sing another song, really."

"No, no, not another song. I want you to sing 'Under My Skin' again. Just for me."

"No, I wouldn't. I couldn't do that. I'm not feeling well, actually. Please excuse me."

He manages to duck his head and extricate himself from her. He retreats back several steps so that he is knee-deep in dermatologists again. Then he pushes onward, away from Dr. Borden, and eventually crosses paths with Dr. Flemming again.

"Vincent. Everything okay, boy? There are some doctors here who want to buy you a drink."

"Oh, Jesus. Another drink? No. Please. Thank you, though."

"Everything okay? You seem a bit frazzled."

"Do you know Dr. Borden?"

"Barbara Borden?" Dr. Flemming said, "Yes, I thought I saw her here."

"She's definitely here," Vincent says. "Is she a dermatologist?"

"She's a dermatologist who does veterinary medicine, or a veterinarian who does dermatology. I've never been clear which it is."

"That's my understanding too, yes," Vincent says.

"I'm sure she hitched her wagon on some dermatologists staying at the El Famous. Very hot, though, don't you think?"

"You think she's hot?"

"Well, she's an astoundingly *smooth* woman. But I think you should stay away from her."

"I'm *trying* to stay away from her," Vincent says. "She wants me dead."

"Dead? I'm sure you're exaggerating. What for?"

"Pigs… It's a long story," Vincent mumbles, while still keeping one eye out for her.

It takes a moment for Dr. Flemming to fill in the blanks. Then he lights up and snaps his fingers.

"Oh, that's right. *That* Borden. *Pigs on a Hot Tin Roof.* That headline. Yes. Everyone still talks about that. We all thought it was very clever. A bit of an overreaction on her part, if you ask me."

Vincent isn't surprised Dr. Flemming knows about it. Every dermatologist who read *Skinformation* seemed to know about it and the fallout that came afterwards. It was probably the story he'd become most known for, or most infamous for.

"I don't know if she remembers who I am, but I don't want to find out."

"She's bad news, Vincent. Borden likes rubbing shoulders—and anything else she can manage to rub—with people in our industry. She turns up at all these events. She's big into Botox, plastic surgery. Nothing wrong with Botox, mind you, but I draw the line when patients overdo it. She's *addicted* to it. No one who's Board-certified will go near her. But I think she's got several cosmetic dermatologists in the bag to help feed her habit. She spends a lot of money on it, I'm told."

This explains her utterly blank expression, Vincent thinks. Behind her Botox she might have been frowning, scowling, glaring, or seething for all he knew. In the absence of a curled lip or narrowing of the eyes, how could he possibly know?

"Still. Kind of hot though, don't you think?" Dr. Flemming reiterates.

"Actually, I'm not really keen on that kind of manufactured beauty," Vincent says.

"Lots of men are. I'll admit, she's heavy into plastic. She also puts big money *behind* it all."

"Behind what?"

"Botox, fillers. She not only uses a lot of it, she funds clinical trials, drug companies, grants. There are some unscrupulous physicians who want to rush their products on the market. They schmooze with her and probably sleep with her in order to squeeze some funding out of her. Although you didn't hear that part from me. I guess she came into a large inheritance when her husband died."

"She had a husband?"

"Don't you watch the news? They called her 'Botox Lizzie Borden' behind her back. Not even behind her back. Sometimes to her face, although it's hard to tell which is which with all the work she's had done. There's a rumor she spiked her husband's cranberry juice with Botox. Tightened and constricted his airways."

"Jesus Christ." Vincent feels his own airways tightening and constricting.

"They couldn't prove it. I think it's because she showed no emotion during a deposition. Frankly, I don't think she *could* show emotion with all that botulinum toxin in her glabellar frown lines. Didn't look innocent, but she didn't look guilty either. Anyway, they let her off. It never went to trial, but all of us in dermatology know about her."

"I can't believe dermatologists are okay with this," Vincent says, pursing his mouth and trying not to swallow.

"I told you. Money. She's a cash cow. And plenty of her cash went into her udders, as well. Sorry. But let's be honest, that's all filler. Kind of hot, though, no? I don't know. I think so. Anyway, I'm glad I never had any dealings with her. I understand she has quite a temper. Well, I guess you know that."

"That's just great." Vincent wilts, feeling weak.

"You don't look well," Dr. Flemming says. "I think you should let me examine you." Under throbbing neon and flashing lights and amid the crowd he begins observing Vincent more closely and touches the burn on his forehead. "It's difficult to tell under these lights, but it looks like a severe case of sun exposure."

"I know," Vincent says. "Can you maybe examine me back at the hotel? Right now, I need to find a way out of here."

"Let me drive you back," Dr. Flemming said. "It's the least I can do. The articles you wrote about me and my work in *Skinformation* did a lot for my reputation."

"I appreciate that. But I can't. I have Mitchell Wallace's rental car."

"At least let me follow you back. I just need to say goodbye to a few people. Can't you go out the side door, through the karaoke room?"

"I could, but there are some Japanese businessmen in there that also seem angry with me. I think I inadvertently embarrassed them or something."

"What about out the back?"

"I've been there. It's a straight shot off the deck into the ocean. Although I'm seriously considering it at this point. Look, don't worry; I'll get out of here. Can I meet you outside in the parking lot?"

"I'll be right behind you," Dr. Flemming said. "I'll see you back at the hotel. If we get split up, I'm in the James Mason suite on 12. Strange room. Looks more like it was designed for a young girl. Strange hotel."

"I'm familiar with it, yes."

Vincent ducks his head down and keeps moving forward from crowd to crowd, keeping his already peeling eyes peeled for any sign of trouble. He considers the unhappy, possibly angry Japanese karaoke posse at the back of the house, and the glamor shot Botox killer in the front. He makes a lateral move into the middle of the dining area, tagging onto a group of restaurant waitstaff delivering cake, helium balloons, and happy birthday wishes to one of the tables. He shuffles in among them, using them as a small protective flank, an army of samurai ballplayers.

He breaks off from this group when he nears the front door. Then he slips outside.

Feeling safe and free, he walks along the edge of the exterior red barn wall of Slammin' Sammy Sushi and waits for Dr. Flemming. Feeling anxious, he reaches into his jacket for a cigarette.

As he is about to light up, however, Dr. Borden appears once again, emerging from the shadows with the flash of her Zippo and a dark cloud from her Virginia Slims.

"Ah. There you are," Dr. Borden says. "Do you need a light? So glad to find another smoker out here."

"No, I don't smoke," Vincent says, dropping his cigarette and already starting to backpedal.

"You didn't need to make any pretenses to find me out here," she said. "I'm just glad you tried to find me again."

"I didn't..."

Vincent glances around quickly and recognizes another dermatologist exiting the restaurant. It is Dr. Constantine Stamospoulos, one of the many doctors he'd interviewed years ago, a mole specialist from Spokane. But it's been a long time. He's not sure the doctor will remember him. He approaches the doctor and tries to engage him in conversation to extricate himself from Dr. Borden.

But not long after Vincent gets into a discussion with Dr. Stamospoulos about the ABCDEs of moles—why asymmetry, borders, color, diameter, and evolving conditions matter in diagnosis—Dr. Stamospoulos stops mid-sentence and looks squarely at Vincent. "Wait a moment, wait a moment." He shakes Vincent's hand. "Of course. It's Vincent, right? *Vincent Cappelini*. I'm sorry I didn't recognize you at first. What have you been up to? It's been a while."

The doctor is louder than Vincent would have liked. He hears and feels his Christian name blaring and echoing through the parking lot as though an ominous air raid siren is wailing.

"You look rather shiny, pale, and red, Vincent," Dr. Stamospoulos says. "You should see someone about that. Good to see you again, Vincent. Keep up with those great articles. Sorry to have interrupted you."

The doctor shakes Vincent's hand again and leaves him alone with Dr. Borden.

"Vincent? You're Vincent Cappelini?" she says.

"Oh, well, you know, every so often, it's a name I use," Vincent stammers.

"You're the man who published my pig photo. But... then you sent me that dreadful letter."

"I did, yes. I'm sorry. I was going through a lot at that time and very upset. Nice to see you again, Dr. Borden. Please enjoy the rest of the conference." He tries to walk away. She puts a hand to his sunburned shoulder. It hurts.

"Hold on," she says. "I'm sorry if I caused you any trouble."

"Oh, gosh no, don't apologize," Vincent says. "That was a terrible letter I sent you. I shouldn't have done that."

"You *were* terribly cruel in your letter to me," Dr. Borden says. "I was very angry. Well, I'm sure you know that. But now that I've met you, now that I've seen you sing... I realize what a sensitive soul you are."

"I'm really not," Vincent says. "I imagine people say all sorts of things behind my back."

"I know people say awful things behind *my* back," Dr. Borden says.

"Not to me," Vincent said. "I don't know anything. Honestly."

"You must listen to me… the stories they tell. About my late husband. I'm sure you've heard about it."

"Nope. Not really."

"All those syringes around the house. Those were mine, yes. But you must believe I'm innocent."

"I didn't know… I don't know any of the details."

"You're a writer. Perhaps you should write a story about *me*. It would help restore my good name."

"Oh, no, I couldn't," Vincent says.

"I know we've had our differences…"

"Just the one, actually. I don't really know you that well."

"You know me better than I know myself."

"I really don't," Vincent says.

Dr. Borden's voice lowers to a whisper.

"I think you know that I've been a naughty girl…"

"Excuse me? Did you say 'naughty'…?"

"… a *very* naughty girl, yes. And I would accept your punishment. I would welcome it."

Vincent has backpedaled as far as he can go, and his back is now braced against the red barn exterior of the restaurant. "Oh. Well, that's… that's not really my place. I mean, that's fine, if that's your thing, but I'm not into all that. I'm sorry."

"Look at you, you're blushing," Dr. Borden says, running a hand through his hair. He tries to extricate himself from her, but he is pinned against the wall. She is still moving in.

"I'm not blushing. I was out in the sun too long," he says. "I usually tan very easily. This is unusual."

"Oh, you're like an adorable baked ham," Dr. Borden says. "It's so refreshing to see someone who's so pink and juicy and not all pale and serious at one of these seminars."

It was supposed to be a compliment, but it has no effect on Vincent, other than to alarm him. He wonders about her comparing him favorably to ham when she could be so easily upset by pigs on a hot tin roof.

"I'm feeling kind of light-headed, actually," Vincent says. "I think I need to get out of here."

"Good idea. We can go back to my hotel room at the El Famous. I'm in the Grand Canyon suite on the National Parks floor. It's very deep and roomy. Like an abyss, really. It's very roomy. I could make us a couple more drinks."

"No, no. Please. I couldn't."

Dr. Borden pushes into him again and her hips brush against the small brown paper wrapped package in his front jacket pocket.

"Oh my, what have we here?" she says.

"It's a present."

"I'll say it is."

"No, no. It's a present I received for the karaoke contest."

Summoning all his strength—and he doesn't feel like he has much left to spare—Vincent manages to duck out from under Dr. Borden again and moves away from her quickly. He has already decided it is in his best interest not to wait around for Dr. Flemming to catch up with him and he sprints across the gravel parking lot looking for Mitch's cherry red Mustang.

He would have had enough trouble finding his car on an ordinary evening and now the parking lot of Slammin' Sammy Sushi is packed with cars. Dizzy, sick, and undoubtedly feverish, and now with a pounding in his brain, he tries to find the red Mustang convertible rental among scores of other anonymous-looking red Mustang convertible rentals. Eventually he finds the only vehicle with a Mason jar of aloe, mint and Kalahari melon seed oil sitting on the passenger seat. He puts the top up on the car, cocooning himself inside the Mustang, then slumps down low in the driver's seat. Then he turns over the engine. It's loud.

Keeping still, he hears the clatter of high heels on gravel. Then he hears his name being called out. He raises his head slowly, checks his rearview mirror, and sees someone rapidly approaching his car. It's Dr. Borden. She's spotted him.

"I'm sorry," he says, rolling down his passenger window

halfway. "I'd like to continue this conversation, but I'm not well, and this is not good for me, and I really have to go."

But Dr. Borden is halfway inside his window before he can get the words out.

"I'm parked just over here as well," Dr. Borden says. "Isn't that funny? Don't tell me this isn't fate. Aren't you adorable? We're so alike."

"We're not alike," Vincent says.

"Well then, we're like fire and ice. You'd be fire obviously, with that face of yours, and I suppose that makes me ice. But opposites attract, don't they? Perhaps we're soul mates. Don't we owe it to each other to find out?"

Chattering, chattering, chattering on, a mile a minute. It may have been a passionate diatribe, but it was hard for Vincent to tell with nary a wrinkle or frown on her Plasticine features.

"We're *not* soul mates," Vincent says.

"We both *love* Sumatra," she says.

"*Sinatra*. It's *Sinatra*," Vincent says, wearily and irritably, anger pushing its way to the surface.

"I'm sorry. It's the injections," Dr. Borden says, running her orange fingernails along her smooth jaw. "That and the drinks. I sometimes mispronounce names."

"Sinatra should not be one of them. And—for your information—lots of people love Sinatra."

"Yes, of course, but when I heard that song and walked into the room and saw you, I felt a connection. Like you were singing that song only to me. Surely you felt it too."

"I didn't *see* you when I was singing. I didn't even know you were out there."

"I feel sure we were put here together at this Sushi sports bar tonight for a reason. I know it. That song is our song."

"Please don't say that," Vincent says. "Don't ever say that again."

"You seem angry. Maybe *I'm* angry, too. I can't decide if I'm angry at you or if I'm falling for you."

"Well, I can't tell by looking at your face," Vincent says.

"Maybe send me another letter when you get back to Roanoke."

"Don't push me away. You can't push me away after all we've been through."

"We haven't been through that much, really. Most of what we've been through has been in the last five minutes."

"I felt the heat from your body back there. Can you deny that?"

"It's the sunburn. And I feel feverish, as well."

"Fever, yes, I feel it, too," she said. "We're both caught in this fever. Must I throw myself at you?"

"Please don't. This isn't my car. It's a rental."

Vincent frantically begins to roll up the passenger window. Dr. Borden puts her fingers in, clawing like a zombie from *Night of the Living Dead*, and with that same dead stare determination. As the window closes, he hears Dr. Borden yelp—or maybe yip, like a puppy—and he sees her extract her right hand and cradle it in her left. He detects a sawn-off blur of orange still against the passenger window, and he pauses long enough to make sure he hasn't captured one of her fingers. He hasn't, but he's clipped off one of her flaming orange fingernails. It was stuck in his rolled-up window like a leftover Cheeto.

"My nail!" Dr. Borden cries out, pressing her face against the glass of the passenger window. "You've ruined my manicure." If she is angry, she doesn't show it. Then Vincent remembers again that she can't.

He feels his throat tightening again. Tighter than his stomach.

He revs the engine, hoping it might spook her, as one might deter an intrusive grizzly bear. Dr. Borden backs away, ranting something, looking neither lovelorn, sad, nor angry. She looks more like an abandoned mannequin in a parking lot. When he turns on the headlights, she's gone, as if she has disappeared. He looks around quickly to make sure she isn't behind the car, maybe sneaking into his trunk. Then he backs out, puts the Mustang in drive and makes his way between lanes of parked cars.

He feels shadows darting between the cars. Vehicle doors slamming and headlights following him. Whether it is Dr. Flemming, trying to catch up to him or stop him from driving, or Dr. Borden coming after him to kill him, or mad Japanese businessmen, he doesn't wait to find out. He high tails it out of the parking lot and back out onto the highway. When he feels he is a good distance away, he rolls down his driver's window and frees the orange fingernail.

Chapter 17

(high beams)

Back behind the wheel, driving south on the highway, Vincent opens the front of his shirt, unscrews the Mason jar with one hand, and slathers more of Paige's balm on his chest and face.

"Better," he mumbles.

But it is only better for a moment. The hot wave returns to his face as quickly as if someone has turned on a sunlamp. Conversely, he still has chills. His palms are now slick on the steering wheel, so he looks for something to wipe the excess goo off his hands. Finding nothing suitable in the Mustang rental, Vincent tears open the karaoke prize in his front jacket pocket and wipes his hands with the brown wrapper. As he does so, he sees that the package contains a compact disc, but he can't identify it in the dim light inside the car. It isn't in shrink wrap. No cover art. *A homemade CD? What kind of prize is that?* He snaps it open and slips the disc into the CD player in the dash.

It was Old Blue Eyes, back with him yet again. "Summer Winds." He assumes it is a best of Sinatra CD, probably something the emcee at Slammin' Sammy Sushi has ripped and burned for the winners of the Mystery Sinatra karaoke contests.

Vincent turns the volume up. He's desperate to reclaim Sinatra for himself, desperate to exorcize the demons that he feels have been closing in on him, threatening his monosexuality. Yes, Paige is sweet, beautiful. She'd felt good in his arms.

Don't acknowledge it.
Play the music louder.

Dr. Borden: downright creepy; all that sick orange hair and that sick orange fingernail and all that business about her husband and how she had probably killed him, and all that business about soul mates, and her ruining Sinatra for him. And not just Sinatra but ruining his experience of "Under My Skin."

Play it louder. Drown it all out.

The harsh glare of high beam headlamps flashes into his rearview mirror and he squints his pained eyelids.

Too close.

Go around. Pass me.

Things are getting too close. He can't make it back off.

He feels feverish. Sick. God knows from what anymore—the blowfish, the odd julep, the kamikaze. Maybe bourbon from Dr. Borden laced with Botox in his throat and stomach. Or perhaps Kalahari melon seed oil and Balsam of Peru. He's lost track of the potions and ingredients in and on his system.

Only Sinatra can heal him. He wants the music to fill the car, the voice to fill his head, and the memories of Melissa to flood into his system fully. He wants nothing to obstruct what he wants to remember, no one to force what he chooses to forget.

But it's all too much. The sickness and the bright lights, the music, the memories, all clogging the arteries in his brain, looking for release. Memories.

A phone call. The evening Melissa left for California. The words: "She doesn't love me. I know she's going to come back to you."

Suppress it. Choose the best of all bad scenarios.

Vincent presses on the gas, trying to escape the car getting ever closer, bearing down on him.

Play the music louder. Try to dilute or drown your brain.

But again, he is increasingly losing his ability to pick and choose which thoughts come to him. How many scenarios has he created to explain the absence of Melissa? Three, four? More? Headlights glaring at him. Too bright. Too close.

Chapter 18

(scenario)

Not long after Melissa has left their Chicago apartment for the airport that morning, Vincent receives a telephone call from Kirsten, Melissa's college friend in California. Ostensibly, Kirsten has called to find out if Melissa's flight has gotten off on time. But Kirsten is drunk. That is clear in the first few minutes of the phone call.

Vincent prefers not to speak to Kirsten, and certainly not when she is jabbering under the influence of alcohol. Kirsten has been the instigator, after all, the one who's made Melissa aware of the graphic arts job opportunity in San Caliente. When he answers the call, Vincent is already missing Melissa, resenting Kirsten, and anxious to get off the phone so he can start some serious misery drinking of his own.

"I'm so sorry, Vincent," Kirsten says.

"I suppose it's not entirely your fault," Vincent says, hoping to appease Kirsten and shorten the phone call. She is sniffling on the other end of the line.

"I'm not ready to think that way yet," Kirsten says, and then she begins to sob, openly. "I know what's going to happen. I know why Melissa is coming here to San Caliente."

"Kirsten...Kirsten...what's with all the tears? You shouldn't drink."

"She's not coming to stay, Vincent. She's coming to say goodbye. I know it. I thought it might be different. She made it sound like she wanted to come here and make something happen. But I know she loves you. She's going to come back to you."

Kirsten sobs some more.

Vincent hates the tears, but he's privately glad to hear what she's saying. "Kirsten… You need to get a grip. I'm sure there are plenty of graphic designers who can fill her spot."

"I don't care about the job," Kirsten cries. "And I don't care about the rest of it anymore. She loves you. She's choosing you, not me."

Like most everything in life, Vincent needs to be hit over the head quite soundly before things sink in. This is one of those times. Even when he begins to realize what Kirsten is saying through all those tears, he still can't wrap his mind around it.

"Choosing me? Over the job?"

"It has nothing to do with the job. I know she's in love with you, not me."

"Wait. What are you saying? You… Melissa? You and Melissa?"

"Oh my God," Kirsten says. "She promised me she was going to talk to you about it before she left." And then she jabbers on before Vincent can stop her.

"It's something that just… happened," Kirsten says. "It started years ago, when we were living here together in San Caliente. We were watching a movie on Lifetime. *Mother May I Sleep With Danger?* It was late. It was cold. We were under the covers. We'd been drinking a lot. And then, you know… things happened."

"Things happened?"

"Yes. But then she got the job in Chicago and moved there and she met you. I thought things were over. But we kept in touch. We talked a lot on the phone and then she said she was coming back. So, I thought maybe she was coming back for me. But now I feel sure she is just coming to say goodbye."

Vincent doesn't really hear all of it because at some point he feels a loud buzzing in his head and grows light-headed. And then the phone drops from his fingers.

Vincent will never know exactly what occurred between Melissa and Kirsten. Or what would have occurred. He hangs up on Kirsten.

When Kirsten calls right back, he doesn't pick up. He closes all the shades in his apartment, retreats to his bedroom with a bottle of Jack Daniels and doesn't come out.

From early morning until late afternoon, Vincent drinks and considers what is happening. Melissa has never spoken to him about an attraction to anyone other than him, and certainly nothing about an attraction to Kirsten.

Maybe Kirsten has it all wrong, he thinks. Perhaps Kirsten had an attraction to Melissa at some point in the past. Maybe it had even gone as far as Kristen touching Melissa. Or maybe there was a misinterpreted hug involved. And maybe Melissa had even acquiesced in some way. In confusion, or in drunken female camaraderie, or whatever. Or maybe nothing at all had happened. Melissa may very well have rebuffed Kirsten's advances and has invented some crazy story around it all, something to do with Melissa going to California specifically to rekindle something from her past.

He will never know.

Vincent figures Melissa must have suspected that Kirsten was offering more than a job when she planned her California trip, but she'd kept it from him.

Why?

The fact that she never told Vincent anything about this matter could have meant one of two things. Either Melissa had something to hide or, conversely, it may have meant that it had never been anything at all, or completely one-sided on Kirsten's part, and therefore not an issue worth mentioning to him. Still, Vincent wishes she would have talked with him about it.

You opened me up to so many things, Melissa had told him on several occasions. She often said it after sex. Maybe she confessed other things; had Vincent not been listening closely enough?

Melissa had never claimed to be a monosexual. That was Vincent's domain. She'd only told Vincent that he was *the only man* in her life. He'd just assumed she felt likewise, and by feeling likewise, she must be monosexual.

Vincent is sure that whatever is happening now, in the wake of this call from Kirsten, is the worst thing in the world that can happen to him. His ideal of monosexuality is not merely bruised, but *shattered*, like the thousand and one pieces of a broken Christmas ornament.

But the worst thing hasn't happened yet. When Kirsten calls again a few hours later, Vincent doesn't pick up and lets it go to voicemail. He doesn't know that Melissa's flight hasn't arrived. He doesn't know that Melissa's flight hasn't made it to California at all. He won't know any of this until the next day when he turns on the television, watches the news, and finally plays the voicemails he has been avoiding.

The information Vincent receives that next day is not entirely clear. Melissa's scheduled flight has crashed, but her name is missing from the flight manifest, and her body (along with several other bodies presumed to be aboard the flight) cannot be found or identified. This leaves room for a lot of speculation.

From that day on, in the absence of knowing (or refusing to know) anything for sure, Vincent will decide from day to day whatever he wants to believe is real. He will pick and choose his facts. He begins to create his own, preferred scenarios.

He has a favorite one.

Chapter 19

(the preferred scenario)

In Vincent's preferred scenario, Melissa's name is missing from the manifest and her body is not found because she misses her scheduled flight. She hesitates at O'Hare. Vincent believes she hesitates because she is not sure whether or not she wants to see Kirsten in California or return directly to Vincent. And so, Melissa takes a *later* plane and misses the fatal crash. In this scenario, Melissa finds her way to Kirsten, tells her that she is not interested in a relationship with her. But she stays in California sorting things out in her head before she will (invariably) return to Vincent.

In this preferred scenario, Melissa is on a journey of self-discovery in San Caliente, always on the verge of reuniting with him. But she is also nowhere, so she could be *anywhere*.

She could be waiting for Vincent poolside at the El Famous. She could show up in the El Famous lounge when Vincent is having beers with Mitch. She could show up out of nowhere and angrily admonish Vincent for letting a strange woman rub Kalahari melon seed oil and Balsam of Peru on him. She could be just behind a red curtain at Slammin' Sammy Sushi as Vincent finishes a perfect Sinatra karaoke. She could be waiting at his hotel. Waiting in his hotel room. In this scenario, Melissa is always just about to make a surprise entrance.

*

Belief in this preferred scenario keeps Vincent's head above water. If he thinks anything less, thinks that Melissa was just plain gone forever, with all his questions unanswered, and all his ideals smashed, he will have to sink into despair. People like Mitch and his pilot friend Glenn, even a lot of dermatologists that he works with—they all know about the plane, and the news, and what happened. When he encounters those who know, they will invariably say how sorry they are about what has happened. He—also invariably—pretends they are talking about something else or someone else.

His acquaintances don't know anything about Melissa's relationship with Kirsten. They don't know why Melissa was going to San Caliente. They only know what they saw on CNN. They know a plane has gone down. It's their understanding that Melissa was on that plane. But that's more than Vincent is willing to accept or admit.

That's how he holds himself together. As long as Vincent never acknowledges exactly what has happened, never acknowledges what he knows or doesn't know about what happened to Melissa that day, no one can affect him with any unwanted, grim, tragic realities.

Chapter 20

(viper)

Oncoming vehicles approach and pass Vincent on the California highway like screaming, streaking meteors. He forces his eyes open wide and concentrates on staying in his lane to avoid hitting the other cars head on. Worse still are the cars following him. He is pushing 65, 70, 75, but no matter how he tries to outgun the vehicles behind him, the headlights invariably creep up and glare harshly and painfully in his rearview mirror before they overtake him.

Vincent's hands are still slick with Kalahari melon seed oil, confounding his ability to navigate the stereo and the steering wheel. He can't see the ocean, just the Mustang's headlamps beating down against the black highway in front of him.

He is blinking more now, his vision getting worse. His head is throbbing to the same ugly beat that seems to be pounding in his stomach. His body, which had craved the open air, now begins to feel chill again. He buttons up his shirt again with one hand, still feels cold and feels anew the sting of his shirt against his sunburned chest.

It is all closing in on him now.

The possible and impossible scenarios of his life with and without Melissa are rushing through him. In a fit of pique, he ejects the Sinatra disc and hurtles forward on the highway in silence.

As the latest car behind him looms closer, Vincent's forward vision becomes obscured by the glare of the car's high beams. Just as he thinks the car might ram him from behind, it swerves into the left lane and moves to pass him.

Vincent takes his eyes off the highway just long enough to look at the vehicle bullying him. It is a red Dodge Viper convertible, and it stays confoundedly and stubbornly at his side. He rolls down his passenger window, puts out his arm and tries to wave the car on, past him. But the Viper slows and gets beside him once more.

He glances toward the Viper again and can just make out the hellish, expressionless face of the driver, who is not watching the road, but staring at him from behind the wheel. Staring but not glaring, because glaring would have involved facial movement. Her hair is a blustering cluster of orange cheese curls. The Viper makes an aggressive move and swerves toward him. Instinctively—with whatever instinct is still operating in him—Vincent turns the steering wheel sharply to the left.

Then something is whirling. The rental car, his head. Maybe both.

And, ultimately, a collision of memory and metal, accompanied by a bone-jarring, unforgettable sound.

Crash.

Chapter 21

(post-traumatic morphine/fever/memory/dream)

Poolside at the El Famous. When he climbs the ladder and comes up out of the water, Vincent walks over to the other side of the pool, where Melissa is on her stomach, in her green (or was it teal?) two-piece swimsuit, untied in the back. She is facing away from him on a fluffy pink towel. He reclines next to her on an adjoining pink towel, on his back, and can feel the sun baking his chest to the point of discomfort, but he doesn't turn over.

It's hot, he says.
Terribly hot, Melissa answers.
She pauses. Then she says, I'd hate for you to get burned.
I won't, he says. Wait, do you mean...? Are you talking about the sun?
She turns her face to him.
Smile, he says to her.
I am smiling, she says.
But she's not.
Can you frown for me? he asks.
I am frowning, she says.
It's all the same to me, he says.
No, she says. It's all the same to me.
He feels the pool water dripping down his body.

Chapter 22

(sponge)

Saturday morning, 7:03 am

The moistness, the droplets. The sensation of being touched. Something moist rubbing along his chest. In his morphine stupor, Vincent is poolside with Melissa. She is looking compassionately into his face and rubbing his chest with her fresh-from-the-pool fingertips. The face slowly blurs, fades, and then morphs into the compassionate face of Paige. He is back in her beach house, being cared for yet again with her blue balm. The face morphs a final time, and it's someone else entirely. A female stranger. But still compassionate.

As his lucidity advances, Vincent realizes that he is not in a lounge chair by the pool at the El Famous, nor is he in a beach house. He is in a hospital bed. And the person in close proximity, rubbing his chest, is not Melissa or Paige but a Japanese nurse. Her straight black hair is tied up into a nurse's cap. She is wearing a starched white top so bright and pristine that it hurts his eyes, as though he is looking into a sunlit snowbank.

Her name tag says "Emiko." Vincent doesn't know if that is her first name or last, nor does he know if she is a registered nurse or a candy striper sent in to fluff his pillow, change his linens, and... rub things on him.

Vincent tries to speak, to ask about his condition, but a weak guttural grunt emerges instead. The nurse pauses and lifts her fingers from his body.

"Lie still," she says. "Don't exert yourself."

This short instruction calms some of Vincent's immediate fears. If the nurse thinks Vincent is capable of *not* lying still and *is* capable of exerting himself, it suggests his body may be largely intact, operable, and capable of exerting, not exerting, and over-exerting. Finally, Vincent croaks out a question.

"How bad is it? What did I lose?"

The nurse smiles. "Not a scratch on you," she says.

"That can't be true."

"I'll show you," she says. Emiko walks across the room. Vincent keeps still but his eyes follow her. She turns up the dimmed lights in the room a few notches and returns. She looks around the room for something specific but appears unable to find it. Then she picks up his empty silver bedpan from his bedside. Emiko places it in front of him, but Vincent can only see the top of his head in the silver reflection. He can only see that his black hair is matted and uncombed.

"I can't see. Can I lift my head a little?"

Emiko assists him, adjusts the pillows under his head. In the bedpan reflection he gains a brief glance at his nightstand. On top of it is his wallet, a Mason jar with the blue balm from Paige, and the Sinatra CD. He wonders how these things have followed him to this hospital room.

Vincent refocuses and squints at the dark image of himself in the bedpan and sees a rough approximation of his haggard, reddened face. His features are—he hopes anyway—partially distorted by the curves in the bedpan. Other than that, he doesn't appear to be bandaged or bleeding. There is no neck brace around his neck. No stitches apparent. No metallic halo pinned into his skull.

"What about further down?" Vincent asks.

Emiko carefully and neatly folds back the covers, exposing Vincent's legs and genitals. In the bedpan, all his parts seem similarly warped, as they might appear in a carnival fun house mirror. But everything seems intact.

While he is exposed, Emiko takes up a sponge and bowl of soapy water from the bedside.

"Shall we finish up?" she asks.

He stares at her, blankly.

"Finish? What have we started?"

When she raises and begins to sponge his genitals with lukewarm soapy water, they react, far more than Vincent would have liked. Or expected. There is nothing to impede the steady rise, no underwear, or adult diaper, or chastity protector. Just Emiko's hands, soapy lukewarm water and the sponge (and her fingers, by default) in direct contact with his genitals, manufacturing an unintended erection.

"Oh... no, no," Vincent says. "I'm sorry. This is bad." He tries unsuccessfully to wish away the growth of his penis.

"It's okay," she assures him. "This happens. It's perfectly natural."

"Not for me," Vincent says. "It's not supposed to happen to me."

He tries to will the thing down, although technically, as a monosexual, he shouldn't *have* to do that. His body is supposed to know better and act accordingly. In any case, his mental powers of penile telekinesis are ineffective.

Apart from the occasional blinking of his tired eyes, his penis represents the lone active element of his body.

His thoughts whirl like a school of trout in a roiling stream of freshwater consciousness. Could this erection have been caused by the lingering dream of Melissa by the pool? Or was it the recent memory of Paige on her deck in the sunset? Or... could it be that it was neither of these, and that Emiko's tender caress with her soft sponge was all that it took? The fact that he didn't know or wasn't sure made him feel unsure of *everything*.

"It's okay," Emiko says. "It shows you're healthy. Coming around."

"No, no... it's not good," Vincent moans, helplessly.

Then the bath is over. She pats his member dry, like a flightless dove, and pulls the covers back up over him. When Emiko stops, so does everything else. Things settle down, nestling into genital stasis. Again, he can't help but observe that the action and reaction run contrary to his monosexual nature. He is supposed to be in complete control of this, not the nurse.

"Why can't I move? Am I paralyzed?" He really wants to ask why the only part of him that moves is his penis, but this seems a better way to pose the question.

"You can move. You've actually been moving a lot in your sleep," Emiko says.

"I have?"

"You should just try not to move too much for a bit. You've had a high fever and you're dehydrated and weak."

She takes his temperature. Vincent waits for the results.

"It's still over 100," she reports.

"How much? Like closer to 200?"

"No. More like 101. But you were lingering at about 105 for a while. It keeps going up and down."

"Because I'm dying?" Vincent asks.

"You're not dying," she says, shaking her head and smiling again.

If he is not outwardly battered, Vincent assumes something internal has landed him in a hospital bed. He wonders if it's something to do with his monosexuality being out of whack. That's it. His monosexuality is hemorrhaging internally. And they will never be able to treat it because they won't be able to find it. Mostly because he has invented it.

"Please be straight with me," he says.

"You're going to be fine," Emiko said. "Really. The doctor will be in to see you soon."

Vincent's head sinks back into his pillow.

Emiko takes Vincent's pulse and checks on his IV drip. When he senses her imminent departure, he speaks again.

"I still don't understand what happened to me," Vincent says, referring to his inability to piece together his mind-boggling journey from highway to hospital bed.

"Please don't worry about it," Emiko says. "It happens all the time."

She is already out of the room when he realizes she was still talking about his penis.

Chapter 23

(havoc)

Despite his surname, René Enrique Havoc, MD, is just the sort of soft, round, shaggy-haired, mustachioed, amiable doctor Vincent might have wished for. He doesn't seem to Vincent like the sort of doctor a hospital would appoint to deliver bad news. Dr. Havoc walks into Vincent's room later that morning, silently examines him, crosses his arms, and strokes his chin.

"So, Doc," Vincent finally says, because Dr. Havoc seemed like the kind of physician Vincent felt he could comfortably address as "Doc." "What's the story here? I've been led to believe all my parts are all still intact and working?"

"You're sick, but you're still in one piece. You've been feverish and sedated."

"Give it to me straight, Doc. What's wrong with me?"

"It's poisoning."

"Poisoning?"

"That's right. I'm assuming—from the looks of you, the bad sunburn—that you've had a lot of sun exposure recently?"

Sun poisoning, Vincent thinks.

"It's called sun poisoning," Dr. Havoc says, as the predicted diagnosis is still echoing in Vincent's head. "An intense overexposure to the sun followed by your immune system breaking down."

"Yes, I'm familiar with it," Vincent says. He could have recited the symptoms chapter and verse: Skin redness. Pain and tingling. Headache. Nausea. Fever and chills. Dizziness. Dehydration. He'd written several articles on the subject and even penned one for *Giornale della Faccia*.

Bad sunburn.

Brutte scottature.

"Your fever is still hovering around 100," Dr. Havoc says, "but I think we're getting it under control. We've got a specialist coming in for your skin. A dermatologist. Apparently, there's a dermatologist convention here in San Caliente. How's that for luck?"

"Lucky, right," Vincent says, lacking the commensurate vivacity in his voice.

"The dermatologist has already recommended a topical treatment for it."

Dr. Havoc retrieves the jar at Vincent's bedside and holds it up. Vincent is certain it is Paige's Ball Mason jar filled with her concoction.

"Is that what you've been using on me?" Vincent asks.

"Something new, apparently," Dr. Havoc says. "A topical skin treatment derived from the regenerative genes of laboratory mice. It's called Topo-Genio. We've been applying it to you periodically around the clock and you seem to be responding well to it. Even when we release you, we'll want you to continue to apply it."

Vincent wants to say, *no, it's not Topo-Genio, but far more likely to be mint, aloe, yogurt, Balsam of Peru, Kalahari melon seed oil, blue food coloring, and all, concocted in a woman's kitchen sink,* but he fears uttering his opinion will prompt the doctor to move him to the psych ward. Then again, maybe he *is* in the psych ward and Dr. Havoc just hasn't told him yet.

"How long do I have to be here?" Vincent asks.

"We're still battling your fever. Like I said, I think we've got it under control, but it spikes up occasionally."

"This is all from sun poisoning?"

"No, partly from sun poisoning but also from food poisoning."

"I have food poisoning, too?"

"Have you had any food that might not have been properly prepared? Undercooked, perhaps?"

The fugu, Vincent thinks.

"I had some sushi," he says.

"What kind of sushi?"

He doesn't say. He already feels stupid enough for having fallen asleep in the sun. He doesn't want to add to his poor judgment by admitting he'd eaten an unknown raw fish.

"You know, there's all those different Japanese names," Vincent says. "I don't think I can remember."

"Based on where the police found your car, up the coast, I'm guessing it was from Slammin' Sammy Sushi. When we pumped your stomach…"

"…my stomach has been pumped?"

"Yes." Dr. Havoc says, his tone becoming sterner. "Look, let's not waste any time here. Did you have the blowfish?"

"Blowfish?" Vincent repeats innocently, doing his best to feign sudden realization. "Oh. Perhaps, yes. A little bit. But you've got it all out of me, right?"

"We got the sushi out. But apart from the sun poisoning and food poisoning, we think there's other poisoning. And when I say 'we' I mean 'me.' I personally think there is—or was—some other toxin in your system."

"Other…?"

"…yes, a potentially more serious toxin, like rat poison or strychnine or something. Hard to tell exactly."

"You're kidding, right?"

"It's nothing to kid about. It could have been very serious."

"*Rat poison?*"

"Or something like that. Just a trace, but still very dangerous."

"Jesus."

"Does someone have it in for you?"

"No, that's impossible," Vincent says, although he is already compiling a top ten list in his head.

"Well, it's also possible that the restaurant was using rat poison or something to keep away vermin or some such and somehow it got into you..."

"So, you think that's..."

"...possible, yes, but not all that likely. That's why I think it could have been just a regular old dose of poison. Possibly in a drink."

Vincent tries to recall the many libations that have crossed his lips in the last 24 hours. The beers at the hotel lounge, the Mai Tais at the sushi restaurant, the juleps on Paige's deck, the drink Paige had served him with "something extra in it" before he left her beach house, the kamikaze shots from the Japanese businessmen, the sip of the highball glass drink from Dr. Borden. Six different drinks and five people, give or take.

He goes over it again.

Would Mitch want to poison him? Would he go that far just to scoop him on a hot dermatology story? Vincent dies and Mitch becomes top dog in the world of skin disease journalism? No. That didn't seem likely. After all, Mitch needed Vincent to write and polish his story. They had a deal. Mitch wouldn't poison him at this conference.

He didn't want to consider Paige, but his paranoid brain could not dismiss her. He had sporadically worried about her turning out to be a crazy California girl, a person that might have lured him to her beach house with underlying malevolent intent. Vincent has also rejected Paige at every turn, and she seemed unhappy with him and definitely frustrated with him.

Hell hath no fury like a woman scorned. Had Paige felt scorned enough to poison him? She offered him food and drink, but didn't eat or drink much herself, which he found suspect. But Paige had also been sweet and engaging. Indeed, it was likely her blue balm that was healing his skin.

Without ruling Paige out entirely, however, he moves on to the events in the wake of his karaoke performance. Perhaps the shamed Japanese businessmen karaoke singers had slipped something into his kamikaze.

You never sing here again, Mr. Frank.

Vincent shudders as he remembers these words.

At the same time, Dr. Borden seems a highly likely suspect. That sip of bourbon offered to him. *Botox Lizzie Borden.* It had been such a small sip. *Still…*

Ultimately, Vincent had to face the fact that many different people could have poisoned him in the last 24 hours. Or even several of these same people. *Perhaps a conspiracy of poisons.* If everyone he'd encountered had given him just a little bit of poison, a little at a time—a touch from Mitch, a touch from Paige, a touch from the Japanese karaoke singers, a touch from Dr. Borden—that would be an effective way to kill him.

Or maybe there is someone he hasn't considered or remembered. Or even some strange person that's anonymously poisoning out-of-towners. Anything was possible. In a nutshell, that was the problem with his addled, paranoid, conspiracy-prone brain—the fact that *anything was possible.*

Vincent also knows that if he shares his theories with Dr. Havoc, the doctor will be compelled to relay the information to someone with a badge, and that badge will end up asking a lot of questions to his list of suspects. Picking on the wrong person could have truly terrible consequences.

"I can't think of anyone," Vincent finally says to Dr. Havoc.

"Well, maybe something new will occur to you when you're feeling better."

He shudders to consider that even *more* suspects might occur to him later.

"So, sun poisoning, food poisoning, and just plain old poisoning," he finally says. "Is that it?"

"I think so," Dr. Havoc says "And like I said, I think we've got it under control. You'll just need some meds and some rest to feel better and we'll keep you under observation until you're safely out of the woods."

Vincent nods.

"And my personal suggestion is that you try to stay out of whatever woods you've been in for a while." Dr. Havoc adds.

Chapter 24

(hallucination Sinatra)

The next thing that happens doesn't seem to Vincent like a dream. He is in his hospital room and all the details of the room remain exactly as he remembers them. The IV is still stuck in his arm. His wallet, the jar of blue balm, and the CD are all still by the bedside, and he can still count the tiles on the ceiling. The shades are drawn.

But in the darkness, in a chair in the corner of the room, he sees a man in a suit and sporty hat. Wisps of cigarette smoke curl and envelop him. Vincent hears the tinkle of ice in a highball glass.

The man walks to Vincent's bedside, his hat cocked jauntily on his head, coat thrown over one shoulder. The man shakes his head sadly, looks up at the ceiling and then stares directly at Vincent.

"Wow, you're everywhere, you know that?" Vincent says.

"Don't I know it, kid," Hallucination Sinatra says. "Do you know, they play my music more now than they did when I was alive?"

Real life Sinatra has been gone since May 1998, lost to the world at the age of 82, but Hallucination Sinatra looks young and vibrant, straight out of a late 1950s album cover.

"You look really good," Vincent says. "What are you doing here?"

"You want a drink?" He offers his glass to Vincent. "Nectar of the gods."

Two fingers of Jack Daniel's whiskey, a splash of water, four ice cubes. Or so the Sinatra legend goes.

"No. Thanks, though."

Hallucination Sinatra sighs, sits next to Vincent, and cocks his hat back on his head. "I'm here to tell you, you're messin' up, kid," he says.

"I know," Vincent says. He doesn't know how, or what Hallucination Sinatra is referring to exactly, but it seems the right response. Hallucination Sinatra turns his head away from Vincent and takes a drag off an unfiltered Camel. The smoke spirals around Vincent's IV bottle. "Could you be more specific?" Vincent says. "How am I messing up?"

"Don't kid a kidder."

"I'm not," Vincent says. "I'm just…you know that I'm working through some things…"

"Working through some things? What kind of crap is that? Your shrink give you that fancy diagnosis?"

"No, I just mean, I'm trying to figure things out," Vincent says. "Love is strange."

"Who said it wasn't? Of course love *is* strange. Women can also do strange things to men's heads. But it ain't a big mystery, kid. Straighten up. Melissa was good. She may have been the best you ever had. Maybe not. Move on."

"You would advise me to move on?" While Vincent wasn't ready to concede this point, he realized it was important to take Hallucination Sinatra seriously.

"I've been there, pal. I'll tell you this—if I wished back all the women in my life, I'd have a room full of headaches. And probably several doses of the clap."

"I'm not sure how helpful it is for me to know all that. But what about that thing between Melissa and Kirstin? What am I supposed to do with that? It doesn't fit for me."

"Maybe that's why she left you. Because it didn't fit for her."

"Is that… I'm sorry, is that some kind of double-entendre joke?"

Hallucination Sinatra chuckles and takes another sip of Jack. "You need to lighten up, kid."

"But—and excuse me for asking, because I don't know how much you already know about me and about all this—Melissa made me a monosexual. You know that, right?"

"How's that? A what? What kind of tutti-frutti Weirdsville crap are you handing me?"

"It's a term I use to describe… it just means that sexually and emotionally, I'm kind of stuck in neutral. And it feels like if I ever got out of neutral it would be betraying Melissa, betraying my monosexuality, I mean."

"Didn't understand a word of that," Hallucination Sinatra says dismissively, taking another slug from his drink, and another drag from his cigarette. "So, who's that doll you had sushi with?"

"Paige? You know about Paige?"

"Cute broad. I wouldn't be so quick to take a pass on that."

"So," Vincent half whispers, "she didn't poison me, right?"

"Don't be stupid, kid. C'mon with that cockamamie crap."

"No, I didn't think so, but I honestly don't know who else to ask about this."

"Put it out of your head. Move on."

"But I have this devotion to Melissa… I *live* by it."

"Yeah, yeah, kid. That's very noble. I'll tell you something, you don't need to know what the score was with Melissa. You just get the hell over it. Sure, it hurts, but you get yourself to a place where your heart doesn't hurt so much anymore. That's all you can ask for."

"I suppose…"

"You want my advice? Life is short. Get 'em in the sack when you can, get your kicks, and move on. That's what I'd do."

"Wow. Look, don't get me wrong, I appreciate you being here, and all, and you were sort of making sense, saying things that sounded like good advice, but that last part doesn't sound anything like me. I don't think I can be like that. I'm not like you."

"Then stop trying to be like me. I saw that stuff you pulled in the karaoke bar."

"You saw that?"

"Don't worry about it. You did a decent job. And it took a lot of spunk."

"Maybe I should have been a singer."

"Let's not go overboard. Your intonation is shit. And you don't have any real stage presence. Tell the doctor to check your meds, kid, 'cause I think your head's gone funny. Stick to writing."

Hallucination Sinatra straightens his hat and drains the last of his Jack Daniels.

"Is that all? You make everything sound so simple, but I'm not sure it is."

"Look, I'm in favor of anything that gets you through the night. Whether it's prayer, tranquilizers, or a bottle of Jack Daniels."

"Yes, I know that's one of your quotes, and I like the way it sounds, but I honestly can't tell anymore if you're an incarnation of Sinatra or some weird cliché ghost in my head that's good at stealing Sinatra quotes."

"Does it matter?"

"Well, yes, I think so. I mean, it would be helpful to make decisions based on reality, don't you think?"

"Now you're getting it. Why not try living your life that way and see what happens. Use your mentality. Wake up to reality."

"Oh. Oh, I get what you're doing. No, you can't turn it around like that. I'm onto you now."

"You don't like my answers? I'll send Sammy Davis Jr. to talk some sense into you. I gotta get going."

He stands and walks to the door.

"Go? Where would you have to be?"

"It's a big hospital. Everyone loves Sinatra. You know that."

He slings his jacket back over his shoulder and saunters out, singing "There's Such a Lot of Livin' To Do."

After Hallucination Sinatra is gone, Vincent is pretty sure the visit had been real and regrets not asking him about Marilyn Monroe and the Kennedy assassination.

Chapter 25

(98.6)

When Vincent's temperature finally drops to its normal level, he finds himself bathed in sweat, coming awake again to the sound of a sharp rap at his hospital room door. Dr. Hugo Flemming enters. He sits down in the chair next to Vincent's bed and sets down his brown leather doctor bag at his side.

"You look much better," Dr. Flemming says, eyeing Vincent from head to chest. "You didn't look so hot the last time I saw you. Or should I say, you looked *very* hot the last time I saw you. Now you just look like you're perspiring heavily."

"I think my fever finally broke. How did you know I was here?"

"What do you mean? I'm the one who got you here," Dr. Flemming says.

"*You* got me here?"

"I knew you were in bad shape back at the sushi restaurant. I wasn't too far behind you in my car. I came up the highway and saw the wreck. Your car was beached in a sand bar by the side of the road and you were passed out. Not injured, just passed out. So, I called an ambulance and got you out of there."

"I don't remember..." Vincent says.

"It wasn't pretty," Dr. Flemming says grimly.

"I remember there was a car racing up behind me, and then it was beside me, trying to run me off the road. I veered to my left and then I heard a crash—or felt it—and then I guess I passed out."

"That crash you heard was the *other* car," Dr. Flemming says. "She must not have been paying attention because she hit a disabled, abandoned vehicle in the right lane."

"She…?"

"Dr. Borden. I don't think she ever knew what happened. If she was trying to kill you, she may have saved your life by forcing you off the road when she did. I can't imagine—in your condition, with your reflexes impaired—that you would have avoided that abandoned car. As it happened, you just plowed into some thick sand. Pretty lucky, I'd say."

"So, Dr. Borden is…"

"… gone, yes. Poor thing. Probably on impact. All that padding in her face didn't save her, apparently."

"Wow. Dr. Flemming. That's horrible."

"Yes, well…you're right, I suppose I shouldn't be glib, but, you know, she was a few sandwiches short of a picnic, you know what I mean? Not a lot of corn on that cob. And she did have a dark side. She was a murderer, after all."

"You said that was just a rumor."

"More than a rumor. Everyone knows she killed her husband. I didn't want to say that flat out before. But she had that OJ Simpson thing going. She was the kind of person that could throw a lot of money at lawyers, beat the rap on a technicality, and still show up at golf outings and high-class events."

"She golfed?"

"No, OJ golfed. I'm just saying. It's a tragedy, sure, but you shouldn't lose any sleep over it. It's kind of a shame, too. Sexy gal like that."

"You thought she was sexy?"

"Didn't you?"

"No. Does everyone know about this? About my accident?" Vincent asks.

"Everyone I've talked to. They all send best wishes."

"I don't expect I'll ever be hired for freelancing again."

"On the contrary. I wouldn't worry about that. You're a good reporter. All the doctors I know like you. Your stories make us important. I'll put in a good word with your boss at *Skinformation*."

"That would help, thanks."

"Plus, the docs all loved your Sinatra karaoke. I'd say your reputation is pretty solid right now."

"That may not last. You know, I came here to write a story for the ICARUS seminar, but now..."

"Ah, yes, I figured that might be a problem for you, so..." Dr. Flemming reaches into his brown leather doctor bag and pulls out a pair of videocassettes from black plastic bags. "Here are all the highlights of the symposium. These are my private copies on tape. Unless you have a DVD player. Or LaserDisc?"

"No, I have a VCR. I'm still not sure DVD players are going to catch on. You still have a laser disc player?"

"They're rare, but they're still popular in some countries. I like to make sure I can watch in any format. Anyway, good. Please use the videotapes to help you write your story. I'd be obliged if you sent them back to me when you're through. I want to transfer them to DVD. And LaserDisc, too, maybe. Can't be too careful. Still popular in Japan. Anyway, I'll contact you from Paris and give you an address to send them to."

"Does Mitch know about these tapes?"

"Mitch? Mitchell Wallace? No, why would he?" On this remark, Dr. Flemming stands up. "I hope you don't mind if I treat and run. I've got some things to do before I fly overseas for another seminar."

"Dr. Flemming. Thank you. For the tapes. And everything else."

"Just make sure I'm prominently mentioned in your article. Two m's in Flemming."

Just as he is about to leave, Dr. Flemming pauses and picks up the Ball Mason jar on Vincent's bedside table.

"This blue stuff seems to be working nicely for you," he says, putting the jar up to his face and inspecting it closely.

"Topo-Genio? I've never even heard of it. Is it something new?"

"Yes. Very new. Well, actually... I don't even know. I probably shouldn't tell you this, but... I don't know *what* this stuff is, exactly. I didn't bring it."

"What does that mean? The other doctor told me you brought this."

"I came here in the wee small hours of the morning, after your accident to make sure you were okay. When I got here there was a woman in your room, applying this blue stuff to your face and body while you were asleep."

"The nurse."

"No, not the nurse. Pretty girl in jeans. I think she works in the bar at the El Famous."

"*Paige?*"

"Paige, yes, that's the one. It concerned me at first, seeing a strange woman in your room. Particularly since it was clear she wasn't the nurse. I was about to alert security. But then she told me who she was. And then I recognized her myself from the El Famous hotel bar. Mixes a mean martini, that girl. And then I remembered you'd told me at the sushi restaurant that you'd been using this stuff on your body. And it did seem to be effectively palliative. Your redness started to lose some of its alarming vibrancy and your skin was responding positively."

"Is Paige here now?" Vincent asks. He raises his head as if anticipating she might suddenly come through the door.

"She wasn't downstairs when I arrived, no."

"So, I still don't understand. What is Topo-Genio?"

"Topo-Genio? I made up that name," Dr. Flemming says. "I told the doctors it was something that I had prescribed for you. I said it was something that worked topically and used regenerative genes from lab rats... or some nonsense like that. Your doctor looked puzzled but thought it sounded legit. I don't know what's in it, actually."

"It's all homemade ingredients. At least I think so. Paige made it herself. It has Kalahari melon seed oil."

"Ah. That explains it. Well, it seems like it's excellent for sunburn. And for its obviously stimulating qualities."

"Stimulating?"

"Well, difficult to tell. Might have been the skin balm. Might have been the fact that the girl was rubbing it on you. But your body seemed to *like* it, if you know what I mean. I'm sure I could market something like that. The balm, I mean. Smart girl. Cute, too."

"Could you tell me again about the part where she's rubbing this stuff on my body while I'm unconscious?"

Chapter 26

(la molta vida)

Mitchell George Wallace paces around Vincent's hospital room. He looks out the window, inspects the walls. Looks at a chart on the back of the door. Looks at the pain level wall calendar. It appears to Vincent like Mitch is doing all he can to avoid the chair next to Vincent's bed and the IV tube next to Vincent's hospital bed.

"It's sunburn," Vincent says. "You know as well as I do that it's not contagious."

Mitch finally pulls the chair out a few inches away from the bed and sits down.

"So, Vincenzo. You gonna live, or what?"

"Looks that way, yes."

"You're lucky, paisano. If I had gotten to you earlier, I might have killed you myself. Thanks for totaling my rental."

"I thought it wasn't badly damaged."

"The body's not bad, but the motor's shot. So much sand you could play a game of volleyball under the hood."

"How did you find me?"

"Paige called me. She couldn't reach you, but she had the business card I gave her. She was frantic. Then Dr. Flemming got in touch with me."

"You talked to Paige?"

"Yeah, she told me everything that went on. Flemming gave me the rest, about the accident. And Dr. Borden. *Man.*"

"Is she here?"

"Borden? I imagine that piece of plastic has been recycled by now."

"Mitch, that's awful. No, I meant Paige."

"Paige? No, I didn't see her downstairs." Mitch frowns and shakes his head. "You know, it's bad enough you leave me stranded at the El Famous hotel bar and take off with my Mustang..."

"I didn't 'take off.' You gave me the keys."

"... and there I am," Mitch continues, "stuck at the El Famous trying to get the keynote speech after the plenary. I can't find any dermatologists, turns out they all hightailed it out of the hotel after the lectures to go do karaoke. So, I can't get my hands on any videotapes, I can't reach you, and all I've got is a handful of bad handwritten notes..."

"... about that..."

"... so, then I give up and go down to the bar to look for Paige, and then it turns out she was with you the whole time."

"Not the entire time."

"What's with the joyride, man? I thought you were just going to go to some local restaurant. Then I find out you're cruising the California coastline in my cherry red Mustang like some kind of Marcello Marscapone."

"Mastroianni."

"... living *la molta vita*, chasing down women."

"It's *la dolce vita.*"

"And then I find out that you've been doing karaoke with all the dermatologists from the seminar. Meanwhile, I'm stuck at the El Famous without a car."

"It wasn't like that. It all happened very fast. And I wasn't chasing down women. Paige usually carpools with Rosalio and asked if I'd take her home."

"Who's Rosalio?"

"He's a barback in the hotel lounge, I guess. I don't know him personally. I just know about him from Paige."

"For a guy who was supposedly lying low, you've sure been busy expanding your social network. You put more than 50 miles on that Mustang. You exceeded the flat rate mileage charges. All so you can bang Paige behind my back? Do me a favor, paisano, next time you bang someone behind my back, do it to my face. That's all I'm saying."

"I didn't bang Paige."

"Well, she definitely seems to have a sweet spot for you, Marcello. I sure as hell don't understand it."

"Is the Mustang going to be okay?"

"They towed it. It's not my problem anymore. The police contacted me after the accident because the papers in the glove box were registered to me, care of the hotel. So, I talked to the police. Then I got charged by the rental company for letting an 'unauthorized driver' operate the vehicle. Plus the towing charges."

"Am I in any trouble? With the police, I mean."

"I heard you had a few drinks in you. They probably could have busted your ass. But under the circumstances, the high fever and all that, and considering that you were being chased down by that maniac, Dr. Borden, they're not going to pursue any charges. They said to tell you not to get behind the wheel like that again."

"I don't plan to."

"But I still have to pay a penalty for letting you drive that rental car. You're lucky there's just the towing involved and no damage on it. No way am I paying for this shit."

"I'll take care of it."

"That's right. You will. And now I've also lost a lot of time working on the ICARUS story. Talking to the police, the rental company, coming here. I'm just saying."

"I hear you. Don't worry about the story. I have videotapes of the lectures. Dr. Flemming loaned them to me."

"Flemming gave the tapes to you?"

Vincent points to the black plastic bag next to his bed. "Yes. Dr. Flemming says the videotapes have all the highlights of the symposium. I'll write it all up when I get back to Chicago. One for you and one for *Giornale della Faccia*. Just like we talked about."

Mitch opens the black plastic bag and carefully inspects the videotapes as if they are rare artifacts from an archeological dig. "I can't believe he gave you these tapes…"

"They're on loan. I have to get them back to him. What did you tell Paige when you talked to her?"

"Oh. About that… yeah, well… we probably need to talk about that."

"What is there to talk about?"

Mitch lowers his gaze, looks out the window again. "I think Paige was worried she had upset you. So, I told her about Melissa."

"*Melissa?* Why would you do that? And what could you possibly tell Paige about Melissa?"

"She was concerned. I don't know, man. I just told Paige some things about how things were with you and Melissa, and about the… you know, the *plane crash*." Mitch whispers this last part and sinks down into his chair. Then he continues. "And, you know, how you get weird about it when you talk about Melissa, and your denial and general instability, and all that good stuff."

"You told Paige about my denial and general instability to make her worry less? Oh, that's nice. No wonder she hasn't come back to see me."

"I think Paige thinks you don't want to see *her*. I don't know. Maybe because of some of these things I said."

"That's terrific, Mitch. Nice job."

"Look, don't put it on me. Your love life is like one of those… Russian jigsaw puzzles."

"Russian…?"

"You know, like those nesting doll things. Chinese finger puzzles. I don't know how the fuck to explain it."

"No one asked you to explain it."

"Paige did."

Vincent sinks his head back into his pillow. "Man, I have to get out of here."

"But you're still going to write the story for me, right? I mean, not now, obviously. When you're feeling better and out of this place."

"Yeah, don't worry about it."

Mitch stands up and eyes the objects at Vincent's bedside.

"Is this your swag?"

"Just some stuff I picked up along the way."

"What's with the CD?" Mitch asks.

"It was a gift. I won it at the karaoke contest."

"Nice for you. And what's with the jelly jar?"

"That was a gift, too," Vincent says.

"From whom?"

"It's from... it's from Dr. Flemming," Vincent says, preferring not to explain the elaborate and convoluted origins of Topo-Genio.

"Lucky bastard. No doctor ever gave *me* jelly," Mitch says. "I didn't even have time to steal any samples from the vendor table outside the seminar ballroom. You get the ICARUS tapes, a CD, a date with Paige and this jar of jelly, and meanwhile, I end up with a shit sandwich and a bunch of extra charges on a rental car."

"I said I'd take care of it."

"And that's it? You're not going to share any of this swag?" Mitch waves his hand broadly over the bedside items.

"I can't give you the jar," Vincent says.

"Why not?"

"I've been spreading that stuff all over my body to make me feel good."

Mitch shook his head. "Sick bastard."

"You can have the CD," Vincent said. "I don't need it anymore."

"What's on it?"

"It's a Sinatra CD."

"Just Sinatra? Or is there some Sammy Davis Jr. on there?"

"Just Sinatra, I think. Greatest hits."

"Lame. That figures."

Mitch gets up, takes the CD, and disappears.

Vincent watches the door to his hospital room for a long time after that, waiting for the knob to turn, waiting for someone to appear. Or reappear.

But Paige never shows up. Mitch doesn't come back either and neither does Dr. Flemming. Nor does Dr. Havoc or even Emiko, the night nurse. Nor is Vincent visited by apparitions of Frank or Dean or Sammy or any of the Rat Pack. All at once, Vincent finally feels a sense of being alone, not alone in a nebulous, unknowing sense, not in the sense of not being sure, or anticipating a long solitude, and not even completely lonely, but truly alone. His loneliness results in tears, and he cries for the first time in a long time.

Sometime later Vincent realizes that of all the people he had been anticipating might appear at his hospital door, he'd omitted Melissa. For the first time, it doesn't occur to him that Melissa will come walking through the door at any moment. He knows now that it's something that's not going to happen.

Moreover, he's hoping for something else entirely.

Chapter 27

(release)

Vincent is released from the hospital with a guardedly clear bill of health around noon the following day. It is a short taxi ride back to the hotel.

As he approaches the front desk to tell them he will be checking out, he sees a familiar face. He can't place her at first, then realizes it's the young mother he'd seen by the pool with her daughters when he'd first arrived at the El Famous. She acknowledges his red features with a grimace.

"Didn't I tell you… *sunblock*?" she says.

"Right," Vincent says, with a shy smile.

"Did you find that woman you were looking for?" she asks.

"No," he says. "No, I did not."

"Sorry to hear that," the woman says. "There is a woman out there now, by the pool. On a pink towel. Well, they're all pink, as you know. But maybe it's the person you're looking for."

"Maybe," he says. Vincent steals a glance in the direction of the door that leads to the pool area. "Green swimsuit?"

"More teal, I'd call it."

"Thanks for the information. Are you checking out?"

"Yes."

"Have a safe trip home."

Vincent feels the familiar pull, a tug drawing him toward the door to the pool area, but it is a tug of a recalled and obsolete obsession. *This is how I always respond in this situation*, he thinks. But now it feels dulled. Still, he heads down a mirrored hallway in the lobby toward the pool. When he catches his reflection in the mirrors in the hotel lobby, he pauses and stares at himself for a moment. He is still very red, and still looking a bit haggard, but better, he supposed, than he was 24 hours earlier. He turns back to continue down the hallway toward the pool, then stops and looks at himself again, more discerningly.

Vincent thinks again about that other poison—the one Dr. Havoc couldn't identify. The one that didn't identify itself clearly on any blood or toxicology test. Maybe it isn't a physiological poison at all, he thinks Maybe it is a toxin that only builds up in the system of a monosexual. He feels the need to purge it.

Instead of going out to the pool area to investigate the identity of the woman in the green (or teal) swimsuit, Vincent turns around, heads to the elevator and goes up to his room.

The tiny James Madison room is very much as he'd left it. He just has to throw a few things in his suitcase and he will be ready to check out again. He makes sure the Topo-Genio is in his carry-on, in case he needs it on the plane.

He calls down to the desk to arrange for a cab to take him to the airport. He never looks out the window, never looks down to see who is at the pool.

There is little evidence to suggest anyone else has been in the room in his absence, except that the bed is pristine, not a wrinkle in the mattress—and this is not how he'd left it. Housekeeping, he surmises. They would have come in and straightened up no matter how clean the room was.

Vincent looks up above his bed. The yellow Post-it note with *fly me to the moon* written on it is missing from the ceiling. Again, he assumes it has something to do with housekeeping tidying up. He wrinkles his face. Then he notices the Post-it note on the carpet in a narrow groove next to the bed.

Vincent opens his wallet, removes the photo of Melissa, sticks the Post-it note to the front of the picture, and props it up against a lamp on his nightstand. He takes $20 out of his wallet for housekeeping and lays it next to the photo and note.

"There," Vincent says. "Now you can be someone *else's* mystery."

He zips up his suitcase and takes the elevator down to the first floor.

Chapter 28

(rota-range)

Vincent decides he is going to wait outside the El Famous for his cab, but when he gets down to the lobby of the hotel, he makes a U-turn and heads instead to the hotel lounge. There is a barmaid on duty, but it isn't Paige. He asks the woman whether or not Paige is scheduled to work. The woman doesn't know. He asks if Paige might be working at Slammin' Sammy Sushi today. The woman doesn't know. He gives up and walks outside, out of the air conditioning. He feels humid and deflated under the fake plastic palms.

His cab arrives, the driver puts his bags in the trunk, and he gets in the back seat.

"San Caliente airport," Vincent says.

The taxi makes its way back north up the California coastline. The driver is good. He stays within the speed limit and signals when he makes lane changes.

About 10 minutes into the trip, as Vincent is gazing idly out the left side of the vehicle, he shudders at what he sees. Long black tire marks are etched into the highway. Skid marks that end in an oddly discolored patch of concrete where flames, twisted metal, and other carnage had likely licked at the pavement. And to the right of the scene, he sees the torn opening in the orange plastic fence—the little escape hatch where he'd been forced off the road. Forced into salvation.

"Geez," he says, his eyes widening at the sight.

"Atsa some bad accident happen here, eh boss?" The taxi driver says.

Vincent nods, silently.

"They say it's a rota-range," the driver says.

"I'm sorry, what was that?"

"Rota-range."

"Rota-range? Oh. *Road rage*."

"Yeah," the driver says. "Rota-range. The driver—she's-a no let go with the angry. That's what I hear."

Soon they are a mile past the accident scene, two miles, five. Still, Vincent's neck continues to crane behind him for a while, out the back window, long after he can see what he is looking at.

When he finally turns around again, he sees the giant samurai baseball player out along the horizon, its sword gleaming above the red barn building in the midday sun.

"We need to pull in here," Vincent says.

Chapter 29

(hair of the dog)

The taxi slows to a stop in front of Slammin' Sammy Sushi. The driver offers to wait, but Vincent tells him he can drive on.

He doesn't see Chrysanthemum, Paige's VW camper, in the lot. He walks into the sushi restaurant, looking for a familiar face. He finds one immediately, but it isn't Paige. Nathan is on duty again, decked out in his samurai regalia.

"My man Vincent is back!" he announces to the restaurant patrons.

No one reacts to this, but then Nathan adds, "Sinatra! Sinatra's in the house."

A wave of recognition passes over some of the regulars at the bar and Vincent gets a smattering of courtesy applause. Nathan clatters over to him on his sandals.

"Hey, man. Back to defend your title?"

"No. God, no. I was looking for Paige, actually."

"Oh. Sorry, she's not here, man."

"Oh." Vincent lowers his head and nods sadly. He wonders how far away his cab driver has gotten.

"I mean she was here, but I think she went out back," Nathan says. "Things are slow today. She's probably out on the deck or down by the shore."

"Oh. Thanks. I'm just going to go see if I can find her, if that's okay."

He walks out onto the deck. Paige isn't there. Then Vincent spots her walking alone along the ocean coastline. With no exit off the deck, Vincent hurries back into the restaurant, down the stairs, through the front and around to the back, heading toward the beach. By the time he approaches Paige, he's trotted a good distance in an uneven terrain of sand and feels ungainly and out of breath.

When she spots Vincent, Paige looks surprised. Not happy, necessarily, he notes, just surprised.

Vincent pants. "I didn't see your... I didn't see your camper in the lot..."

"I came in with Rosalio again, the barback," Paige says. "What are you doing here? I thought you'd be on a flight back to Chicago by now."

"I just came from the hotel. Would it be okay if we sat for a minute?"

They walk a short distance and locate a blue-and-green park bench that faces the ocean. Paige leans forward, elbows on her knees, hands on her chin, staring ahead of her. Vincent leans back, content for the moment to talk to the back of Paige's head.

"I wanted to make sure you got the voucher. From Nathan. For the free Mai Tais," Vincent says.

"He gave it to me, yes."

"Good, good."

"Is that what you came to tell me?"

"Not exactly. I wanted to thank you for all you did."

"Not necessary. I'm sure I heard a 'thank you' when you dashed out of my beach house," Paige says.

"Yes. Well, I also wanted to tell you that I don't think you poisoned me."

"Poisoned?" She turns her head up toward Vincent and looks at him incredulously.

"Yes, I had food poisoning, maybe from the blowfish, I don't know. And then the doctor said there was some other poison in me, and they weren't able to pin it down, but I definitely don't think it was from you."

Paige sits upright. "Jesus, Vincent. You actually thought that I *poisoned* you?"

"No. Well, yes. Just for a moment. But you were last on the list."

"Is that supposed to make me feel better?"

"I've not been in my right mind, Paige."

"I heard about that awful Dr. Borden," Paige says. "You could have been killed."

"It's okay. I think there's just a lot of sand in my engine."

"You're telling me."

Vincent smiles. Paige manages a smile herself. A cautious smile, Vincent thinks, but a smile nonetheless.

"You look better," she says. "I'm glad you're out of the hospital."

"That blue stuff is pretty amazing. Dr. Flemming—I guess you met him in my room—anyway, he's a famous dermatologist and he was very impressed with you."

"I wish I could have made that kind of impression on *you*."

"You did. You *do*, I mean. I think you're very special, Paige."

"Special enough to poison you."

"No. That's just something I thought. For a second. I don't think that anymore, that's the important thing. Maybe I shouldn't have mentioned it at all."

"Maybe not."

"Forget I mentioned it, then."

"Vincent, I talked to Mitch…"

"*Mitch*? Mitch doesn't know anything about me."

"He seems to know a lot, actually. I'd say he was even a bit more forthcoming than you've been." She stops and looks down at her sandaled feet in the sand. "I found out some things about Melissa that I didn't know."

"Yes, Mitch told me what he said. That's fine. I don't care that you know, or if you think I'm crazy or delusional or whatever.

But I don't want you to hear it from Mitch. I want you to hear it from me."

"I would find that refreshing, as well," Paige says. "Vincent, I need to tell you. When I was in your hospital room… I did something. While you were unconscious or asleep or whatever."

"I know," Vincent says. "Dr. Flemming told me. You were rubbing that blue stuff on my face and chest. It's okay. That was incredibly sweet of you."

"No. Not that. I went into your wallet. I saw the picture of Melissa. I had to see for myself." Paige's voice catches. "She was *very* pretty." She lowers her voice to a whisper. "I'm so very sorry about what happened to her."

Vincent nods, grimly. "Yes. It was a horrible thing that happened." He breathes in deeply again, taking in some ocean mist, and expels a large, brine sigh. "But she's not in my wallet anymore. I left her at the hotel."

"I'm sorry, I don't know what that means coming from you, Vincent."

"I'm saying I left it behind. The photo, I mean. And when I was alone in the hospital, I was waiting for someone, and I had always been waiting for Melissa to turn up, but actually, I wasn't thinking about her at all, I was hoping *you* would show up."

Paige pauses, then speaks again. "I think that ship has gone out to sea," she says, looking far out into the ocean.

"I understand," Vincent says, lowering his head. "I wish you didn't feel that way."

"No, I'm talking about that boat out there. The gray one." She points towards the ocean. "It's been going west the entire time we've been out here."

"Oh."

"You thought I meant…?"

"… well, under the circumstances…"

"… oh. Yes," she says.

"There have been a couple times lately when I… wait, do you even want to hear this?"

Paige folds her hands in her lap and sits up, calmly and attentively.

"I do, yes."

"There have been a few times lately—notably at your beach house and then in the hospital room—when my body has been… reacting in ways that it hasn't for a long time. And particularly when your hands are touching me. You know? I don't mean like… I mean, even when I'm sleeping. I think maybe it says something. Don't you think that says something?"

"You could have been dreaming about Melissa. Or maybe Cindy Crawford visited you in a hallucination."

"Not Cindy Crawford. But I did have a hallucination."

"About Melissa?"

"No, it was Sinatra. He encouraged me to straighten up and get past all this. He wasn't entirely convincing, but some of the things he said made sense."

"Sinatra? Frank Sinatra?"

"Hallucination Sinatra, I think. But I think talking to him did me some good.

"Did he say anything about your monosexuality?"

"Yes, he said he didn't understand it at all."

"I'm not sure I understand it either."

"I don't think I understand it myself anymore," Vincent says. "And to the extent that I understand it, it's not doing me any good now, is it? Living in denial. Chasing after phantoms, ideals…"

"Sinatra's pretty smart," Paige says.

"Well, Sinatra didn't say all that, actually. I'm just interpreting."

"What *did* Sinatra say?"

"He said something about Jack Daniels, and about getting women into bed and moving on."

"Oh."

"No, I know, that's not cool, but that advice doesn't work for me, either."

"Good to know."

"No. And what's really strange is that since the accident and being in the hospital, I keep hearing how 'lucky' I've been. Mitch thinks I was lucky. The nurse, the doctors. They tell me I was lucky. And I'm not sure how I feel about luck. But when I think about meeting you, then… I think I *do* understand luck. I know I feel lucky having met you, Paige."

"I understood that part," Paige says, now fully attentive to him.

"And I like how you know things," Vincent says. "You know what you're doing. You're all put together."

"Me?" Paige says. "You think I know what I'm doing? I don't know if you realize this, but you weren't the only one affected by Melissa's plane going down. I know about that flight. Yes, I watched CNN. Everyone knows about it. I'd already had one bad experience in the air. When Melissa's flight went down, it affected *me*, too. It's one of the main reasons I won't get on a plane."

"I didn't know that," Vincent says.

"I mean, I know what you went through is a lot worse. All I'm saying is that you shouldn't hold me up as some sort of ideal person. I don't always know what I'm doing."

Vincent muses for a moment, then speaks. "This might be something I can help you with," he says.

"What are you talking about?"

"The plane. I can help you get back on a plane again."

"I thought we were talking about you," Paige says.

"I *am* talking about me. I think you should come back with me."

"Back?"

"Back to Chicago."

"What? No."

"Not forever. Just fly back with me. I'll take a later flight. You can pack a bag pretty quick, can't you?"

She laughs. "Vincent… Don't be silly. Did they check you for a concussion when you were in the hospital?"

"I'm fine."

"I can't leave now."

"Why not?"

"I just got a gift certificate for a month's worth of free Mai Tais."

"Paige..."

"... I can't just up and leave."

"You can. Then you can come right back here to San Caliente, if you want. Maybe *I'll* even come back here to San Caliente with you. If you want. But for now, I have to go back to Chicago. I have to write my story and maybe even see about getting my old job back. But I'd like for us to keep talking. So, I think you should definitely come back to Chicago with me."

"We could talk on the phone. We don't have to arrange an entire flight to have a conversation."

"I don't want to talk on the phone. I'll put the flight off a day. I have a friend who's a pilot. He can get us on standby. Pack a bag and come with me."

Paige pauses again, shakes her head, slips out of one of her sandals and traces a polished toenail back and forth in the sand. She looks up in the air, observing a jet flying above them and out over the ocean. She follows the jet stream with her eyes.

"I guess you missed your flight," she says.

"I doubt it was *that* plane, exactly. But yes, I probably missed my flight."

"It's past lunch time. Have you eaten? Are you hungry?"

Vincent looks up toward Slammin' Sammy's. He frowns. "Maybe not sushi."

"Oh. Right. Maybe not sushi. Chicken wings?"

"Maybe. Do you have the gift voucher for free drinks with you?"

Paige opens her purse and brandishes the envelope that holds the gift certificate.

"What do you say we go up and have a month's worth of Mai Tais?" he asks.

Vincent stands, offers Paige his hand, and she rises from the bench.

"I'm not saying yes to anything yet, mind you," Paige says, taking his hand.

"Understood," he says.

They walk down the beach towards the restaurant.

"I don't see how you think you can get me to fly," Paige says.

Chapter 30

(lift)

"Let's go over it one more time," Vincent says.

"Lift. It all has to do with lift," Glenn says. "The Bernoulli Principle states that when air speeds up, the pressure is lowered. The wing will move towards the least pressure. In this case, up."

The explanation hasn't varied—it is, almost word for word, the same one Vincent heard before his flight from Chicago to San Caliente. Captain Glenn Buck patiently delivers the speech again in anticipation of flight 803, nonstop from San Caliente to Chicago.

Vincent has the talk memorized; he could have delivered it himself. But he thought Paige might benefit, as he had, from hearing it directly from an airline pilot. Paige sits next to Vincent in the airport lounge at San Caliente airport. They both sip Bloody Marys. Paige is hanging on Glenn's every word.

"Why do planes have to fly so high?" Paige asks.

"That's for your safety," Glenn tells her, and then he gives the full spiel about how the greater the altitude, the better it is, since you are moving out of the range of mountains, clouds and high-flying birds. The dreaded Asian geese.

Glenn's good at this, Vincent thinks. And he thinks maybe airlines should always have a pilot prepared to talk to nervous people like this before a flight.

"What's on the agenda when you get back to Chicago?" Glenn asks.

"I've got to write up the ICARUS story for Mitch and for *Giornale della Faccia*. And then I'll see where I'm at," Vincent says. He turns to Paige and they exchange glances, as if seeking out or confirming a satisfactory response between them that might satisfy Glenn.

"Apparently, I have a pile of letters at my parents' house from schools that still want to interview me for teaching positions," Paige says.

"And I have to see a board-certified dermatologist back in Chicago about my face," Vincent says. He is still quite red, but his chest is starting to peel. Peeling is good, Vincent thinks. Shedding some old skin and acquiring some new skin couldn't hurt him any.

"Yes, I couldn't help but notice your face," Glenn says. "What happened there?"

"Long story," Vincent says.

"So, you two are...?" Glenn looks from Vincent to Paige and back to Vincent again.

"Paige and I are...we're going to hang out for a while," Vincent says. "See how that goes. Right?" He looks over at Paige for confirmation.

"Right," Paige says. Not smiling exactly but appearing resolute.

"I see. I see." Glenn nods slowly.

"We can talk about it when we get back," Vincent says to Glenn.

"Yes, I think you should," Glenn says. "Come by and see Cookie and the boys. They'd love that. And bring Paige. Right? Paige, you're welcome to come. Right, Vincent?"

"Of course," Vincent says.

"Thank you," Paige says. "I'm anxious to get back home to Chicago. Tie up some loose ends."

"Our ends have gotten very loose," Vincent says.

*

Vincent knows from experience that flying standby has its advantages if you are patient and willing to take a risk. This time it pays off. Vincent and Paige are upgraded to business class with seats next to each other.

"This could be okay, I think," Paige says, settling into her seat and stretching her legs as far as she can. She has been clasping Vincent's hand since the airport lounge, and as Glenn begins to taxi the airplane, he feels her hand tense up in his.

"Glenn's a good driver," Vincent assures her. "A good pilot, I mean."

"Okay," Paige says. "Okay."

Vincent has the window seat. Paige prefers not to look out the window but asks for updates. So, Vincent assures her when the plane has safely cleared the San Caliente airport and safely cleared the San Caliente mountains. He lets her know as they ascend the crucial lines of elevation—those places where they became safe, or safer, at least. Past clouds, past Asian geese.

When they reach cruising altitude, Glenn's voice crackles over the intercom and he goes into his spiel. When Paige hears Glenn's voice, she smiles and nudges Vincent conspiratorially.

"We know him," Paige says.

"It's kind of strange, isn't it?"

"Glenn sounds so serious, but his voice is kind of calming," Paige says.

For a while, all is quiet, then Glenn's voice can be heard over the intercom again to give some particulars about the flight time and wind conditions. It might get a little bumpy as they push east, he says, but nothing serious. Then he talks about what they might expect back in Chicago.

The forecast for Chicago is overcast and cold. Glenn doesn't say this, exactly. He tells passengers that the temperature is 29 degrees at O'Hare and that there are wind gusts of up to 30 miles per hour.

What had the temperature been when he'd left Chicago? Twenty-six? But it was February and the days were getting longer again, not shorter. What had been 26 degrees when Vincent left was now closer to 30 degrees. And what had been eleven hours of sunlight would now be getting closer to twelve. Yes, Chicago would be cold and dark. But not quite as cold and dark as when he'd left it.

"Still nervous?" he asks Paige.

"Aren't you?"

"Yes. But are you doing okay?"

"I think so," she says. She slips her in-flight headphones over her head. She pecks at the buttons for a few moments, then stops and settles back in her seat. She points to the buttons on Vincent's armrest. "Check out audio channel eight," Paige says.

Vincent puts on his own headphones and punches buttons until he stops at channel eight. It's Dean Martin. It's an all Dean Martin station, apparently.

"You like Rat Pack music?" Vincent asks her. "Sinatra?"

"Frank will always be chairman of the board," Paige says.

"Right."

"But you know, sometimes, I feel like Dino is having a little more fun."

Paige nestles back in her seat and closes her eyes.

Vincent purses out his lower lip and nods back at Paige, even though she can't see him. He turns up the volume.

He slips his hand back into hers and she holds on, tightly.

Before long, the plane levels off, the engines grow quieter, and it becomes easier to hear the music and not all the other noise.

About the Author

Dean Monti started writing at age two, but nothing legible until age five. Since then, his fiction has appeared in several literary journals in print and online. His critically-acclaimed novel, *The Sweep of the Second Hand*, was published by Academy Chicago Publishers and reprinted in paperback by Penguin. In addition to other novels, he is the author of several full-length and one-act plays and has had works staged in Chicago and Norfolk, Virginia. His short story "Why Dogs Don't Talk" was adapted as a stage play and short film, and he is currently adapting one of his novels as a screenplay. Additionally, Monti has taught creative writing at Columbia College in Chicago and at College of DuPage. He lives in a 105-year-old house in Glen Ellyn, Illinois, with his wife, Julie and two difficult but sometimes loveable cats.